PRAISE FOR CAROLYN BROWN

Hummingbird Lane

"Brown's (*The Daydream Cabin*) gentle story of a woman finding strength within a tight-knit community has just a touch of romance at the end. Recommended for readers who enjoy heartwarming stories about women overcoming obstacles."

—*Library Journal*

Miss Janie's Girls

"[A] heartfelt tale of familial love and self-acceptance."

—*Publishers Weekly*

"Heartfelt moments and family drama collide in this saga about sisters."

—*Woman's World*

The Banty House

"Brown throws together a colorful cast of characters to excellent effect and maximum charm in this small-town contemporary romance . . . This first-rate romance will delight readers young and old."

—*Publishers Weekly*

The Perfect Dress

"Fans of Brown will swoon for this sweet contemporary, which skillfully pairs a shy small-town bridal shop owner and a softhearted car dealership owner . . . The expected but welcomed happily ever after for all involved will make readers of all ages sigh with satisfaction."

—*Publishers Weekly*

"Carolyn Brown writes the best comfort-for-the-soul, heartwarming stories, and she never disappoints . . . You won't go wrong with *The Perfect Dress!*"

—*Harlequin Junkie*

The Magnolia Inn

"The author does a first-rate job of depicting the devastating stages of grief, provides a simple but appealing plot with a sympathetic hero and heroine and a cast of lovable supporting characters, and wraps it all up with a happily ever after to cheer for."

—*Publishers Weekly*

"*The Magnolia Inn* by Carolyn Brown is a feel-good story about friendship, fighting your demons, and finding love, and maybe just a little bit of magic."

—*Harlequin Junkie*

"Chock-full of Carolyn Brown's signature country charm, *The Magnolia Inn* is a sweet and heartwarming story of two people trying to make the most of their lives, even when they have no idea what exactly is at stake."

—Fresh Fiction

Small Town Rumors

"Carolyn Brown is a master at writing warm, complex characters who find their way into your heart."

—*Harlequin Junkie*

The Sometimes Sisters

"Carolyn Brown continues her streak of winning, heartfelt novels with *The Sometimes Sisters*, a story of estranged sisters and frustrated romance."

—All About Romance

"This is an amazing feel-good story that will make you wish you were a part of this amazing family."

—*Harlequin Junkie* (top pick)

the Devine Doughnut Shop

ALSO BY CAROLYN BROWN

CONTEMPORARY ROMANCES

The Sandcastle Hurricane
Riverbend Reunion
The Bluebonnet Battle
The Sunshine Club
The Hope Chest
Hummingbird Lane
The Daydream Cabin
Miss Janie's Girls
The Banty House
The Family Journal
The Empty Nesters
The Perfect Dress
The Magnolia Inn
Small Town Rumors
The Sometimes Sisters
The Strawberry Hearts Diner
The Lilac Bouquet
The Barefoot Summer
The Lullaby Sky
The Wedding Pearls
The Yellow Rose Beauty Shop
The Ladies' Room
Hidden Secrets
Long, Hot Texas Summer
Daisies in the Canyon
Trouble in Paradise

CONTEMPORARY SERIES

The Broken Roads Series
To Trust
To Commit
To Believe
To Dream
To Hope

Three Magic Words Trilogy
A Forever Thing
In Shining Whatever
Life After Wife

HISTORICAL ROMANCE

The Black Swan Trilogy
Pushin' Up Daisies
From Thin Air
Come High Water

The Drifters & Dreamers Trilogy
Morning Glory
Sweet Tilly
Evening Star

The Love's Valley Series
Choices
Absolution
Chances
Redemption
Promises

the Devine Doughnut Shop

CAROLYN BROWN

Published by Montlake, Seattle

www.apub.com

Amazon, the Amazon logo, and Montlake are trademarks of Amazon.com, Inc., or its affiliates.

ISBN-13: 9781542038492 (paperback)
ISBN-13: 9781542038485 (digital)

Cover design by Leah Jacobs-Gordon

Cover images: © ronstik, © New Africa, © NG-Spacetime, © Al.geba, © MaraZe, © EPS, © LumenSt, © schankz, © LilaloveDesign, © Bokeh Blur Background / Shutterstock

Printed in the United States of America

To my family, all forty-five of you—kids, grandkids, and great-grands—for your love and support

Chapter One

"here's the nearest convent or boot camp?" Grace Dalton stormed into the kitchen of the Devine Doughnut Shop that Friday morning. "This daughter of mine needs to spend some time in whichever one that will take her."

"What has Audrey done now?" Grace's younger sister, Sarah, asked.

"She sent me a text last night after I'd gone to bed and said that she had been suspended for today," Grace answered as she slipped a bibbed apron over her head and tied the strings in the back. She tucked her hair up into a net and moved over to the sink to wash her hands.

Their cousin Macy, who was a partner at the doughnut shop, set the bowls up on the counter to get the dough made and rising. "Good Lord! What did she do?"

Grace flipped the hot doughnuts into a bowl of powdered sugar glaze, turned them over, and set them out on a different rack to cool. "She got caught with a pack of cigarettes and one of those little sample bottles of whiskey at school. When she goes back after spring break, she gets to spend two days in the in-school suspension building. I'm paying for *your* raising, Sarah June, not mine. I was the good child."

"Thank you for that. But, honey, you were every bit as bad as me. You just hid it better." Sarah turned around, saw what her sister was doing, and pushed a strand of platinum hair up under a net. "I appreciate you glazing those doughnuts, but you've got severe memory-loss problems if you think *you* were the good child."

"None of us can brag about shiny halos and big white fluffy wings," Macy said.

"Amen to that," Grace said, "and I have to remember that Audrey's father was one of those bad-boy types that mamas warn their girls about. She's got his genes as well as mine, but she wasn't this rebellious until she started running with those two girls, Crystal and Kelsey. She was so much easier to live with when she hung out with Raelene Andrews and that group of kids."

"I'm glad that Neal and I have decided to have all boys when we start our family," Macy said as she punched down a bowl full of dough, flipped it out on a floured board, and began to knead it. "This is the last of what we're making this morning. If we hadn't sold out early to those fishermen, we wouldn't have had to make more."

"Good luck with only having boys." Grace grimaced. "You might remember that Justin did not have a halo. Your boys might grow up to be like him."

Macy gasped. "No!"

"Could happen," Sarah said.

Grace nodded. She and Sarah both had a thing for the bad-boy type. She'd gotten over hers when Justin deserted her, but Sarah still walked on the wild side. An unlikely bunch of roommates, the three women and Grace's daughter all lived in the same house, not far from the back door of the shop. Grace felt that she was in the middle of the scale and Sarah was on the far-left end. Tomorrow night, since it was Saturday and the shop was closed on Sunday, her little sister would be off to a local bar to drink, dance, and maybe even go home with a two-steppin' cowboy.

On the opposite end of the scale—the far right—Macy was a Sunday school teacher and engaged to be married in June. Dozens of her bridal magazines cluttered up the old yellow chrome table in the back of the Devine Doughnut Shop—the Double D, as the folks in town had called it for years.

"What's that supposed to mean?" Macy rolled out the dough and cut out the doughnuts.

"It means," Sarah piped up, "that you've got a fifty-fifty chance of having boys, but you could have all girls. Look at our family. We haven't had a boy in it since before Texas became a state. There's us three, and before that there was our Mama, Liz, and Aunt Molly; Granny and her sister, Gloria; and Great-Granny, who started this shop, and her sister, Edith. We are a family of sisters."

Grace thought of their great-grandmother, who had inherited a chunk of money from a land sale when her father died. She'd used the funds to buy the acreage, build a small house, and start a pastry business. She was already famous all over town for her pastries by the time her husband was off to fight in the war. Now the fourth generation was reaping the financial benefits of that small endeavor.

"And a couple of girl cousins thrown into the mix back along the way." Grace nodded toward Macy. "Four generations of us have lived in the house and run this business, and now I have a daughter who hasn't got enough ambition to pick up her dirty socks. She's more interested in being as popular as her two new friends are than thinking about running a business in the future. We may be the last group to keep this business alive."

Grace was glad that she'd lived on her salary from the bakery all these years and put her profit-sharing check at the end of the year into savings and investments. Not that she was patting herself on the back for being frugal. Her sister and cousin had done the same thing. The one thing she missed was having the time to spend a small portion of that money on vacations, but the shop had been open six days a week since it began, and none of them could bear to break the routine.

Audrey pushed the back door open, slouched down in a chair, and opened a bridal magazine. Her blonde hair hung down to her shoulders and looked like a brush hadn't seen it in a week. She tucked a strand with a blue streak behind her ear when it fell down over her right eye. Her jeans had holes all up and down the legs, and her T-shirt looked like something a stray dog would have tried to bury in the backyard.

Grace shook her head. "Oh, no, little girl. You don't get to sit around and do nothing. See that bucket over there? Your first job is to go clean the windows, and after we close up, you get to mop the floors. You will work all during your spring break for what you've done."

"Good grief, Mama," her daughter whined. "I could break a nail, or someone might see me cleaning windows or mopping."

"Honey, that's the least of your worries. Starting tonight, we aren't going to clean the dining area after work. You will be getting up and coming to work with us at three o'clock in the morning. From then until five, you will mop the floors, clean all the glass, wash dishes, and do whatever else needs to be done until we close the doors."

"No!" Audrey crossed her arms over her chest. "Getting up at that ungodly hour is child abuse!"

"Maybe so, but that's what you'll be doing," Grace told her.

"I hate you," Audrey whispered.

The air in the shop seemed too heavy to breathe. Then Grace got a second wind and smiled at her daughter. "Well, darlin', I love you every second of every day, but today I don't like you so much. I wouldn't call it hate. It's more like mild aggravation at your choices this past year. With every choice comes a consequence. Your choice to hide cigarettes and booze for your friends means getting up at three o'clock every morning and working right here in the shop with me all through your spring break."

Audrey drew in a long breath and let it out in a huff. "I might as well be in prison."

"Shh . . ." Grace shushed her and held out her hand. "I wasn't finished. Your phone, please."

"What? Why?" Audrey sat up a little straighter. "You can't go through my phone. That's an invasion of my privacy."

"I pay the bill on it, so legally, it is *my* phone, and since you hate me . . ." Grace shrugged. "I won't pay an expensive phone bill for anyone who hates me, so give me your phone."

"No!" Audrey raised her voice.

"All right," Grace said. "Have it your way." She pulled her own cell phone from her pocket, tapped the screen a few times, and went back to work. "Get busy, girl. There were a bunch of little kids and fishermen with grimy hands in here just before closing yesterday, and the display cases and windows need shined up."

"I hate to do windows," Audrey complained.

"We do, too, and we're really glad you're in trouble and have to help us," Grace told her.

Audrey stood up and pulled her phone from the hip pocket of her jeans. She hit the screen several times but nothing happened. Then she whipped around to glare at her mother. "What did you do?"

"Remember when I gave you that phone for your thirteenth birthday?" Grace asked in a calm tone, even though she was anything but that inside. "I had two apps put on it: One that tells me where you are, always. The other is so I can turn the phone off whenever I want. I'll turn it back on at the end of spring break if I feel you have learned to show some respect."

"That's not fair," Audrey sputtered. "I can't believe you are interfering with my privacy."

Grace held out a hairnet. "Fair is in the eye of the beholder—or in this case, the one that pays the phone bill. Put this on and get busy."

Audrey continued to glare at Grace as she pulled her tangled hair up into a ponytail and took a few slow steps toward the utility room.

"Just a minute, kiddo." Grace shook the hairnet at her. "You forgot your hairnet. If an inspector comes in, we could lose our license, so put it on."

Audrey gasped. "What if one of my friends comes in?"

"Then they'll see you wearing a net and shining windows," Grace answered.

Audrey put the thing on but left the blue strand of hair hanging out the side. She turned her back on her mother and opened the small utility room.

Grace tapped Audrey on the shoulder and didn't even flinch when the girl turned around and gave her another dirty look. "*All* of your hair goes under the net—and if it falls out while you are working, I'll either confiscate your tablet and computer when we go home or you can cut that blue streak off at your scalp. Your choice. And, darlin', I love you. This hurts me as much as it does you."

"I hate this place, and I'll sell it when I inherit it," she spat. "And when I'm out of this godforsaken town, I'm going to get a belly ring and a tattoo. I don't know why I can't have one now. Crystal has a butterfly on her shoulder and Kelsey has a rose, and they both have belly button piercings. The only thing we have alike is our blue streaks."

"When I don't pay your bills anymore, you can do whatever you want. And, darlin', who says you'll inherit it?" Grace asked. "Macy is getting married in three months. Her children may be the ones that we name when we make up our will. The blue stuff in the spray bottle is for cleaning the glass, and use paper towels to wipe it off. Don't leave streaks."

Audrey mumbled under her breath as she headed inside the utility room, grabbed the cleanser and paper towels, and headed for the dining room in a huff.

"That was some badass tough love," Sarah whispered and then turned to Macy. "Are you sure you want to have kids after seeing this?"

"I told you, Neal and I are having boys," Macy answered with a smile.

"And if God has a sense of humor and gives you girls?" Sarah asked.

"I'm sending them all to Grace to raise." Macy's blue eyes twinkled. "She makes a good drill sergeant."

Grace wiggled her fingers in front of Macy's face and raised her voice to a high-pitched, eerie tone. "I hereby bless you with five daughters, and all of them will make Audrey look like she has a halo and wings."

Macy's eyes snapped shut, and she covered her face with her hands. "Don't do that! I hated when you did that when we were kids."

"Why wouldn't you want five daughters?" Sarah teased. "I liked growing up in the house with y'all, even if there was only three of us and not five. We had so much fun together."

"Neal and I are having two sons," Macy declared. "We have already named them and are planning to have the first one when we've been married two years. The second one will be born two years after that, and then we'll have our family. I'm the one who is going to break the daughters-only streak." She shot a look across the room at Grace. "Your silly fortune-telling isn't going to work this time."

"We'll see," Grace said and smiled. There had been a few times when her prophecies fell flat—especially when it came to Justin, Audrey's father. Grace had insisted to her mother that Justin would always be there for her, but she had been dead wrong.

"That sounded just like Mama." Sarah giggled.

Grace nodded and did a quick curtsy. "Thank you."

Sarah picked up a tray of glazed doughnuts and carried them to the front of the store. She placed them in the glass display case and glanced up at the clock. An hour ago, the parking lot had been empty, but now she counted several vehicles out there. They didn't close until noon, so Macy might be making more doughnuts after all.

Folks depended on the shop being open until noon. She glanced around to be sure that the four tables were cleaned off and all the crumbs had been swept up from the floors. The black-and-white-tiled floor hadn't changed in more than fifty years, and neither had the four red chrome table-and-chair sets—two on the east end of the long room, two on the other end. The glass doughnut case stretched across the length of the room, with the old cash register sitting at the far end. Pictures of the women who had run the shop in the past hung on the walls, along with old pictures of the town of Devine—from back when the railroad had come through the area and all the way up to the newest sign that had been put up to welcome folks to their small town.

Audrey ignored Sarah but stopped every few minutes to sigh loud enough to raise the dead right up from the Devine Evergreen Cemetery.

"I'm not your boss, as you have told me many times, girl," Sarah finally said, "but you might take a word of advice here. If you will notice, there are folks coming in, and you've already had more than enough time to clean the front of the display case. Get a move on it, and once everyone is inside, work on the door. When they leave, you can clean it again because there will be smudges on it. Your mama wasn't joking when she said she'd make you snip off that strand of blue hair that is sneaking out from your hairnet right now. You might want to put more muscle into work and less into pouting."

"I'm not pouting," Audrey snapped. "And I thought you'd be on my side."

"Own your mistake and do the time for it. That will teach you to be accountable," Sarah told her.

Audrey stomped her foot, tucked her hair up under the net, and went back to work. "They weren't even my cigarettes. I don't smoke, and I told Mama that."

"Who did they belong to?" Sarah asked.

"I'm not a rat," Audrey grumbled.

"Was it *your* whiskey?" Sarah asked. "And if so, where did you get it?"

Audrey shook her head. "Like I said . . ."

"Well, then, your friends are getting off free and probably having a good time over spring break while you are doing chores and will be getting up every morning before daylight," Sarah told her.

"But they're still my friends, and they wouldn't be if I ratted them out," Audrey answered as she finished the door.

"And, honey," Sarah said, lowering her voice, "if they were really your friends, they would take responsibility for their own actions. They're using you, and true friends don't do that."

Audrey shrugged. "It's my life, and I'll live it the way I want to."

"Yep, you can, and you can learn all your lessons the hard way." Sarah turned and went back to the kitchen.

Audrey had been a pretty baby who'd grown up into a cute teenager. She wouldn't ever be tall, not with her genetics. Grace was barely over five feet tall, and Audrey's father, Justin, was only about five feet, six inches—or at least, the sorry sucker had been when he was twenty-one and left Grace to raise his child alone. She'd gotten her long blonde hair from her mother, her brown eyes from Justin, and her smart mouth from her Aunt Sarah.

"I wish I'd given her something other than genes that are constantly getting her into trouble," Sarah muttered as she picked up two more trays of doughnuts.

"What was that?" Grace asked.

"Nothing," Sarah answered. "I was just talking to myself. Do you ever wish that Justin had stuck around and been a father to Audrey?"

"Of course I do, especially on days like today." Grace got started on filling a dozen doughnuts with a fluffy cream cheese pudding. "But he disappeared when he found out I was pregnant. Remember the story of the frog and the scorpion?"

"Yep," Macy answered, "and the moral is that you can't change a person's nature. Justin was the best-looking guy I've ever seen, but he really was a bad-boy type. He probably hasn't grown up or accepted responsibility for anything, even yet."

"And that's why I have to make Audrey accountable," Grace said. "She's got his genes as well as mine. From the time she was three months old, she could flash that smile of hers and bat those brown eyes, and we'd do anything to make her happy."

"Just like you did with Justin, right?" Sarah headed toward the dining room.

"Yep." Grace nodded. "But I learned my lesson about bad boys the hard way. No more of that type ever for me again. If I hadn't been past twenty-one, Mama might have put *me* in a convent during those few months that Justin was around."

Sarah remembered those days well. She had just finished her first year of college and would have been on probation in the fall if she hadn't quit. Grace was pregnant, Justin was in the wind, and they had no idea where he had gone. Macy was a sophomore in high school, and Sarah was needed in the doughnut shop. She had loved the party life at college—but the classes, not so much. She had managed to pass a couple of basic business classes, and those had helped when a blood clot went through her mother's heart, killing her instantly, two months before Audrey was born. She was resentful, angry, and grieving all at the same time; but after a while, all that passed, and she had settled into the family business and routine. Sometimes she wished for a few days off, but that just wasn't possible.

"What are you thinking about so seriously?" Grace asked.

"Life in general and how things can turn around in the blink of an eye."

She carried the trays into the dining area and noticed that Audrey was trying to hide behind the counter. "What's going on here? That door hasn't been cleaned."

"That is"—she pointed toward the door—"Crystal's and Kelsey's mamas coming this way."

"So?"

Audrey rolled her brown eyes toward the ceiling. "They'll see me cleaning windows."

"So?" Sarah asked again, then said, "Good morning, Lisa and Carlita. What can I get you today?"

"Two coffees, black, and half a dozen maple doughnuts," Carlita said.

"We'll take them to go," Lisa said. The woman was a short brunette with brown eyes, so much like her daughter, Crystal, that she often referred to the girl as her mini-me. "Audrey, we heard that you were caught with contraband at school. Our girls are good churchgoing kids, so we can't have them affiliated with someone who smokes and drinks. We've told them to end their friendship with you."

Anger rose in Sarah's heart so fast that she got light-headed. "Sorry, ladies, but we're all out of maple doughnuts."

"I'm looking at a dozen right there," Carlita said.

"We had a call-in order just before you arrived, and they are taken," Sarah said through clenched teeth. She would bet silver dollars to doughnut holes that the contraband belonged to Crystal and Kelsey.

"Then forget the whole order," Carlita snapped and whipped up a forefinger with a perfectly manicured nail to point right at Audrey. "You stay away from our girls. They don't need your kind as friends."

She had jet-black hair, brown eyes, and a temper—something that Kelsey had inherited right along with her mother's hair and eyes. The two women left the shop in a huff, slinging dirty looks over their shoulders and whispering back and forth all the way out the door.

Audrey covered her eyes with her hands and started to cry. "Look what y'all have done."

"Honey, you brought all of this on yourself. We didn't do anything but make you accountable for your mistake," Sarah told her. "Dry your eyes and wait on these next folks coming in here. And you probably won't listen to me, but you need to reconnect to your old friends. They would never ask you to do something like take the rap for a crime you didn't commit."

"I've lost all those friends," Audrey whined. "Raelene doesn't even speak to me anymore."

"Is that the truth, or did you throw her friendship away and quit talking to her when you started running with this new crowd?" Sarah asked.

"It doesn't matter—and besides, I'm not going back to them anyway. Crystal and Kelsey are my real friends," she huffed.

"I'm going to get the last of the doughnuts that Macy and your mama have made. You take care of orders and hold your head up. You don't need those girls in your life." Sarah hurried back to the kitchen.

"How's Audrey doing?" Grace asked.

"She's about to have a meltdown, but Mama told us that whatever doesn't kill us will make us stronger," Sarah said and went on to tell them what had happened. "My first instinct was to tell her to go on to the house and drown her sorrows in ice cream, but she has to learn to own her mistakes."

Grace's face went into what Sarah called her "mama bear" expression and got worse with every second. "I shouldn't hate anyone, but I'm coming real close to that point with both of those girls and their mothers."

Her hands knotted into fists, and Sarah was glad that Carlita and Lisa had left the shop, or she might have been bailing her sister out of jail that afternoon.

"She has to accept responsibility, but it sure don't make it easy on me," Grace said through gritted teeth.

"I understand, and that just about blows holes in what little righteousness I have, too," Macy said. "We all love her so much that it's hard not to feel sorry for her."

"What kind of advice would Mama be giving all of us right about now?" Grace asked. "I could sure use some of her wisdom to help me get control of my temper."

"She would tell me to have a beautiful wedding and wonderful life with Neal." Macy tucked an errant strand of her red hair up under her net. "She would tell you"—she pointed at Grace—"to be tough and make Audrey accountable." Her blue eyes twinkled again as she glanced over at Sarah. "And she would tell *you* to settle down, stop hitting the bars until they shut down on Saturday nights, and to be a better example to your niece."

"Two out of three ain't bad." Sarah picked up the last two trays. "And maybe I will settle down someday soon." She bypassed the opportunity to tell them about the man she'd been seeing for a few months. She wanted meeting him on Sunday to be a surprise. "I see our old guys parking their truck."

"Dependable old Frankie, Ira, and Claud," Grace said as she shed her apron and picked the keys off the rack beside the kitchen door. "They must have been at a cattle sale, or they would have been here when the doors opened this morning."

Macy hung her apron beside Grace's and crossed the kitchen floor. "I was seventeen when they retired and started coming in for breakfast every morning, so it's been fifteen years. I'll make a fresh pot of coffee for them."

Audrey had just finished waiting on a family of six, who had pushed two of the tables together and were having doughnuts and milk. She gave her mother the old stink eye and started toward the kitchen.

"Where do you think you're going?" Grace asked. "You and I are going to stay up here in the front and wait on customers until noon."

"Do I have to wear this thing on my head?" Audrey's tone dripped icicles.

"Today you do because your hair looks like a rat's nest. Tomorrow, if you brush it out good and wear it up, you can take the net off, but if

13

you're needed in the back to work on making doughnuts, then the net goes back on," Grace answered.

"What if my friends come in?" Audrey whined.

"If any of your friends come into the shop, then they'll see you with a net on your hair—unless you have a brush in your purse. If that's the case, then you can go to the bathroom and pull it up into a bun on top of your head, but make sure all the hair is tucked in tight," Grace answered. "I see more customers coming this way, so you better hurry."

Audrey dashed through the door leading into the kitchen, and Grace bit back a smile.

"Not funny," Sarah teased as she arranged the white coffee cups with the Devine Doughnuts logo on a tray.

"It is a little bit," Grace said. "I'm remembering when you had to work one whole summer to pay Mama back for the damage you did to the car when you snuck out and wrecked it on a back road."

Sarah filled three cups and put them on a tray. "I hated that summer almost as bad as Audrey does having to work through her spring break."

Grace nodded. "Maybe she'll think twice before she does something stupid like this again. Did she tell you who she was covering for?"

Sarah shook her head. "Nope. She swears she's not a rat, but we both know it's Crystal and Kelsey. But never fear—they have been banned from ever being her friend again."

"Those girls are nightmares in my Sunday school class," Macy said. "I can't imagine them listening to anything their parents say."

A teenage girl opened the door and glanced around the room as if she were lost or in trouble. She looked like she could break into tears any minute, and her hands were trembling.

"Who do I talk to about applying for a job?" she asked.

Sarah motioned for her to come inside. "Raelene, it's been a while since we've seen you."

"Yes, it has, but . . ." She scanned the room. "But Audrey and I . . . ," she stammered. "We kind of aren't friends anymore, but I'm in trouble and I need a job, and I was hoping that you might need help. A job here would mean I could work in the mornings on a work permit from school and still finish up my classes in the afternoons so I can graduate." She finally stopped for a breath.

"I'm sorry to hear that you're in trouble. We don't need help, but is there something else we can do to help you out?" Grace asked from behind the counter.

"I'll do anything you want. I can clean or wash dishes . . ." Tears began to flow down her cheeks. "I'm sorry. I shouldn't have bothered you." She turned and started out of the store just as the three old guys pushed their way inside.

"Whoa!" Grace said. "Wait just a minute. Don't go yet. Let's talk. Want some doughnuts and milk?"

Raelene shook her head. "No, ma'am. I'm not looking for a hand-out. I *need* a job."

"You come with me." Sarah motioned toward one of the tables to the left. "Sit down and tell me what's going on since your grandmother passed away." Even though she'd never been as desperate as Raelene, she could feel her pain, and she patted the girl on the shoulder.

Raelene didn't argue. "Yes, ma'am," she said and pulled out a napkin from the dispenser to wipe her wet cheeks.

"Did you walk all the way from your house down here? That's four miles, at the very least." Sarah eyed Raelene.

She looked a lot like her mother, whom Sarah heard had left town a few weeks ago with her current boyfriend. At eighteen, Raelene was even shorter than Grace, had thin brown hair that she'd pulled back to the nape of her neck in a ponytail. Her clean but well-worn jeans—no holes in the legs—were a little baggy on her, and her T-shirt was slightly frayed around the neck.

"Tell me what's going on," Sarah said. "Your mother and I graduated together. We didn't stay friends, but we knew each other pretty well back in the day."

"My mama and her new boyfriend moved to California and left me behind. The rent has run out on the house we live in. The food is all gone, and . . ." She closed her eyes, took a deep breath, and went on, "And I'm a straight-A student, and . . ." She opened her eyes and nodded toward Audrey, who had just emerged from the kitchen, her hair wrangled into a sloppy bun perched atop her head. "I figure if she's working here, then I don't have a chance."

"Whether we hire someone or not doesn't have anything to do with Audrey," Sarah said. "What happened between you and her, anyway?"

"She told me that in order to run with the popular crowd, she couldn't be friends with me or any of the little group we've been a part of since we were all in elementary school."

"I see," Sarah said with a nod. "I'm going to get you a glass of milk and a couple of doughnuts to eat while we talk about a job for you. I can tell you right now that you won't make enough money at your age to pay rent and utilities on a house."

One of Raelene's thin shoulders raised in a half shrug. "I'll figure out something if I have a job. I've got a scholarship for the fall, but I have to get through graduation first. I'll sleep in the park, if I have to. The weather is getting warmer, and there's showers in the bathrooms for the campers."

"Don't go anywhere. I'll be back in five." Sarah crossed the room, picked up two glazed doughnuts from the case, put them on a disposable plate, and poured a tall glass of milk.

Audrey rolled her eyes when Sarah came around the counter. "What's *she* doing here?"

"Looking for a job," Sarah answered.

16

Audrey gasped. "You can't hire her! I'd be the laughingstock of the whole school if my friends find out she works here. Crystal and Kelsey will turn their backs on me."

Grace frowned. "Why?"

"She's weird, and a tech weenie," Audrey whispered.

"And what is that?" Grace asked.

"It's what you old people would call a *nerd*," Audrey said with another of her pitiful sighs.

Sarah turned away from Audrey and lowered her voice. "Grace, she's got three months until she graduates, and she's a straight-A student. We heard that her mother had moved, but I had no idea she had left Raelene to fend for herself. The rent has played out, as well as the food."

"Mama, please! Don't do this," Audrey begged.

"I will not turn away a kid in need, especially one of your former friends," Grace said. "Sarah, you do whatever you think is best."

"Mama! I'll work harder, but please . . ." Audrey's hands went into the prayer position.

"We've got an extra bedroom in the south wing," Sarah said. Her niece needed to crawl out of the hole she was digging for herself, and having someone like Raelene around might be just the answer.

"No! Good Lord!" Audrey's hands went to her cheeks. "She can't live in the same house as I do."

Sarah patted her niece on the shoulder. "If *you* needed a home and food, I would hope someone would help you out."

"Speaking of *you* . . ." Grace turned toward Audrey and pointed to the tray on the counter. "Take those three cups of coffee to those guys who are getting settled at their table, and get their doughnut order."

Sarah carried the milk and doughnuts she'd gathered over to where Raelene was waiting. She put them on the table and then sat down across from her. "I've got a deal for you. We have an extra bedroom at our house. The school bus runs right out here on the road every morning at seven thirty, so you can catch it and make all your classes, not just the afternoon ones. We don't really need any help here at the shop, but we do need someone to help with housework and laundry and general cleanup jobs at the house. We can pay you a little bit and give you room and board until you graduate."

Raelene took a sip of the milk and then bit into a doughnut. "Why would you do that for me?"

"Two reasons," Sarah answered. "You are a smart kid who deserves to graduate, but I don't think it's safe for you to sleep in the park. The second thing is that I hate to dust and do dishes. How does fifty dollars a week and room and board sound? You would only need to work about two hours a day for the money, and Sundays will be your free day. I can go with you right now to get your things and move you into your room. You can start by dusting and vacuuming tomorrow morning while we are here at the store. Sound good?"

"It does. You can depend on me," Raelene said. "May I finish my doughnuts first?"

"Yes, of course," Sarah said, and with an inward wince, she continued, "Why did your mama leave you behind?"

"Her boyfriend didn't like me, and she loves him," Raelene answered. "My grandmother was the one who raised me, not Mama. She died a few months ago, and I had to move in with Mama. We didn't know each other so well anyway, so it wasn't hard for her to leave me . . ." She paused. "Or for me to refuse to go with them, either. Mama said that I was eighteen and old enough to make my own way."

"I see." Sarah felt so sorry for the girl that she had trouble keeping tears from her eyes. "Well, you finish up here, and then I'll take you to get your belongings."

"Thank you, and I'd work for room and board. You wouldn't have to pay me," Raelene offered.

Sarah stood up and patted the girl on her shoulder. "That wouldn't be fair. You'll need lunch money and a little bit to buy personal items."

"I don't eat lunch," Raelene said under her breath.

No wonder you are so thin, Sarah thought, but she said, "Why don't you eat lunch?"

"The kids are kind of mean, especially the girls that Audrey is running with these days, so I just go to the library during that hour and do my homework." She shrugged again.

Sarah gritted her teeth to keep from swearing. "Well, you can take your lunch for the rest of the year. There's always sandwich makings in the fridge or leftovers from supper."

Raelene finally smiled. "Thanks again."

Sarah crossed the room and poured herself a cup of coffee. "I just hired a maid for the next three months. She's going to work for room and board and fifty dollars a week."

"Audrey is going to be mortified," Grace whispered, and then went over to sit down across the table from Raelene. She reached out and laid a hand on Raelene's. "I'm glad you are coming to live with us, and we'll be very grateful for your help."

"I hope it doesn't cause problems with Audrey and your family," Raelene said in a low voice.

"My mama used to say that everything works out the way it's supposed to," Grace said.

"I hope she was right," Raelene said.

"You enjoy your breakfast, and this afternoon we'll get you settled into your new room." Grace patted her hand and then headed back to the kitchen, with Sarah right behind her.

"Is that as good as a convent or boot camp?" Sarah asked.

"Pretty dang near," Grace answered.

Chapter Two

*C*laud, Ira, and Frankie were the first in the shop, as usual, on Saturday morning, despite the rain pouring down. They removed their yellow slickers and hung them on the line of hooks to the left of the door and set their cowboy hats on the empty table next to theirs. Grace filled three mugs with coffee and was rounding the end of the counter when several more customers arrived. Then a tall man with dark hair pushed his way into the shop. He set his umbrella by the door and then headed over toward Claud and the other guys' table.

Grace got a little zing when she looked up and saw him. There was something about his smile when he saw the older men, and the pure joy in his expression at seeing friends. But that wasn't anything compared to the immediate attraction—something she hadn't felt in many years.

"This is crazy," she muttered. "I don't even know this man."

"Travis Butler!" Claud exclaimed and pushed his chair back. He met the man halfway across the room for a handshake that turned into a hug. "Come on over here and sit with us. We ain't seen you in a month of Sundays."

"Been a minute, hasn't it? I saw your trucks parked out here and figured this had to be the home of the famous doughnuts you used to bring to the ranch when I was a kid." Travis's deep drawl boomed all over the shop—which had gone quiet as soon as he walked inside.

"Bring another cup of coffee, Grace. We'll share our doughnuts with Travis while we catch up," Claud said.

Grace arranged a dozen doughnuts in a box and set it on a tray with a mug of coffee, a handful of tiny containers of cream, and a couple of packages of sugar. Then she added four forks, a fistful of paper napkins, and four saucers, and carried it to the table.

"I want to introduce you to a friend, Grace," Claud said. "This is Travis Butler. His granddaddy and all of us served on several committees together for the Texas Cattlemen's Association. Holt used to bring Travis with him to the conferences, so we've known him since he was knee-high to a grasshopper."

"I don't think I was ever that short." Travis smiled up at Grace.

"Pleased to meet you," Grace said and set about unloading the tray. Another spark of attraction flashed, and she wondered where and why such feelings were hitting her now, after all these years. Perhaps the way the shop had fallen silent when he entered reinforced it.

"Pleasure is all mine." Travis's smile widened, and chatter picked back up around them. "Claud and these fellows used to bring a couple dozen of these pastries to the conference. Granddad and I always looked forward to getting them. What's your secret?"

Ira chuckled. "Her great-granny started this place, and believe me, there ain't enough money in the state of Texas to make her give up that recipe."

"Are you sure about that?" Travis teased as he reached into the box and brought out one with chocolate icing.

"As sure as anything or anyone can be. It's written in my mother's will that we cannot sell the recipe. And trust me, it would be impossible to mass-produce our doughnuts, anyway," she told him.

He took a long drink of his coffee. "Why is that?"

"Because we make them from scratch. We do not buy the usual premix for the dough, and we make them in small batches—somewhere around two to three dozen each time, depending on whether we leave the middles uncut so we can fill them with our own special cream cheese mix or fruit fillings, or cut the holes out," she answered. "But all that is a moot point since I cannot sell our recipe, and I wouldn't even if we could." Grace took the tray back to the counter.

Then she went to wait on the two women who currently held the top position on her shit list. Her first instinct was to ignore Carlita and Lisa after what they'd said about Audrey not being friends with their hooligan daughters, but Macy would tell her to take the higher ground and be nice. Crystal's mother and Kelsey's mother had grown up in Devine and were Sarah's age—both had always been the town's biggest gossips—and now seemed to be reliving their teenage years through their two girls.

"What can I get y'all this morning?" Icicles dripped from Grace's tone.

"We'll have four maple doughnuts and two cups of decaf coffee," Carlita said with a fake smile. "We like having our coffee here . . . and now that we understand each other—"

Grace cut her off by throwing a palm up so close to her nose that Carlita had to take a step back. "We don't understand each other at all. I've told Audrey repeatedly that your girls were trouble, and I didn't want her hanging out with them."

"Why would you say that?" Lisa asked. "Our girls have been good enough to take your child into their group."

Grace lowered her hand. Arguing with these two would just bring her down to their level. "Yes, they did, and they should be grateful to have her."

She walked away, filled their order, and took it to them. Then she picked up a full coffeepot to take to the men's table to refill their cups. "I wondered if y'all would be out in this nasty weather," she said as she gave each of them a warm-up.

"We're tough," Ira said. "We ain't sugar or salt neither one, so a little rainwater ain't goin' to melt us. Besides, we're cranky if we don't get our coffee and doughnuts in the morning," Ira told her with a broad grin. "You've outdone yourself on these glazed fellers today, darlin'."

"I'm paying today. What we don't eat, I'll take home," Frankie said. "These are good enough to eat even on the second day."

"How do you know that?" Ira asked. "We ain't never had them last that long when I take them home."

"You caught me." Frankie winked at Grace. "But I was just tellin' what I've heard folks say about them. Hey, you want to sell this shop, Grace? What with Macy getting married this summer, y'all are going to be shorthanded. Travis here is in town looking for some land to buy to use for a housing development. You girls could sell your acres and this place in one fell swoop and retire while you're still young enough to travel and have fun."

"Nope," Grace answered without hesitation. "You know I'm not interested in selling. But are y'all thinking about selling all your cows and buying a doughnut shop? You could eat all you want for free and not have to go out in the blistering-hot summer sun or the freezing winter weather to feed the cows or take care of them. Are you planning to learn the art of making doughnuts, or are you going to put your wives to work?"

"Honey, we'd all shrivel up and die if we didn't have cows to gripe about and ranchin' to keep us from getting old," Ira answered. "But Travis here could hire folks to keep the shop open and build a nice development on your land. He's got his fingers in a lot of pies—we've not only bragged about your pastries, but we've taken dozens of them to his grandpa through the years. We think it would be wonderful if folks from coast to coast could get the best doughnuts in Texas, so we've been trying to talk him into buying your recipe and . . ."

Grace shifted her eyes over to Travis. "Are you a baker?"

"Lord no!" Ira answered for him. "He's a businessman. His grand-daddy was a friend of ours and owned a huge ranch, one of the biggest in Texas. Like I said, he's got his fingers in a lot of pies all across this state. Land, oil, construction, and even a car dealership or two."

"*Was* a friend?" Grace asked.

"He died a couple of years back," Travis said.

"I'm so sorry." Grace remembered when her mother had passed and folks said that. She often wondered if they meant it or if it was just words. How could a person be sorry for losing someone that they never knew?

"Thank you," Travis said with half a smile and a nod.

Claud went on to explain more about the man not two feet from her elbow. "Holt—that would be Travis's granddad—sold the ranch when he found out he didn't have long to live, and Travis's daddy decided he wanted to enjoy a few years of life that didn't involve sitting behind a desk, so he retired and turned his corporation over to Travis a while back."

Grace noticed that telling all his personal business was embarrassing Travis and tried to shift the conversation over to something else. "Think it's going to rain all day?"

The expression on his face thanked her even if he didn't say the words.

But Frankie mowed right over her question. "He goes into a small town, sets up a factory or maybe a car dealership, and hires folks to run it for him. We been tryin' to get him to bring something to Devine for over a year."

"Well, y'all can forget about this business. If he wants to put in a factory, I'm sure that would be good for our economy, but the Double D isn't for sale," Grace told them. "I'll make sure Audrey keeps your coffee heated up. Looks like this rain is going to last all day, so you'll need to be warm when you go back out in it." She sure didn't want to have to tell them again and again that her shop was not for sale.

Claud nodded and held up his mug in a toast. "Might be a little muddy or messy, but a rancher never complains about the rain."

"Amen to that," Ira and Frankie said in unison and touched their mugs to his.

Grace went over to warm up Lisa's and Carlita's coffee. She wished they would take their orders to go, but evidently that wasn't going to happen.

"We couldn't help but overhear that there might be some new business coming to town," Lisa said.

"Maybe so," Grace said. "What has that got to do with you?" She turned to walk away.

"We've got to get home and tell our husbands." Carlita's whisper carried far enough that Grace heard it. "They could get in on the ground floor and make millions. Just think, we might have a summer home in France in a couple of years."

"Leave the coffee," Lisa said. "This news is too hot to let sit on the back burner."

Grace just shook her head and went on into the kitchen. Those two women hadn't changed a bit since they were in high school.

"Hey," she said.

Both Macy and Sarah looked up from what they were doing.

"Y'all want to sell the business?" she asked. "Seems that our old cowboys out there are trying to talk a businessman into buying us out. Carlita and Lisa are already planning to talk their husbands into getting in on the deal so they can have a summer home in France."

"No. Not just *no* but *hell no!*" Sarah said.

"Not in a million years," Macy added.

Audrey looked up from the sink, where she was washing dishes. "Yes! Can we move tomorrow?"

All three women whipped around to face her.

"Why would you say that?" Macy asked. "This is your inheritance."

"If you're lucky," Grace added.

Audrey made a sour face at her mother. "You've moved Raelene into our home. I have to face my friends at school after spring break, and by then they'll all know—that's even if they're still my friends after what their mothers said. Now that they know Raelene, the queen of tech weenies, is living with me, they'll turn their backs on me for sure. So, yes, sell this place and let's move. Can we move to Paris, France, maybe even get a house right next to Crystal and Kelsey?" Audrey asked. "The shopping there would be wonderful."

"We're not selling," Grace said without a hint of a smile.

Macy frowned. "If he did make us an offer and y'all were willing, I *might* sign on the dotted line. I wouldn't have to drive down here from San Antonio every day, and I could use some of the funds to buy the home of my dreams for me and Neal to live in and not feel guilty about spending that much money."

"Honey, you've got enough money stashed away that you can buy a mansion, if that's what your dream house is," Sarah said.

"Well," Audrey huffed and went back to washing dishes, "if I owned this place, I'd sell to the first person who showed me the money."

Grace's mama's voice popped into her head. *Bite your tongue if you have to, but don't argue with her. She's got some growing up to do—just like you did at her age. In time, she'll change her mind.*

Macy changed her clothes three times that Sunday morning before she finally decided on a simple blue dress and a white cardigan. Neal always complimented her when she wore blue. His romantic nature and kind heart were just two of the many things she loved about him. She held out her engagement ring—a sweetheart-cut carat set on a wide gold band—to catch the sunlight flowing through her bedroom window.

"I'm just the luckiest woman in the whole world." She smiled as she moved her hand to make the heart-shaped diamond sparkle even more. Neal had promised her a ruby necklace—to match her hair—for their first anniversary. She had told him that his love was enough of a present and that he didn't need to buy expensive gifts for her, but he'd just smiled and given her one of those kisses that made her go weak in the knees.

She hummed "Amazing Grace" as she followed the aroma of coffee and bacon wafting down the hallway from the kitchen. The original part of the house was almost a hundred years old and had started out as a small two-bedroom place built of fieldstone not long after the town was named after Judge Thomas Jefferson Devine. One of Macy's first memories was sitting on her mother's lap and hearing the story of how Devine had been the inspiration for the name of their doughnut shop.

One of the grandparents had added three more rooms and another bathroom onto it, and then another grandparent had built a second wing with two more rooms and another bathroom on the other side. Macy had always loved the sprawling feel of the place and would miss it when she moved into Neal's tiny efficiency apartment in a prominent San Antonio hotel. But that was only for a few months. He already had his eye on a couple of houses that he wanted them to look at to buy as soon as his year of being the assistant manager of the hotel was finished. At that time, he would have learned the job and could move to wherever he wanted.

She breezed into the kitchen to find Grace and both girls at the table. The tension was so thick that a machete would have trouble cutting through it, and the air around them was cold enough to freeze every barbed-wire fence in hell. "Good morning. Who's going to church with me this morning?"

"That would be me and Audrey," Grace said, "and Raelene, if she wants to go."

"Mama!" Audrey cut her eyes over at Raelene. "I don't want to go to church."

"You need some Jesus right now." Grace used her fingers to pick up a piece of bacon from the platter in the middle of the table. "Consider it your only day to see your friends since you will be working at the shop the whole week. You'll know by the way they treat you if you've been kicked out of the mean-girl club."

"That's harsh, even for you, Mama." Audrey pouted. "We are not mean girls. We are popular, and next year Crystal and Kelsey are going to help me get a place with the cheerleaders."

"I'd love to go to church, if I'm not needed here," Raelene said.

Macy pulled out a chair and sat down. She slathered a biscuit with butter and then scooped scrambled eggs and bacon onto her plate. "I love Sundays, when we can have breakfast food and sleep later than two thirty."

"And go to church and sit beside Neal, right?" Grace teased.

"That's the best part. God is so good to have sent Neal into our shop at Christmas," Macy said. "I still can't believe that he loves me. And speaking of that, we're spending the whole day together, and he says he has a surprise for me. I'm hoping that we're going to look at a house. His apartment at the hotel he manages is so small that . . ." She paused and smiled.

"You couldn't cuss a cat without getting a hair in your mouth," Grace finished for her. "Mama used to say that all the time."

Raelene giggled and Audrey shot another dirty look down the table at her.

"What?" Raelene raised a dark brow. "That was funny."

"Yes, it was," Grace agreed. "And it was really nice to come home to a clean house yesterday and not have to spend our entire afternoon stripping beds and doing laundry."

"Or dusting and vacuuming," Macy added. "I even got my own personal laundry caught up, so now I can spend the whole afternoon with Neal and not feel guilty."

"If you girls are finished, you should go get dressed," Grace said.

Audrey pushed back her chair, put on her best hangdog look, and shuffled out of the kitchen.

Raelene picked up her plate and Audrey's and carried both to the sink. "Macy, I really should stick around here and do these dishes. The flower beds look like they could use some help, and the porch needs a good mopping."

"The flower beds are Sarah's bailiwick," Grace said, "and the porch can wait until next week. We'll all go to church together."

Raelene grimaced. "But . . ."

Grace stuffed the last of the eggs and bacon into two biscuits. "There's no buts, Raelene. Get ready. Macy teaches the teenage class, and she's asked me to sit in on it today, so you'll have friends there."

"Y'all have been too good to me"—Raelene's glassy eyes were about to spill tears when she turned around to face Grace and Macy—"for me to be an embarrassment to Audrey. She was a good friend to me. High school gets us all riled up."

"Audrey will be fine," Grace said. "She's pouting because of her decision to take the rap for her friends. That was her choice, and now she has to be accountable for it."

"My granny used to tell me that kind of thing all the time," Raelene said as she left the room.

Macy poured herself another cup of coffee and sat back down. "Think Raelene and Audrey will ever be friends again? She was sure easier to live with back when she ran with that group of girls."

"Probably not, but it would be nice if they were," Grace answered. "Raelene's grandma, Hilda, was not of the upper class here in Devine, but she was a wonderful person. She's done a good job of raising that child. Raelene's mother, Geneva, was a handful and pretty much gave the baby to Hilda to raise from the time she was born."

"Mama used to take a couple dozen doughnuts up to her about once a month," Macy said. "I went with her one time when I was a little girl, and Hilda was worried about Geneva even back that far. I had forgotten all about that until you mentioned it."

"She had a right to be worried," Grace said. "Geneva has always had a wild streak."

"Wilder than Sarah?" Macy whispered.

"Oh, yeah," Grace replied and nodded. "She would make Sarah look like an angel. But I've got a confession to make. When Geneva got pregnant with Raelene, I was just like Audrey and her little buddies, and I gossiped behind her back. A year later, I was in the same predicament. That taught me a valuable lesson about judging."

Macy took a sip of her coffee and set the cup back down. "Is that why Sarah gave her a job and took her in?"

Grace finished off her coffee and took the cup to the sink. "Probably. She would have remembered Hilda and Geneva—and I feel like at one time, they were friends."

"Small towns," Macy said with a sigh. "I'm glad that I'm moving to San Antonio this summer."

"You'll miss Devine. I know you will." Grace chuckled.

"I'll be coming back every day to work in the shop," Macy said, "at least until Neal and I start our family, and then I'm giving you and Sarah my part of this place."

Grace held up a palm. "We're not going to have that conversation for a while. We've still got a wedding to plan and lots of doughnuts to make between now and the end of June."

"Do you think you and Sarah will ever get married?" Macy asked as she stood up and took the first step out of the kitchen.

"Can't speak for my sister, but not me," Grace answered. "Audrey wouldn't adapt well to a stepdad, and there's not a man on the earth who could endure raising a teenage girl that wasn't his child."

"But what if a guy like Neal came along and swept you off your feet, and what if Audrey loved him?" Macy pressed.

"Jesus is in heaven," Grace told her.

"What's that got to do with anything?" Macy asked.

Grace raised an eyebrow and shook her head slowly. "Think about it."

Macy gasped. "Oh! I get it. A man would have to be as perfect as our Lord and Savior to ever put up with Audrey. Well, miracles do happen."

"But not for me—and, honey, just a word of advice . . ." Grace lowered her voice. "Don't put Neal up on too high of a pedestal. He's human, but he's also a man. He's not perfect, and when he falls off that pedestal, if it's all the way up in the clouds, it could easily tear apart your relationship. And I am definitely speaking from experience."

"He's not Justin," Macy snapped. "He would never hurt me like Justin did you."

Grace crossed the room and patted Macy on the shoulder. "I hope not. He wouldn't want to face the consequences of his actions if he did. If we're going to make Sunday school, we'd better put a rush on things."

"I'll meet all y'all at the car in ten minutes," Macy said. "I'm glad you're sitting in on my class this morning. I need you there, Grace. The kids have gotten out of control, and I don't know what to do. Only one boy even participates, and he acts like it's an embarrassment to speak up in front of the rest of the class."

"How long has this been going on?" Grace asked.

"Weeks, maybe months," Macy admitted. "I didn't want to say anything because Audrey is in the class, and I didn't want to get her in trouble."

Grace gave Macy a quick hug. "Well, today's the day she'd better be on her best behavior, or she might not get her phone back until summer. Meet you at the car in ten."

Later, Macy and Grace met in the living room at the same time and were heading out the door when Audrey yelled, "Shotgun!"

"Too late," Grace told her when she reached the porch. "I've already reserved it for myself."

"But that means . . . ," Audrey sputtered.

31

"It means you and Raelene will have to ride in the back." Grace led the way to the car, where Macy was sliding in behind the wheel and Raelene was in the back seat.

"Mama, why are you being so mean to me?" Audrey whispered, but the chill was there, as clear as if she'd yelled.

"Be careful, my child," Grace warned her. "I won't tolerate you being hateful." She wrapped her arm around Audrey's shoulder and gave her a hug all the same. "I love you too much to be mean to you, darlin' girl. Did you ever think back when Raelene was your friend? Did *she* ever ask you to lie for her?"

"I've chosen different friends—true friends, thank you very much," Audrey said out the corner of her mouth, "and Raelene will never be my friend again. I have to share *my* bathroom with her and let her live in *my* house, but she's just our maid."

"That is enough. If I hear you say she's just a maid again, you will be very, very sorry," Grace cautioned her daughter. "And be forewarned, if you go to school and bully her because she works for us, there will be consequences."

"I'm not a bully, but I won't sit with her on the bus or be all sweet to her at school, either. My friends and I don't like her kind." Audrey stomped her foot.

"Seems like that was about what Crystal's and Kelsey's mamas told you—they didn't like *your* kind. You might remember that they feel about you like you do about Raelene these days. Now, go get in the SUV and quit arguing with me," Grace told her.

"Crystal and Kelsey will never feel like that, no matter what their mamas say," Audrey hissed under her breath, then crawled all the way back to the third seat to avoid sitting beside Raelene.

She looked out the side window all the way from the house to the church parking lot. As soon as the car stopped, she bailed out of the vehicle and practically jogged across the parking lot to where a group of her friends had gathered.

Macy looked up at Raelene in the rearview mirror and said, "Come on with me and Grace. We'll take you inside and show you around. This church is a little bigger than the one where you and Hilda went."

"I miss my granny so much," Raelene said.

"I know you do. I still miss my mama, and she's been gone for years. Your granny was one of her dear friends," Grace answered. "This is a small town, sweetie. Everyone knows everyone, and there's a lot of folks who loved Hilda."

"That's the problem a lot of times, isn't it?" Raelene whispered.

Macy looped her arm through Raelene's. "Or the blessing. It all depends on how you look at it."

Bright sunshine came through the window of Travis's penthouse apartment on Sunday morning. He laced his fingers behind his head and stared at the ceiling. He had no doubts about buying land for a housing development in Devine. The houses would probably be sold before they could finish building them. Folks—especially those with children—were looking for smaller towns that weren't far from San Antonio. A thirty-minute commute wouldn't be much different from going home during rush hour when they lived only across town.

But the idea of owning a doughnut shop? Even if Grace Dalton would sell him the shop and her recipes for what had to be the best pastries he had ever eaten . . . He sat straight up in bed and grabbed his glasses from the bedside table.

"What if I went really big with it?" He always talked to himself when he was plowing through a problem. "What if I put in a factory and turned out her doughnuts in mass production and shipped them all over the United States?"

She said very emphatically that she would not sell, the annoying voice in his head reminded him.

"Everyone has a price," Travis argued as he got dressed and called his best friend and CEO, Calvin.

"Are you coming to church with us?" Calvin asked.

"Not this morning," Travis answered. "I'm going to open up the office and work on some figures about a business opportunity. I just wanted to let you know that I wouldn't be there."

"Maggie will be disappointed. She invited a really sweet woman to go to lunch with us," Calvin said.

"Sorry about that, but I've told you both time and time again that I'm not interested in dating," Travis said.

What about Grace Dalton? Would you go out with her? the voice in his head whispered.

"Hush," Travis said.

"I didn't say anything, but I will now. You need to get back out there, my friend. You are too young to do nothing but work," Calvin warned him for what seemed like the millionth time since Erica had walked out on him.

"I wasn't talking to you," Travis said.

"Point proven." Calvin chuckled. "You talk to yourself to have company! You have to be lonely, even if you won't admit it. See you tomorrow at work, and we'll discuss this new venture you're thinking about."

"Yes, we will," Travis said. "Give Maggie and the girls a hug for me."

"Will do," Calvin said.

Now, about Grace Dalton, he thought. Yes, he would go out with her in a heartbeat. She was beautiful—and more importantly, she had grit.

Chapter Three

Sarah propped her chin up on her elbow and looked her fill of Joel McKay. Sunlight streamed in between the blinds on the motel window, leaving stripes of shadows on his handsome face. His black hair was all messy, and he sported a day's worth of dark whiskers—all that only made him sexier in her eyes. They'd been seeing each other every week since right after Thanksgiving, and today she was going to ask him to go to Sunday dinner with her. She wanted her family to meet him, to get to know the man she had fallen in love with over the past four months. She touched the little gold heart necklace he'd given her for Christmas. The romantic note that she had put away with her other keepsakes said *I'm giving you my heart and all my love.*

No one, not even Audrey, had noticed her necklace; but then, Sarah loved jewelry, so they probably thought it was one of the many that she owned. She wanted to wake him for one last bout of sex before she asked him to meet her family, but she wanted a shower and coffee even more. She eased out of bed, pulled on her jeans and a shirt, and made her way to the motel lobby. They always had coffee—if you could call it that—and packaged pastries. After the hunger she'd built up the night before, neither tasted too bad.

She filled two cups with coffee so thin, she could see the bottoms of the disposable cups; put lids on them; and picked up a couple of Danish rolls. "Not as good as Devine Doughnuts, but this will hold me until

Sunday dinner," she muttered and thought about Grace's pot roast that was probably already in the slow cooker.

Joel was still curled up, sleeping soundly, so she set his breakfast on the nightstand, and stumbled and spilled a little bit of her coffee on the carpet. She set the cup down and grabbed a fistful of tissues. She dropped down on her knees to clean up the mess and noticed a phone under the bed. Thinking it might be hers, she picked it up and stared at the picture that popped up on the screen. She tapped it and found a message that had arrived right after midnight: Happy Anniversary, my darling Joel. Your folks are keeping the kids for us this afternoon and tonight, and I've booked a room for us at our favorite hotel. We'll have room service and spend the whole day in bed. Chocolate strawberries and champagne have already been ordered. It was signed with a heart emoji, from a contact labeled *Camille*.

This couldn't be true. Sarah Dalton did not date married men; that was the first question she had asked Joel when he sat down beside her at the bar. He had said that he wasn't, and never had been, but that someday he wanted a family. She looked at the picture again, and those three children looked just like Joel. She noticed that the woman was wearing the same heart necklace she was. She jerked the chain around her neck so hard that it broke. Anger boiled up like hot lava in her heart. She glared at Joel, amazed that the heat flowing from her didn't turn him into nothing but a greasy spot on the sheets. She was way too mad to cry—both at him for duping her and at herself for not checking the man out before she fell in love with him. She glanced down at the broken necklace in her hand and thought about using the chain to strangle him. Jail for the rest of her life might be worth it, but she couldn't leave three kids without a father—no matter how worthless the cheating son of a bitch was.

She couldn't choke him or smother him, so she laid the broken necklace on her pillow, along with his phone. Then she pulled on her cowboy boots, picked up her purse, and walked out of the motel room.

She got into her truck and slapped the steering wheel until her hands turned red. Afterward, she just sat there, almost drowning in anger. "There's no fool like an old fool—or one that's ready to settle down, either," she moaned. "At thirty-five, I should be smarter than this."

Her mother's voice popped into her head. *Nothing to do now but get past it. Fool me once, shame on you. Fool me twice, shame on me. Remember that and move on. He's not worth fretting about.*

"But I loved him . . ." Sarah blinked several times to keep the tears at bay and then folded her arms over the steering wheel and rested her forehead on them. The squeaking noise of a door opening and shutting made her sit up straight. If Joel had found the necklace and phone, and was coming with an excuse about his behavior, she didn't want to hear it. But it wasn't Joel. She blinked a few more times, but the couple practically having vertical sex right in front of her didn't change.

"Sweet Jesus and all the angels in heaven," she whispered. "That's Darla Jo and Neal."

There was no doubt about who they were when Darla Jo walked Neal to her little blue sports car, kissed him a couple more times right there not ten feet away from Sarah. Then the two of them got into the car and drove away. Sarah was stunned speechless and couldn't even blink until she heard a vehicle come to a screeching halt and park in the spot that Darla Jo had just vacated.

A car door slammed, and a tall woman with blonde hair marched from the vehicle up to the motel door that Sarah had just come out of not five minutes ago. She pounded on it, but when Joel didn't answer, she went back to her car, opened the trunk, and threw garbage bags toward the motel.

"I know you are in there with some hussy, and you promised me after the last one that you wouldn't cheat anymore!" The woman's screams pierced the air. "Don't come home begging for another chance. You've had enough."

Sarah slid down as far as she could in the pickup's seat. She was peeking up over the dashboard and hoping the blonde wouldn't find her when Joel opened the door.

"What's going on out here?" he asked. "Have you gone stark ravin' mad? And what's all these garbage bags?"

"They're your things," the woman yelled. "I hope your mistress loves you enough to take your sorry cheating self into her place because you don't have one at our home anymore."

"Come on in, Camille." Joel stood to one side and motioned her into the room. "No one is in here. We played poker in this room last night, and since the boys rented it, I slept here. Look in the bathroom and under the bed. I didn't have a woman in here."

"You lyin' bastard," Sarah whispered.

Camille brushed past him, but before he could even take a step, she was storming back out. "I found this on the pillow. It's just like the one you gave me. I'm seeing a divorce lawyer tomorrow morning. We are finished." She threw the broken necklace in his face and stomped over to her car, leaving him standing there with the chain hanging on his ear.

He's all yours now, the voice in her head said loud and clear.

"What would I want with someone who cheats and doesn't even think about the effect it will have on his family?" she asked as she started the engine and left the parking lot, glad that she hadn't left her vehicle right in front of the room like she usually did.

She didn't want to think about Joel or his wife but let her mind drift to how hurt Macy would be when she found out about her darling Neal cheating on her with Devine's black widow—the very one who'd married two elderly men and then cashed in on insurance and property when they each died less than a year after the weddings.

Sarah felt like she needed a long, hot shower after everything that had gone on in the past hour. She was the Darla Jo in the situation with Joel, even if she hadn't known the man was married. Darla Jo had to know that Neal was engaged to Macy. Everyone in town had been talking about it—calling it a fairy-tale story—for months. She could barely wrap her own mind around everything she'd just witnessed; how in the world was she ever going to convince Macy of it? One thing was for sure: she wasn't going home until the family had left for church, because she needed some time to think.

"What do I do now, Mama?" she pleaded softly. "If that Travis person came to the shop today and offered to buy it, I'd sign on the dotted line just like Audrey would to get out of town when the crap hits the fan. Is this an omen that all three of us need to start over somewhere other than Devine, Texas?"

Her mother didn't have any answers, but Sarah knew she would have to tell Macy eventually. Maybe not that day—but before long so that she could figure out what to do. Knowing Macy and how much she loved Neal, if this was a one-time fling, she would forgive him and the wedding would go on as planned.

She wondered if Joel would sweet-talk Camille into one more chance—maybe for the children's sake.

With a heavy heart for herself and for Macy, she drove south toward Devine. From the lights flowing out of the kitchen window, she knew the family was probably having breakfast. Sarah usually got home in time to shower and change for church, but she wouldn't be attending services this morning. She had to work up the courage to face Macy and try to muster the willpower not to do bodily harm to both Neal and Joel.

She parked her truck in the pasture surrounding their house, got out, and sat on the tailgate. She and Joel had watched a lovely sunrise through the motel window that morning and talked about how in love they were. Then he had drifted off to sleep again. Did he use the same lines on all his women? What kind of lies had he told his wife about not coming home on Saturday nights for the past four months?

She hopped down from the tailgate and opened the passenger door to her truck, took out a warm root beer, and pulled the tab.

She would have preferred a beer, or even a glass of white wine, but she was grateful that Audrey had failed to unload the six-pack of soda the day before when she had helped take in the groceries. She went back to the tailgate, finished her root beer, and crushed the can with her bare hands. She almost smiled when a cottontail rabbit ran out in a blur at the sound. Not even a cute little scared bunny was enough to get her out of her mood this morning. The last time she'd felt this much rage and disappointment all rolled up into one big ball had been when she was a teenager. She had cried for a week when her boyfriend broke up with her two days before prom so he could take another girl. She was a grown woman now, and she didn't want to shed another tear—but she did want to crush Joel and Neal both like she had the can, throw them under the mesquite bush, and let the coyotes have them for supper.

"I bet Grace felt like this when Justin left her high and dry," she muttered as she hopped down off the tailgate, slammed it shut with a force, and rounded the truck. She slid in behind the wheel and started the engine, but she didn't put the truck in gear until she saw the rest of her family come out of the house and get into Macy's car.

She drove down the rutted pathway grown up with weeds and parked close to the back of the house. The aroma of pot roast wafted out across the yard when she unlocked and opened the door, but she didn't even stop for a cup of coffee. She headed straight for the bathroom, stripped out of her boots and clothing, adjusted the water, and stepped under the spray. Until then she had been too angry to cry, but there was no controlling the tears at that point.

"Men!" she said under her breath when there were no more tears to cry. She got out of the shower, dried, dressed in a T-shirt and a pair of underpants, and fell into bed. In minutes she was dreaming of moving from the house where she'd lived her whole life to a huge mansion in a gated community.

"Hey, girl, dinner is on the table." Grace's voice woke her, and for just a split second, she was still in that big, beautiful house all alone. She didn't want to live in a huge place by herself, but it made her happy that Grace was there.

"Dinner?" she mumbled as she sat up. "What time is it?"

"Twelve thirty. Your eyes are bloodshot and swollen. Have you been crying, or are you hungover?" Grace asked. "We missed you at church this morning."

Sarah slung her legs over the edge of the bed. Everything from a few hours before washed over her, bringing with it all the emotions again. She felt herself age ten years in those moments, and she still couldn't imagine telling her sweet cousin what she had seen. "We need to talk. Where's Macy?"

"With Neal," Grace answered. "Are you all right? You look horrible, Sister. Has someone died?"

"Are you sure Macy isn't here?" Sarah asked.

"Positive," Grace replied with a worried look on her face. "Neal is with her, so she's okay. They were going out to dinner; then she was hoping that they would look at some houses to buy. She can't stand the idea of living in a hotel permanently, even if the room is like a small apartment. Neal says that his job requires him to be on call all the time, especially after-hours at night, but Macy wants to raise a family in a house with a white picket fence and a yard."

"Give me five minutes to pull on some pajama pants," Sarah said after a long sigh. "We'll talk after we have dinner—and it's got to be somewhere that Audrey can't eavesdrop."

"You are scaring me. Did you have an accident and hurt someone?" Grace asked. "That's the only thing I can think of that would make you look like a ghost."

"Nope, but let's have dinner and then take a drive." Sarah pulled a pair of sweatpants from a dresser drawer and stepped into them.

"Maybe a hint?" Grace asked on her way to the door.

"Don't ever fall in love," Sarah answered as she led the way down the hall to the kitchen. Her own heart was breaking, but she would get over it. She wasn't sure that Macy—with her sweet nature—ever would.

When Sarah sat down at the table, Raelene raised her eyes and smiled. Audrey looked like she could chew up railroad ties and spit out toothpicks.

Grace settled into her normal place at the other end and said, "Audrey, you can say grace today."

"I'd rather not," Audrey said.

"I'll do it, if that's okay," Raelene offered.

"Thank you," Grace said with a nod.

Raelene said a short prayer and thanked God for giving her a roof over her head and new friends, and asked that the hands that prepared the food be blessed.

"That was sweet," Sarah said, her voice cracking a little. She'd been wallowing in her own misery so much that she'd forgotten all the blessings in her life—family, a new friend, and a chance to live another day. Poor little Raelene hadn't had any of those things, and now Audrey was treating her like she had the plague.

"So how did church go this morning?" Sarah didn't care about the sermon or even the hymns, which were her favorite part of the service, but she did want to talk about something—anything—to get her mind off Joel and Neal.

"The preacher talked about how important it is to forgive like Joseph did his brothers, and we discussed the different attitudes of his brothers in Sunday school," Raelene said. "I enjoyed being in that church. If I was staying in Devine, I might even change my membership."

Audrey's head raised a little, and she shot a look across the table. "Where do you think you're going?"

"I have a full two-year scholarship to this little junior college in Oklahoma." Raelene took the platter from Grace and loaded her plate with pot roast, potatoes, and carrots. "I get to live in the dorm, and I'll have enough grant money to even pay for my cafeteria-meal ticket."

"How did you get that?" Audrey's tone had changed very little.

"Lose the attitude or pay the price. You really are acting like a mean girl, and that's not acceptable in this house," Grace said in a low voice.

"I applied for it and sent them a demo tape. The choir director helped me make it," Raelene answered.

Audrey took the platter when it came her way and scooped a few potatoes and some pot roast onto her plate. "What if I don't care about living in this house, Mama?"

Raelene blushed. "Maybe it would be best if I moved out."

"You will not," Sarah said. "Audrey, you're being a mean little snot. This girl was your friend until last fall, and she's done nothing to warrant you treating her like dirt."

"You're not my mama," Audrey countered.

"Yes, but *I* am," Grace said, "and this is going to stop. You can be civil, or you can suffer the consequences."

"Yes, ma'am," Audrey said, but her tone was far from sweet.

"What kind of demo tape?" Sarah asked.

"Songs. I will be singing in the choir," Raelene said. "In addition to my scholarship, I get a small stipend for living expenses, and I get to travel with the choir on out-of-state trips. I've never been anywhere outside of Texas, so that's pretty exciting."

Sarah's heart felt a little lighter just thinking that this kid was finally getting a lucky break. She would get out of the small town where she'd been branded as weird—*a tech weenie,* as Audrey had called her.

"But the nursing program is what I'll be enrolled into. In two years, if I pass my state tests, I will be an RN," Raelene said. "It's the only place I know that I can finish in that time and be able to get a job and support myself."

"That's fantastic," Grace said. "I hope that someday Audrey can get a good scholarship like that. Right now, she's failing algebra."

43

"I'd be glad to help you, Audrey," Raelene said. "Math and science are my strong points. If you want, I might be able to catch you up over spring break."

"Not in a million years," Audrey said with a sneer. "I'd rather flunk."

"If you do, you get to repeat all the classes that you've failed, and it might even keep you from having enough credits to graduate," Sarah said.

"Raelene's offered you free tutoring lessons," Grace added. "You should take her up on that."

"Well, maybe," Audrey agreed, "but that doesn't mean we're friends. I don't know why I have to take algebra, anyway. When I inherit the doughnut shop and this house and all the land we own, I'm going to sell it to the highest bidder. Then I'm going to travel the world. I'll shop in Paris and Rome and London, and send gifts to Crystal and Kelsey."

Raelene looked across the table at Audrey and didn't even blink when she said, "I don't want to be your friend, Audrey. Why would I want to hang out with someone who treats me like you do?"

Audrey looked like she had been hit by a streak of lightning. "But . . . everyone wants to be popular," she sputtered.

"Not me. Popularity is overrated," Raelene said.

Sarah chuckled for the first time that day. "Good for you for figuring that out, Raelene. And, Audrey, I would like to know: What will you do when the money runs out? It won't last forever with that lifestyle."

"I will marry a rich man," Audrey said with half a smile.

"Good luck with that," Grace muttered.

"Amen!" Sarah agreed.

Chapter Four

*G*race felt as if a stone were sitting in her chest where her heart used to be when she and Sarah left the house to go for a drive that afternoon. The only thing she could imagine was that whatever her sister had to tell her must concern Audrey. All kinds of scenarios played out in her mind: Sarah had seen Audrey with a fake ID at the bar she frequented on Saturday nights. Or she'd heard that Audrey had been smoking more than cigarettes. She had been such a problem child since she began her sophomore year that nothing would surprise Grace—and yet she sent up a prayer that the news Sarah had wouldn't be anything to do with her daughter.

"Okay, spit it out," Grace said the moment that her sister had driven around to the front of the doughnut shop and parked in the middle of the gravel lot.

"This is probably far enough that no one can sneak up on us and eavesdrop." Sarah checked the rearview and side mirrors, turned the engine off, and faced her sister. "First of all, I'm sorry for the way I treated you when Justin left. And for the way I talked to you when Mama passed away. Blaming you being pregnant for her death wasn't right."

"Good Lord!" Grace gasped. "What brought all this on fifteen years after the fact? And I don't remember you treating me so badly or blaming me for anything."

"I didn't verbally, but I did in my heart, and that's just as bad," Sarah said after a long sigh. "I thought you were a fool to even date Justin in high school. Then Mama died, and I needed to be angry at someone. My whole life changed. You were supposed to be old enough to know better than to get pregnant. And I might have been on probation the next semester of college, but at least I wouldn't have been in Devine, Texas, working at a doughnut shop for the rest of my life."

Grace grimaced. "Again, what brought all this on now? I thought we were all happy running the shop together."

"We are now, but here lately I've been itching to settle down and have children of my own. I've loved helping you raise Audrey, but . . ." Sarah paused. "I was hoping for someone to share my life with, and maybe even have a daughter or two to carry on the family business since Macy is determined to have all boys."

A little of the rock in Grace's chest chipped away. "Boys can make doughnuts just as well as girls—and from the expression on your face, this isn't just about me getting pregnant or raising Audrey as a single mother. I can tell something is wrong. Are you pregnant? Do you have a boyfriend that you've been keeping secret? Maybe a bad boy like . . ." Grace gasped. "Don't tell me that Justin has come back and you're dating him."

"Good Lord, no to most of that!" Sarah answered. "But you nailed it on the secret boyfriend. Right after Thanksgiving, I met a guy named Joel at a bar up near Hondo, and we hit it off from that first night. He said he didn't usually go to honky-tonks. I said I was there to have a few drinks and dance some leather off my boots, like I do every Saturday night. By Christmas, we were skipping the bar and going straight to a cheap motel that I usually paid for. I rationalized it by telling myself that I would spend that much or more on drinks."

"And you fell in love," Grace said with a smile.

"I did," Sarah whispered, "and I fell out of love this morning. Evidently, Joel's phone came out of his pocket and had slid up under

the bed. I spilled coffee and was cleaning up the mess when I found it."
Her voice cracked, and a single tear rolled down her cheek.

Grace laid a hand on Sarah's shoulder. "Go on."

"I understand what you must have felt back then." Sarah covered
Grace's hand with hers. "I found out this morning that he was married.
I've been seeing him every Saturday for almost four months, and we've
talked and texted every day. I was going to ask him to come to Sunday
dinner and meet y'all today."

"What happened?" Grace could feel her sister's pain so much that
she wanted to find this Joel man and kick his ass.

"I grabbed the phone, and a picture of a woman and three kids
popped up on the screen. The text said *happy anniversary* and that they'd
be going to a hotel to celebrate," Sarah went on softly. "I've been sleeping with a married man who was telling his wife that he was playing
cards all night with his buddies."

"What did *you* do?" Grace asked. "Did you beat him to death with
a hotel lamp? Do I need to provide an alibi for you?"

"I laid the phone and the heart necklace that he had given me for
Christmas on my pillow and walked out the door. His wife was wearing
the same necklace, so evidently, he gave us each one—the sorry bastard. I went out to my truck with intentions of coming straight home,
but . . ." Sarah took a breath. "I was mad at myself for being duped, mad
at Joel for conning me. I was shaking too bad to drive, so I just sat there
in my truck for a few minutes and tried to calm down. That's when
the door to the room right next to Joel's and mine opened. A woman
and man stepped out and made out like a couple of teenagers for a few
minutes. Grace, it was Neal! The woman was Darla Jo!" She went on to
tell Grace about Joel's wife showing up and what had happened.

"Are you sure it was Neal?" Grace could barely whisper. "Macy is
going to be devastated, and with Darla Jo . . ." She slapped a hand over
her mouth.

"Oh, yeah, I'm sure it was Neal. No doubt about it," Sarah answered and nodded with every word. "The sunlight lit him up real good, and I'd know Darla Jo anywhere. What are we going to do?"

"We have to tell Macy, but we should have proof," Grace muttered. "Did you think to take a picture with your phone?"

"Nope, I was too stunned. But there was no mistaking that it was him and Darla Jo—or their vehicles, either. She's been in the shop enough that I could identify that bright blue sports car of hers, and he's been to the house in his red SUV," Sarah said. "She's buried two husbands and gotten rich off each of them. Do you think he's after her money, or are they in this together and he's after Macy's money?"

The heaviness in Grace's chest was overwhelming to the point that she had to remind herself to take a deep breath. "Why would he need her money? He's the assistant manager of one of the biggest hotels in San Antonio."

"Is he, or is he just an employee who has a room so he can be on call 24-7?" Sarah asked. "Do we tell Macy today or do some checking so we have more facts?"

Grace's nerves got the best of her, and she giggled.

"This is not funny," Sarah scolded.

"No, it's not," Grace agreed. "I was laughing at myself for thinking I'd done so good to offer help to Macy in her Sunday school class. Then I get the props knocked out from under me with this news. I'm so sorry that you've had to go through this, Sister. I hope Joel's wife takes him to the cleaners. I'm not sure if Macy would even believe us if we told her. Maybe we should try to help her find out on her own."

Sarah nodded. "But we can't let her buy a dress and flowers, and we've got an appointment to look at both at the end of the month."

"That gives us a little more than two weeks," Grace said.

Macy had never dated a lot, and until Neal came into her life, she had never been in a serious relationship. Grace couldn't bear to see her heartbroken.

"I wonder what game he's playing," Sarah said. "Why would he string Macy along if he's planning on going after Darla Jo? And everyone in town knows that Macy is engaged to him, so why is Darla Jo even seeing him? None of it makes a bit of sense."

"They both came from Houston," Grace said. "Maybe they knew each other before she moved to Devine and got involved with Wesley and then Henry."

"And Wesley was barely in the ground when she took up with Henry and wound up inheriting that big ranch of his when he died. I've always wondered if she had a list of prospective older guys that she could fleece," Sarah said. "Do you think Neal is doing what they call a *long con?*"

Grace shook her head. "Surely not. Why would he be engaged to Macy if he and Darla Jo are getting rich off her husbands?"

"To cover up their relationship," Sarah suggested.

Grace giggled again. "We've both been watching too many cop shows in the evenings. He's probably just having one last fling before he has to settle down and be a faithful husband."

Sarah laughed with her. "Look at us—sitting out here, thinking that there's a real black widow in our little town. Wesley died of a heart attack, and Henry's diabetes killed him. You're right. Neal is just having a last fling. You can tell by the way he looks at Macy that he's in love with her."

"Let's go home and get out the rocky road ice cream and two spoons," Grace suggested. "That will help you get over Joel."

"It might. Ice cream heals everything from broken hearts to the desire to smother a man with a cheap hotel pillow." Sarah started up the engine and drove back to the house. "But I'm not sure I'll ever trust a man again—and in my defense, he wasn't wearing a ring. He didn't even have a pale spot where a ring might have been. I always check for that before I even let a man buy me a drink."

"There are a few good men out there," Grace said, "but I don't think they hang out in bars."

Sarah shook her head slowly and parked in front of the house. "You met Justin at *church*. Of course, you were both just kids at the time, but still . . ."

"Point taken, but do you realize that Justin and Joel both start with a *J*? Maybe we should avoid any men from now on that have a *J* name," Grace told her as she got out of the truck and made her way to the porch, where Macy was sitting in the swing.

Grace was about to open the front door when Macy called out to her, "Hey, I'm glad y'all are back. I need to talk to you about something really important, and there's no time like right now to get it off my chest."

"She knows," Sarah whispered, so close behind Grace that it startled her. "Can I get a beer first?"

Grace grabbed the handle to the screen door. "And I'd like an iced tea. Do you want one, Macy?"

"I'd love one," Macy said and flashed a brilliant smile.

"She doesn't know," Grace whispered on the way to the kitchen. "If she did, she wouldn't be smiling like that. She would be crying until her eyes swelled shut."

Audrey slipped into the kitchen and went to the refrigerator for an ice cream sandwich. "Know what?"

"Nothing," Grace answered and felt guilty for lying to her daughter.

"We were talking about Darla Jo," Sarah answered.

That wasn't a total lie, since they had been discussing the woman earlier.

"She *is* probably crying," Audrey said and closed the freezer door. "Dillard Wilson got married yesterday to his old high school sweetheart. Talk around town says that he was the next man she was going to seduce."

Grace almost dropped the tea pitcher. "Good grief! Where did you hear that?"

Audrey shrugged. "Crystal babysits for her on Saturday nights and usually stays over. Darla Jo's got a young, good-lookin' boyfriend, according to Crystal, but she marries old men so she can get their money when they die. But she and her boyfriend go out on Saturday night and don't come home until early Sunday morning."

"What else did she tell Crystal?" Grace asked.

Audrey peeled the paper off her ice cream sandwich. "Darla Jo said that she and her boyfriend were going to move away from Devine and live on a tropical island. Someday, I'm going to be rich enough to live like that."

Sarah pulled the tab on her beer and took a long drink. "Has Crystal met the Saturday-night boyfriend?"

Audrey took a bite of her ice cream. "Nope. He don't pick her up at the door. She meets him somewhere and doesn't come home until daylight or after most Sunday mornings. She has to be home by ten so Crystal can go to church. That's her parents' rule. Darla Jo pays Crystal a hundred dollars. I told Crystal if she ever needs a relief sitter that I would do it in a heartbeat for that kind of money. The little boys are in bed by nine—and when Darla Jo cleans out her closet, she gives Crystal what she doesn't want. Last month she gave her a purse that cost five hundred dollars brand-new."

"That's pretty generous," Grace growled.

"Yep, and that's why I'm going to marry a rich man someday," Audrey said with a smile. "When I do, you all three can come and live in my mansion with me."

"Well, thank you for that." Grace was amused by her daughter's statement—and glad that Audrey was talking to her at all, to tell the truth. She picked up the two glasses of tea and headed outside.

"You are welcome, but"—Audrey followed her mother across the kitchen—"don't expect to run my life for me when you live with me."

"Wouldn't dream of it once you are grown," Grace told her.

Macy was still smiling when Grace handed her a glass of tea and then sat down beside her on the swing. "Isn't today just beautiful? I believe spring must be coming early this year."

"Could be," Grace agreed.

Sarah sat down on a chaise longue and stretched out her legs. "I noticed that the willow tree up by our fishing pond is beginning to leaf out. I hope you're right. It's been a long winter, and I'm ready for warm weather."

Macy put the swing in motion with her foot. "Neal and I talked about buying a house today, and we even drove past a couple that are listed. If we buy now and pay cash, we should be moved in and settled by the time we get married. I'm so excited that I just had to share the news with you."

Grace shivered despite the warmth of the sun. "Is the hotel going to be all right with him living outside the place?"

"He's talking to them tomorrow, but he thinks it will be fine. His contract says he has to live at the hotel until the present manager retires, which is June 1. He's got a friend who works for the real estate company that is listing the two houses, and he thinks he can get us a good deal since I'll pay cash for the house," Macy replied.

"Isn't Neal going to pay for part of the house?" Sarah asked.

"He's going to buy all the furniture. We're going to go to the bank in San Antonio next week and set up a joint account for all that, and for the honeymoon. We've agreed to do a cruise to Alaska. It will be so romantic." Macy's blue eyes glittered. "I'm going to get it booked soon."

There were two things in the world that Grace hated, and a rat was both. Her mother used to say that she could hear one chewing cheese a hundred miles away. That might have been an exaggeration, but there was one thing for sure that Sunday afternoon: she could sure enough smell one, and it was named Neal.

"Have you told Neal about your funds from your mama's insurance policy and what was left to you when she died?" Sarah asked.

"Neal and I have no secrets," Macy answered. "He's told me all about his salary, which isn't a lot right now, but it will be when he steps into the manager's position. And he does have a healthy savings account—enough to buy the furniture for whichever house we decide on. And I also told him about selling the business. He has already put a call in to Travis and is working on getting us a good deal. If y'all don't want to sell, then you can buy me out. I just have to give him power of attorney over my part of the business for him to get the ball rolling. This is a good thing." She flashed a brilliant smile. "And don't worry—I don't want the half I'm entitled to from Mama's will when she left me her part of the business, but I do think a third would be fair. Neal thinks it would be a wonderful idea. Then we could start a family right after the wedding, and I could stay home with the babies."

"Hey, Mama." Audrey came out of the house and sat down on the end of the chaise longue with Sarah. "I've been messaging with Crystal on my computer. I miss getting to see her in person every day."

"It was your choice to take the rap for your friends and then to tell me that you hated me," Grace reminded her.

"Do you want to hear my newest gossip or not?" Audrey snapped.

Sarah patted her niece on the shoulder. "I want to hear it. Does it have to do with what color eye shadow you and Crystal are wearing to church next week?"

Audrey shook her head. "Nope. Crystal is so bummed that she's crying. Darla Jo forgot to pay her this morning when she came home, and when Crystal went by to pick up her money, she learned that Darla Jo is moving and won't need her to babysit anymore. Her ranch has sold, and she's all excited because her boyfriend—the one she spends Saturday nights with—has asked her to marry him. There goes Crystal's babysitting job." Audrey closed her eyes and sighed, then opened them. "I feel so sorry for her."

"Darla Jo—her older husband died a bit ago, right? She has two cute little boys," Macy said.

"That's the one . . ." Audrey let out another dramatic sigh. "And I won't ever get a chance to do substitute babysitting now. She and her boyfriend are moving to a romantic tropical island. I wish I lived near the ocean and that I could lay out and work on my tan every day."

"When is this move going to happen?" Grace asked.

"Real soon," Audrey answered. "Darla Jo told Crystal that her boyfriend has to finish up some kind of a legal job before they can leave, but they've already bought a house and hired staff on the island. They're going to get married on the beach in their bare feet, but Darla Jo is still going to wear a white dress with a train, and the little boys are going to carry it for her. Doesn't that sound so dreamy? Someday I'm going to be able to say that I've got staff in my huge mansion house on an island just like that."

The heavy feeling in Grace's chest was back. Neal wasn't just having a fling—he was going to fleece Macy out of her inheritance and break her heart at the same time. Now she and Sarah had no choice but to tell her what was going on. Hopefully, she would believe them and not do something as stupid as Audrey had done the past week—like sign the papers to give Neal power of attorney.

Chapter Five

*W*hat are we going to do without Macy to help us? Sarah thought when she awoke from a nap that afternoon.

The shop had always been run by family, and bringing in an outsider to learn their recipe could be disastrous. Until Macy talked to them about giving Neal power of attorney over her finances, Sarah had had no idea just how far Neal had manipulated her sweet cousin. She and Grace owed it to Macy to press charges against the man.

Exactly what would you charge him with? the niggling voice in her head asked as she threw back the covers and sat up in bed. *He hasn't done one illegal thing. And if she does sign the papers to give him access to everything she owns, or if she sells her part of the shop either to you and Grace or to a stranger, that's not against the law.*

"Where's the justice in that?" she muttered. When she opened her bedroom door, something sweet-smelling filled the house. She followed her nose to the kitchen, where Raelene was taking peanut butter cookies from the oven, and Grace was sitting at the table. Several dozen cookies were cooling on the counter, and a loaded plate sat in the middle of the table. Audrey was beside Grace and had one of her poor, pitiful me expressions on her face.

"Did you have a good nap?" Grace asked.

"I did." Sarah sat down and picked up a cookie. "Where's Macy?"

"One of her horrible migraines just hit. Those things come out of nowhere and always start with blurred vision," Grace said and then gave Sarah a look that said they needed to talk.

Sarah hated that her cousin was in such pain, but she breathed a sigh of relief. This would give her and Grace a little longer to figure out how to break the news to Macy.

Rip off the bandage in one fell swoop. Macy is stronger than you think, her mother's voice said loudly in her head.

I don't think so, Sarah argued.

"Are you having a mental conversation with someone?" Grace asked.

"Yes, I am," Sarah answered. "With our mother."

"My granny still pops into my head sometimes," Raelene said and glanced over at Audrey. "I'm glad to know that I'm not the only one who hears voices."

"Not me," Audrey said. "The only thing I hear is my algebra teacher fussing at me for not getting all my work in on time."

"How many lessons are you behind?" Grace asked.

Audrey cut her eyes to her mother. "Maybe ten. Crystal said he wouldn't dare flunk her or Kelsey because their dads are on the school board, and since I'm their friend . . ." She let the sentence hang.

"They're wrong," Raelene said. "Mr. Randolph is a tough teacher, and you get what you earn in his class."

Audrey looked toward the ceiling, sighed dramatically, and finally said, "Is the offer still on the table for you to help me to get caught up?"

"Are we friends?" Raelene asked.

"Nope," Audrey said without a moment's hesitation.

"Then it will cost you. I only help friends for free," Raelene told her. "I get ten dollars an hour for tutoring. I figure we can get you in good shape for about twenty dollars a day."

"That will wipe out what I've saved from my allowance. I wanted to buy Crystal something nice for her birthday with that money." Audrey gasped.

"Then flunk algebra and take it again." Raelene shrugged and turned off the oven. "Your choice. You can either hire me and get a decent grade, or buy something for your friend and maybe not have enough credits to graduate. You do know that those two girls are using you and making fun of you behind your back."

Sarah bit back a giggle. "If I was in your shoes, I'd pay Raelene."

"Right up front, the end of each lesson," Raelene said.

"Okay, okay!" Audrey agreed. "But you're still not my friend. And Crystal and Kelsey are not using me or talking about me behind my back."

"That's fine by me, but now let's talk about Macy." Raelene turned away from Audrey. "Granny called what's ailing Macy a *sick headache*. She had them pretty often, and I know what to do to help. I'll watch over Macy and take care of her this afternoon. I've got some chamomile oil that I rubbed on Granny's temples. That and a couple of over-the-counter pain pills seemed to work for her better than anything."

"I'm sure she'd appreciate any help you can give her," Sarah said and hoped that someday she'd have a daughter as kindhearted as Raelene.

"I'll get the oil, then. I'll need to do it every hour until she is feeling better." Raelene disappeared down the hallway.

"We'd better get on to the shop," Grace said.

"Why are you going now?" Audrey asked.

"Once a month we deep clean the kitchen. You never know when a health inspector might pop in," Grace explained. "But you don't have to be a part of this job. Work on your algebra. Be sure to pay Raelene. Since you created this problem, then you get to use your money."

"I hate mopping floors, cleaning windows, wearing one of those dorky T-shirts, and everything about that shop, but I hate algebra even more," Audrey griped, getting in the last word before hurrying off to her room.

Sarah waited until she and Grace were away from the house to bring up the subject. "How do you feel about Raelene charging Audrey for tutoring?"

"I'd rather my kid spend her money for that than buy a present for a girl that I'm almost positive is the guilty one for having either the cigarettes, booze, or maybe both at school," Grace answered.

"Amen to that," Sarah agreed. "And now what about Macy? I hate breaking her heart even worse than getting mine broken."

"You didn't break her heart," Grace said. "Neal will be responsible for that all on his own. Just like Joel is responsible for his own bad behavior. It wasn't your fault. I'm never letting either of you go out on a date again until we have a private detective check the man out, though."

"You've got a PI on retainer?" Sarah teased.

Grace opened the shop's back door and flipped on the lights in the kitchen. "Not yet, but I will have when y'all get over your broken hearts."

"What about you? Are we supposed to have any man you date checked out?" Sarah got the cleaning supplies out of the utility room.

"You don't have to worry about that for a few more years," Grace answered. "All I have to do is introduce a guy to Audrey, and he won't stop running until he reaches the ocean."

"Hey, what's going on?" An older woman with dyed red hair and enough wrinkles to prove her four-hundred-dollar face cream did not work, flung open the back door. "Audrey said y'all were down here cleaning up."

"How was the cruise, Beezy?" Grace asked.

Beatrice Larson, better known in Devine as Beezy, had grown up with Sarah and Grace's mama and had been her best friend. When their mother passed away, Beezy had stepped in to be a surrogate mother to them. They both left what they were doing and wrapped her up in a three-way hug.

"Lord, I'm glad you're home," Sarah said.

"Cruise was fun, but once is enough on a big old floating hotel." Beezy sat down on a tall stool and frowned. "I can tell by both your faces that something isn't right. I knew I shouldn't have gone and left you. Where is Macy?"

Grace pulled out three coffee mugs. "She's got one of her headaches. Raelene is helping take care of her."

"Liz and Molly both had headaches like that," Beezy said. "Raelene? Is that Hilda Andrews's granddaughter? Why is she taking care of Macy?"

"We should start at the beginning," Grace said as she put on a pot of coffee and sprayed foamy cleaner inside the ovens.

Sarah told her the story of Joel and about being at the motel and seeing Neal and Darla Jo while she emptied the refrigerator and wiped down all the shelves. "Grace and I have to tell Macy, don't we?"

"Of course you have to tell her," Beezy said and then poured each of them a cup of coffee. "It wouldn't be right to keep it from her and let her fall into a life of misery with a cheating husband. I've said from the beginning there was something wrong with that man. He's too perfect, with his chiseled cheekbones and his long, dark lashes and all that romantic tomfoolery. Macy fell in love too fast. If he's trying to talk her into giving him power of attorney, he might be more than just a philanderer."

"We know. What are we going to do?" Grace groaned before taking a sip of her coffee.

"Do you think Neal put something in her food that would cause her to have this migraine? Is he going to take advantage of her addled state and ask her to move money even without power of attorney?" asked Sarah. "She hasn't had this kind of headache in at least six months. It seems strange that one would pop up after she's been out to eat with him."

Beezy took a sip. "Honey, he wouldn't do something stupid like that until she puts his name on her bank accounts. But we do need to make sure of his motives and even more sure he really is who he says he is. You girls are computer savvy, so get on it."

"I tried looking him up this morning . . ." Sarah paused. "On the internet . . ." Another pause. "After you told me. But the Neal Monroes I found didn't look a thing like him. There was one who was ninety-two years old and died last year," she admitted.

"Then I guess he's clean—or maybe he's stolen the identity of a dead man," Beezy said in a low voice. She leaned over to scan the room, as if looking for someone to pop out from behind the bread and sugar bins. "We'd make good detectives. Maybe we should give up the doughnut shop and open a PI business."

"I hate to tell her that there's even a possibility she's been conned on top of everything," Grace grumbled. "But right now, the thought of him talking her into moving money today is downright scary."

Beezy shook her finger at Grace. "She hasn't jumped into the fire yet, darlin' girl. We can save her if this man is cheating on her, or trying to swindle her, or both."

Sarah headed straight for the small office where she did all the bookwork for the business. It had been a storage closet at one time and was just big enough for a desk and chair. The modem for the internet service for both the business and the house was in the desk. She opened it and pulled all three of the plug-ins.

"What are you doing in there?" Grace asked.

"Unplugging the internet to make it tougher for Macy to transfer money," Sarah answered.

"She's got unlimited data on her phone," Grace said.

"Crap!" Sarah fussed. "I'd forgotten about that."

Beezy chuckled. "Smart girl for trying, though."

"We can't leave it off forever," Grace said with a sigh. "Macy's got such a big heart that she'll forgive him if he begs and says his indiscretion was just a one-time thing and that Darla Jo seduced him."

"Maybe for cheating *one time*, but if he's not who he says he is and he and Darla Jo are running a scam, I think she'd have better sense than to forgive him for that. We need to tell her, and I mean really soon. That way she can deal with him."

"I'm wondering about all those weekends that Macy had plans and Neal had to work," Sarah said. "Seems really fishy, doesn't it?"

Audrey came through the back door, out of breath and wide-eyed. "I was trying to message Crystal and the internet went out!"

Beezy opened up her arms. "Come here, baby girl, and give me a big old bear hug. The internet is no big thing. We all lived without it, and you can, too."

Audrey ran across the room and hugged the older woman. "Did you have a good time on the cruise? I wish you'd have taken me with you."

"You would have been bored to tears, my child, around all of us old people. It was a senior-citizen cruise, and I got to admit, I was tired of hearing about aches and surgeries by the second day," Beezy said. "Aren't you on spring break this week?"

Audrey shot a look over at her mother. "I'm in spring break jail, and just when I thought things couldn't get worse, I can't even get into my Facebook page on my computer."

"She got caught at school with cigarettes and liquor," Grace said. "Her punishment is that she has to work in the shop during her break, and then she has to go to in-school suspension for a few days when she goes back. It could have been more, but this is her first offense."

"You do the crime, you do the time," Beezy told her.

"But they weren't even my cigarettes and booze," Audrey whined, "and my friends will all shun me if I get them in trouble."

"Honey, that kind of people ain't real friends." Beezy patted her on the back. "But you have to figure that out all by yourself. If Macy is still under the weather tomorrow, I could come in and run the register for y'all."

"Thanks, Beezy, for the offer, but I think we've got it covered," Sarah said.

Audrey heaved another of her dramatic sighs and headed out the door. "I guess I'll start on my algebra since the internet is down. Did you call up the service and cut it off just to punish me more, Mama?"

"I did not, but that's a wonderful idea if you do something else that gets you suspended from school," Grace told her.

Audrey flipped around and started out the door, then stopped as Grace began to tell Beezy about Raelene.

"From what I've heard about that girl, she is more like Hilda than Geneva. She's a sweet kid," Beezy replied with a nod. "She's got a kind heart like her grandmother. I'm glad y'all took her in. If I'd known about her, I would have done the same thing, but she'll be happier in a house with another teenager, I'm sure."

"Nobody, not a one of them, asked me my opinion about it!" Audrey slammed the door on her way outside.

"I take it she's not happy with this arrangement." Beezy giggled. "How are the girls getting along?"

"Not good," Sarah answered.

"Those new friends of Audrey's are turning her into a mean girl," Grace said.

"Leave her alone as much as possible and let her hit bottom. Those girls are just teenage versions of their mothers. Audrey is smart, and she will take off the blinders someday," Beezy said. "And who knows? They might even be friends by summertime."

"When pigs fly." Sarah laughed.

"I'm so glad to get back to normal life," Macy said Wednesday morning when she reached the shop in time to roll out the last two raisings of dough. "This has been the longest I've ever been away from Neal in the four months that we've dated. We've barely had time to even talk this week. I told him that I was ready to give up my dream wedding with the white dress and go to the courthouse for a quickie marriage."

"Does that mean that you are selling your half of the business?" Sarah asked.

Grace's phone pinged. She dried her hands and pulled it out of her hip pocket to see a message from Travis: Good morning. Travis here. We met in your shop when I came in to visit my old friends. Neal Monroe has approached me with the offer to buy half interest in your shop, and the land. He is acting on your cousin Macy's behalf. Is this true?

Grace sucked in air so quickly that Sarah, Macy, and Audrey all whipped around to look at her. She wondered how Travis had gotten her number but then remembered that it was on the business card in case of emergency.

Audrey turned back to Macy. "You can't do that. I've already picked out my dress."

"I can and I will. Neal says that he loves me and misses me, but he has to be gone on a trip for his job until late Saturday night, so it'll be another four days until I see him again. I'm going to tell him I want to go to the courthouse on Monday morning. We'll be married on his birthday," she said with a smile. "He shouldn't have trouble remembering our anniversary that way. I think all this stress of worrying about a dress, the reception, who to invite, and all that is what caused my headache. But I have to admit, the oil that Raelene put on my temples sure took the edge off it. I'm so glad that y'all hired her."

"Can we go to the courthouse with you?" Audrey asked.

"Of course you can," Macy answered. "All y'all and Beezy. Neal has no living family, so he will appreciate having y'all there when we say our vows as much as I will."

Grace's heart pounded in her chest. Would Travis jump on the opportunity to buy half interest—not even a third, like Macy had told them? What on earth could—or even *should*—she tell him since they had no real proof that Neal was anything but a cheating fiancé?

She thought of Neal Monroe, the old man who had died. His obituary hadn't listed any relatives—not a wife or kids or even a special friend—and she wondered exactly what name was on Neal's official birth certificate.

"Time to unlock the door and let in the early birds," Macy said.

"Don't they get the worm?" Audrey asked.

"No, they get the freshest doughnuts," Sarah answered.

"That's a good one," Audrey said as she was about to leave the kitchen. "I'll get their coffee poured and their orders this morning. Do they ever order the same kinds two days in a row?"

"Nope," Sarah said. "They like variety."

Grace needed to talk to Sarah—alone. They couldn't wait another day to tell Macy what was going on. She needed time to think before the two of them spilled the tea, as the kids said today. She followed Audrey to the dining room and wiped down the already-clean counter around the cash register.

"I figured you'd be off doing fun things with your friends during spring break," Claud said as he led the way into the shop and headed to the table on the far right.

"I should be," Audrey answered with one of her signature sighs, "but my mama has me in jail, and I have to work during my vacation."

"What did you do?" Ira asked.

"Long story, but I'll sure be glad when this week is done." Audrey carried a tray with three mugs of black coffee to the table.

"Aw, we're going to miss you, girl," Claud said with a smile. "You've been good to keep our coffee cups filled."

"Thank you," Audrey said. "Will you tell my mama that I've done a good job?"

"Sure will," Frankie replied as he settled into his normal spot.

"Your mama knows that you've done a good job and is proud of you for it," Grace said from behind the counter.

The door swung open, and Darla Jo, along with her two little boys, made her way to the table at the other end of the dining area. Grace felt all the color drain from her face. If what they suspected was true, then why would Darla Jo come to the shop—especially this early in the morning?

The woman had long blonde hair, green eyes that couldn't be that color without help from contacts, and a curvy figure—everything to attract an older man.

"What's she doing here?" Sarah hissed in a low voice when she brought out a tray of doughnuts to put in the display case.

"Having doughnuts for breakfast, I guess," Grace answered just as quietly. "She's only been in here a few times. Last time I saw her was before Henry's funeral."

"Looks like our guys on the other end of the room aren't paying a bit of attention to her," Sarah said. "Think she's lost her appeal?"

"Maybe they are whispering about their two friends who died in the past three years and deciding they don't want to be next," Grace said.

"I wonder who her kids belong to." Sarah picked up an order pad.

"Do you really have to ask? Look at those brown eyes and dark hair. They are the spitting image of Neal," Grace answered. "He and Darla Jo had to have known each other in Houston, and they're working this con together."

Macy grabbed an order pad and crossed the room. "Good mornin', Darla Jo. What can I get you and these sweet boys today? Y'all are up awfully early."

"Coffee for me, juice for the boys, and half a dozen glazed to share. We've got to go to an early appointment and get caught up on vaccinations and travel shots. They promised to be brave, so we're having doughnuts for breakfast, and later, they will get prizes," Darla Jo answered.

"I heard that you're planning on moving in a few weeks," Macy said. "Are you going to a big city?"

"Oh, no!" Darla Jo said with half a giggle. "It's a small tropical town that's not much bigger than Devine. I want to raise my boys to be wild and free, not cramped up in tradition. They'll have a nanny who will homeschool them until they're old enough to make up their own minds about doing something different."

"That sounds amazing," Macy said. "Your sons are so cute. I can just see them making sandcastles and—" She gasped, threw up both hands, and dropped the order pad on the floor.

Grace and Sarah gave each other a look, cleared the end of the counter, and were headed that way when Macy said, "Sweet Lord, that is one big diamond!"

"It is, isn't it?" Darla Jo held up her left hand to catch the light from the sunrise just coming over the horizon and through the shop window. "I picked it out myself, but it was a surprise when Edward bought it for me and got down on one knee and proposed. Three carats in a pear shape. My hands are too small to wear anything bigger. I just love it. Your *little* engagement ring is pretty, too."

Macy's face lit up in a smile. "Neal did good when he picked it out."

"Yes, he did," Darla Jo said with a smug grin that sent Grace's blood pressure soaring. They were right.

Macy picked up the order pad and started back toward the counter. "I'll bring your order right out. You have a nice day."

Darla Jo flipped her hair back over her shoulder. "Oh, honey, I will, and I'll think of you when I'm living on the island."

Grace bit back a smart remark and picked up the coffeepot. She crossed the room and topped off the three old guys' mugs and whispered, "Guess y'all are all out of luck. She's moving off to an island."

"Don't bother me one bit," Claud said. "My wife told me that she would come up out of the grave and haunt me if I ever got remarried when she was gone. We been together more'n fifty years, and I believe her."

"Got to admit," Ira said, "that I'm scared of my dear Martha Jane. She lets me come to town and have coffee with these two, but she thought poor old Wesley and Henry had both lost their minds."

Grace glanced over at Frankie and raised an eyebrow.

He raised both palms in a defensive gesture. "Honey, my get-up-and-go got up and went a long time ago. I'd have to buy a how-to book to even know what to do with a woman like that. I don't imagine there'll be a lot of tears shed when she leaves Devine. Could you bring us three more of them glazed doughnuts, please?"

"You betcha," Grace said and carried the pot across the room to the table where Darla Jo was sitting with her sons. "Need a little warm-up?"

Darla Jo held up her half-empty cup. "Love one. How long have y'all had this cute little shop? I heard through the grapevine that y'all are about to sell it, maybe to some big corporation up in San Antonio?"

"My sister and cousin and I are the fourth generation to run this doughnut shop," Grace answered. "Our great-grandmother built it right after World War II. It started out almost a hundred years ago as an office for the land management business that my ancestors had in this area, but then my great-grandmother turned it into a doughnut shop—and it's not for sale. That's just a rumor."

"And this little bitty place supports all of you?" Darla Jo asked. "That's amazing."

Grace used the rest of what was in the coffeepot to top off Darla Jo's mug. "Yes, it is, but then, we don't have a lot of overhead. We all live together in the house where we were raised, and it's not fancy."

"Oh, I *must* have fancy," Darla Jo said.

"So you're going to have a mansion on your island, not a little grass hut?" Grace asked.

"Of course," Darla Jo answered. "We've bought a huge furnished villa, and the staff has agreed to stay on. It's my dream house."

"Well, I hope you'll be very happy." A rock that was half the size of the one in Gibraltar was back in Grace's chest, and she fought the urge to cross her fingers behind her back for telling such a blatant lie.

"Oh, I will be," Darla Jo said. "I haven't had such good luck with husbands, but maybe that will change with Edward."

Lady, do you realize what nickname this town has given you? Grace wondered. *You are a black widow. I bet you already had your second rich man picked out when you buried the first one. I'd be willing to lay a bet that they didn't die of natural causes.*

As if Darla Jo could read Grace's mind, she blinked several times and her chin quivered. "You know how couples are. I loved Edward at one time, but we broke up, and I moved here for a fresh start. But bless him, he and I have worked toward this moment for a decade. Now it's our turn to be together."

A decade!

Those words added more weight to the heavy feeling in Grace's chest. Macy was most likely just the tail end of a long line of cons that would end with Darla Jo and Neal on some island where they couldn't be extradited back to the United States.

Grace turned around, slipped her phone from her pocket, and sent a text to Travis: It's not true and it's a con. Could we talk tonight?

The last dozen doughnuts went out the door at eleven thirty that morning, and Sarah locked the door behind their final customer. "We don't have time to make more doughnuts, and we're sold out. I'm going to run up to San Antonio for supplies. The restaurant-supply store closes at three, and we need flour, yeast, and sugar."

"I'm going home to use some more of Raelene's oil on my head," Macy said. "It still feels like one big bruise. Neal is in the air, on his way to California, so we can't talk until he gets there. I'll be so glad when we get all this legal stuff done. Y'all are still going to buy out my third of the business, aren't you?"

"Let's give that some serious time when I get back," Sarah said and then shot Grace a look across the room.

"A long nap is calling my name." Audrey jerked her apron off and tossed it into the bin with the dirty clothes.

"Right after you gather up that load of aprons to take home, wash, and fold for tomorrow. When they're all done and you've had your two hours of tutoring, then you can take a nap," Grace told her.

"That's Raelene's job, not mine," Audrey protested.

"Raelene takes care of the housework for us. We are responsible for the shop, so this is your job, young lady." Grace pointed to the laundry bin. "When you get done with those things, then you can have the rest of the day to do whatever you want."

"What . . . ever!" Audrey said with a head wiggle.

Sarah decided that maybe the universe had been good to her after all in not giving her children back when she was in her early twenties. Sometimes she wanted to wring Audrey's neck for being so disrespectful, especially to Grace, but she had to admire her sister for the way she handled her daughter.

Audrey can say what she wants about her and her little buddies. They really are mean girls, and Audrey is getting more and more like them. I liked her better before she got tangled up with Crystal and Kelsey, she thought as she added her apron to the bin and headed outside.

She took a moment to breathe in the fresh spring air before she got into her truck. She put all the drama going on at home out of her mind and enjoyed looking at the minty green leaves popping out on the trees as she drove seventy-five miles an hour toward San Antonio. A deer ran across the road far enough ahead of her that it made it safely to the other side. Dark clouds gathered in the southwest, promising rain and possibly a thunderstorm.

"An omen for sure," she said as she drove through congested traffic to the supply house. The clouds looked even angrier as they rolled toward San Antonio. When she hopped out of the truck, she saw the first streak of lightning and heard the distant rumble of thunder.

She handed her order to the salesclerk, and two young men quickly loaded what she needed into the back seat of her truck. Drops of rain almost the size of saucers splatted on her windshield at the first red traffic light, which seemed to take forever to turn green. Her windshield wipers were going so fast and furious that every form of vehicle—cars, semis, and even motorcycles—seemed to blur together as they crawled to the next red light.

At the sixth one, she slapped the steering wheel and glanced over to the left to see the entrance to the underground parking lot for the hotel where Neal worked as assistant manager.

"Well, well, well!" she grumbled, and on impulse whipped into the underground parking garage. Beezy had said that they should check him out. What better place to start than the place that he managed—or said that he did?

"Why didn't I think to do this before now?" she asked as she got out of her truck, glad to be out of the downpour and hoping that the storm would have passed on by the time she got through with her little job. She made her way through the parked vehicles to the hotel entrance.

Her mother's voice popped in her head: *Because you were raised to trust people, and he has been so sweet and romantic to Macy this whole time.*

"You are so right, Mama, but after this past week, my trust is gone," she said and then realized that she was talking out loud again. "That's one good thing about all this technology. Everyone is talking on their phones so much that no one realizes when someone is talking to themselves."

She caught the first elevator going up and got off on the lobby floor. People wearing lanyards and badges that identified them as members of a technical convention were everywhere. She made her way between the groups and went straight to the check-in desk, got in line, and waited for her turn to talk to someone.

That someone turned out to be a middle-aged lady with gray hair slicked back into a bun at the nape of her neck and a name tag identifying her as *Linda*. "Checking in?" she asked.

"No, ma'am, I'm here to talk to the assistant hotel manager. We have some issues to resolve," Sarah answered.

"We don't have an assistant manager, but our manager was just here a few minutes ago." Linda scanned the lobby and then pointed. "Maybe he can help you find the person you need. There he is, talking to Edward—our technical guy—over there by the elevators. He's the one with the blue shirt and red tie. You could probably catch him if you hurry."

Sarah followed the lady's finger and saw Neal talking to a bald-headed man who looked to be about sixty years old—the only one of the two wearing a tie. She whipped around to face the lady again. "That's Edward with him, right?"

"Yep, he lives here at the hotel and is on call for any techie problems we have. If that's what you need to talk to the manager about, you can bypass Mr. Anderson and go straight to Edward. He'll get you fixed right up," she said.

"What's Edward's last name?" Sarah asked.

"Carlson," Linda snapped. "Now, if that's all, I have more customers to take care of. This is a busy time of day."

"That's all, and thank you so much." Sarah made a hasty retreat to the stairs that led down to the parking garage. She whipped out her phone and googled the hotel, pulling up pictures of the staff. There was Edward Carlson, only the name appeared under a picture of Neal. His title—just like the woman had said—was *technical engineer*.

This should be enough to take to Macy as a start, Sarah thought and took a screenshot of the image. But she took no satisfaction in what she'd found out. To her, it was just proof that Macy's heart would be shattered, and thinking of that made Sarah want to cry or go back in the hotel and do bodily damage to whoever Neal really was. She wondered how many other aliases the man had had—or, for that matter, how many Darla Jo had burned through since they started on their ten-year mission to buy her dream house on her own private little island. Was Macy's money supposed to be the final deposit in their account? She got into her truck and drove out of the garage and into the bright sunshine.

The roads were still wet from the downpour, but traffic was light once she cleared San Antonio. Sarah made the thirty-minute drive home without noticing anything around her. Aliens could have dropped out of the sky, and she wouldn't have even seen them. One scenario after another played out in her head as she thought about how she was going to tell Macy what she had found out. Finally, she turned the radio on to her favorite country station and hoped that the music would soothe the roller coaster of emotions going through her mind.

The DJ said that it was time to start the five-for-five contest. He would play five songs in a row, and the fifth person who called the station with the names of the five artists would win tickets to a Blake Shelton concert in San Antonio. "And to start you off," he said, "we'll give you the first one with 'Goodbye Time' by Blake himself."

"Well, that's an omen for sure." Sarah kept time to the slow music by tapping her thumbs on the steering wheel.

When she arrived in Devine and parked behind the shop, she still hadn't figured out a way to start her conversation with Macy. Every breath tightened up her chest even more. The anger she'd felt at the hotel was nothing compared to what was boiling in her heart right then. She carried all the supplies for the next week into the shop, then went on up to the house. Macy was on the porch, with her Bible beside her and her Sunday school lesson-plan book in her lap.

The time had come, but Sarah wished she were back in the truck. She wanted to put it in reverse and simply drive away without even looking back. The storm that had dumped a deluge on their area was nothing compared to the emotional hurricane about to shatter Macy's heart.

"Like Humpty Dumpty," Sarah muttered.

Grace came out of the house and sat down on the chaise longue and then waved at Sarah.

"Got to do it," Sarah muttered and slowly walked up to them.

"Something wrong?" Macy asked.

"You look like you've seen a ghost," Grace said before she could answer.

"I kind of did." Sarah picked up the Bible, laid it on the longue beside Grace, and then sat down on the swing beside Macy. "Macy, we've been keeping a secret from you . . ."

"You are scaring me a little bit," Macy said. "I've never heard your tone like it is right now. Did someone die? Please don't tell me that Claud or Ira or Frankie has passed away."

"They are fine," Grace answered. "Are you sure about this, Sarah?"

"Very sure." Sarah pulled out her phone, tapped it a few times, and handed it to Macy. "This is Edward Carlson. He works as a computer engineer at the hotel where Neal told you that he was working toward being the manager."

"But that's not possible. That's my Neal. They must have gotten the staff pictures and titles all mixed up," Macy argued.

"This is Mr. Anderson, the hotel manager." Sarah scrolled up through the employees and found his picture with a long list of his credentials. "I saw him talking with Neal at the hotel."

"But that would mean Neal lied to me." Macy frowned. "We're always honest with each other. I'll ask him about it. I bet he wanted me to think of him as something better because I have a lot of money.

Bless his heart—he doesn't understand that I don't care about money. It can't buy love."

"Just how honest were you with him?" Grace asked.

"I told him that . . ." The frown deepened.

"Macy, what did you tell him?" Grace asked again.

"Everything," Macy said. "From our second date, he's known that we are wealthy from our inheritance from our parents, and that we run the doughnut shop because we love working together and, besides, that way we don't touch the capital. He laughed and said that folks in Devine probably didn't know they were living in the same town with millionaires."

"Since he's a tech expert, he had probably figured all that out before he even walked into the shop that first day," Sarah said.

"That would mean"—Macy's blue eyes floated in tears—"that all of this wasn't real, but there could still be an explanation. I need to talk to him and give him a chance to explain. He has that right. He's innocent until proven guilty, isn't he?" She put her hands over her face and began to sob.

"There's more," Grace said and nodded toward Sarah. "I got a text this morning from Travis Butler, and I've talked to him on the phone this afternoon. Neal offered to broker a deal with him on your behalf to sell half of our land and the shop to him. He would have our recipe, and that would give him the right to build a housing development right next door to us."

"But I haven't signed any papers for him to have that kind of power," Macy said. "And I wouldn't sell half of it—just a third, and only to you and Sarah, not to a stranger." She hiccuped. "Is he really just scamming me?"

Sarah began to weep with her. "He is, darlin'. Believe me, he is." She told her cousin the story of how, the previous Saturday night, she had been with a married man and ended up seeing Darla Jo and Neal coming out of a hotel room next to theirs.

"And Darla Jo mentioned this morning that she and her *Edward*"—Grace threw up air quotes—"had been working on buying their house on an island for ten years. This has been what they call a *long con*."

"I just can't believe all this. Maybe there's an explanation for . . ." Macy tried to justify and yet, at the same time, make sense of the bomb that had been dropped on her. Everything around her seemed to stand still and move at warp speed simultaneously. She felt like she might faint, but the one thing that was positive was that she was going to have another migraine. The aura that preceded her headaches had already begun. "I want to go there and see for myself. It's the only way I'll believe this horrible story. He said that he was leaving early this morning and wouldn't be back until Saturday night, late. Why would he be at the hotel this afternoon? He sent me a text that he had landed in San Diego." She pulled her phone from her shirt pocket and handed it to Grace. "See for yourself."

Raelene brought a tray with three glasses of sweet tea and a plate of cookies out to the porch. "Is everything all right? Why are y'all all crying? Did something happen to Audrey?"

Macy closed her eyes and covered her wet face with her hands. "No, darlin'. It's possible that I've been living a fool's dream, and I gave my heart to the wrong man. And I've got another headache coming on."

"Don't they say something about it being better to have loved and lost than never to have loved at all?" Raelene asked. "I can bring the oil to rub on your temples, if that thing really hits."

"I'd rather to have never been loved if it was all fake," Macy sniffled. "If all this is true, and I hope it's not, I wish I'd never met Neal Monroe."

"Want me to make him disappear?" Raelene asked without a smile. "I've watched *Criminal Minds* with my grandmother and taken enough chemistry classes that I can do it."

"No, because there is an explanation. No one could be as . . . ," Macy stammered, "as loving and sweet as he's been and have it not be real. Whoever this Edward is, he has to be a doppelgänger. We're going to look at houses on Sunday, go by the bank to get our joint checking account and his power of attorney set up on Monday morning so I don't have to worry with finances, and then get married that afternoon." When she heard herself say "so I don't have to worry with finances," her stomach dropped even further.

"Why the rush on houses?" Grace asked.

Macy rubbed her forehead. "It's my idea. I told him that getting to have a new home and being with him would be his birthday gift that Monday."

"That's probably what he and Darla Jo are waiting for. They would wipe you out completely if he got his hands on your accounts, and he wouldn't show up at the courthouse at all. With what she's gotten from Henry and Wesley and all your money, they would probably have enough to buy that island she keeps talking about, not just live on it," Grace said through gritted teeth.

"It can't be true." Every emotion from disappointment to anger flashed through Macy's body, leaving her limp and feeling numb. "I love him so much and . . ." She stopped and stared out over the mesquite trees and cattle in the pasture. "There has to be a logical explanation."

"I hope we're wrong about the money," Sarah answered, "but I have no doubts that Neal and Darla Jo spent the night together."

Chapter Six

*M*acy received several texts from Neal on Thursday saying that he was too busy in meetings and networking with the hotel managers to get five minutes free for a phone call. He ended each one with a heart emoji.

"There is no way he can be this sweet and not be real," she kept telling Grace and Sarah when she shared every text with them.

"The first step in grieving is denial—and, honey, you *will* grieve for what could have been. You are denying it now, but somewhere deep in your heart, you know he's been conning you." Sarah wasn't sure if she was talking to Macy or herself.

"After you found out that your fellow was a married man, did you deny it?" Macy snapped.

"No, because I had too much proof in my hands. I did fight the urge to either strangle or smother him for about five minutes. Then I got dressed and walked out of that motel room in a cloud of anger. That's what I was feeling when I got into my truck and came home," Sarah answered.

"Did he even call you to apologize?" Macy asked.

"He sent me a text. No apology. Just a text to tell me he'd planned to end it that morning, and I'd saved him the trouble," Sarah replied. "His wife had forgiven him, and he vowed to be on the straight and narrow from now on. He was sorry if he hurt me, but it was just a con-sensual affair as far as he was concerned."

"That's a coward for you," Grace muttered. "He's no better than Justin. He left me a note on the windshield of my car."

"I know the steps involved with grieving, and the final one is accep-tance," Macy said, "but I just can't accept that Neal has been unfaithful or that he's out to swindle me. He's not that kind of man."

The tinkling of the bell above the shop door told them someone had arrived. Macy left the kitchen and found Darla Jo standing in front of the display case with a broad smile on her face—or was it a smug look? Otherwise, she seemed as innocent as a newborn baby lamb in her pink gingham-checked sundress. Her hair looked like she'd just walked out of the beauty shop, her pink fingernails didn't have a single chip on them, and her makeup was flawless.

Suddenly, Macy felt downright dowdy in her Devine Doughnut Shop T-shirt and jeans. Her red hair, tucked up into a net, made her look like an old woman. When she had washed her hands in the bath-room just minutes before, she had noticed that her eyes were still dull from the migraine she'd had earlier in the week and the one that had threatened the day before.

"Well, good morning," Darla Jo said. "Macy, isn't it?"

"That's right. What can I help you with this morning?" Macy could hear her icy tone in her own ears. Surely, if what Sarah thought was going on was really true, Darla Jo wouldn't have the nerve to come into the shop and flash brilliant smiles at her.

"I need half a dozen glazed, four of those with cream cheese filling for Edward, and two with sprinkles for the boys," she answered.

"Neal likes the ones with cream cheese filling, too," Macy said as she put the doughnuts in a box. Playing on words, the sign on the door, their T-shirts, and the bags all had the same logo—the D in *Devine* had a halo sitting on top of it and angel wings peeking out the sides. Underneath were the words "As light as clouds and sweet as angels."

Their great-grandmother had come up with the whole thing, and even though it was outdated and slightly sacrilegious, no one had had the heart to change it over the years. Macy had thought it was something divine from God when He'd put Neal into her life, but that morning she wished she could erase the logo—there was nothing as sweet as angels about the place.

"Where are those precious boys of yours?" Macy asked as she rang up the sale.

"They are at home with Edward." Darla Jo laid a bill on the counter. "We've booked a flight from San Antonio this afternoon. We'll get married on the beach on Saturday morning at sunset. Doesn't that sound so romantic?"

Darla Jo's information seemed to prove to Macy that she had been right all along. She felt guilty for ever doubting Neal and yet relieved at the same time. Edward was leaving with Darla Jo in a few hours, so he couldn't be Neal, who was in San Diego right now and coming back to her on Saturday. It was all a misunderstanding.

"How old are your boys?" Macy asked as she made change.

"Six and eight, and they look exactly like their father," Darla Jo answered. "They have Edward's dark eyes and hair."

"You and Edward were married before?" Macy asked.

"No, but we had the boys together." Darla Jo took the change from Macy and picked up the box of doughnuts.

"Well, I wish you all the best," Macy said, with a lighter heart than she'd had in the past twenty-four hours.

"You too," Darla Jo said.

"And tell Edward that I hope he can find cream cheese–filled doughnuts on the island that will satisfy his taste," Macy said with a smile.

"I'm sure he will." Darla Jo waved over her shoulder.

Macy took a moment to float on air before she told Grace and Sarah how wrong they had been. Then her phone rang. She slipped it out of her hip pocket, accepted the FaceTime call, and Neal's face popped up on the screen. He looked terrible, as if he hadn't slept in days.

"Hello, darlin'," she said. "How are things in San Diego?"

"Not so good," he said. "I have a problem, and I'm ashamed to ask you for help, but I don't know where else to go. After Monday, we'll be sharing everything we have, but . . ." He paused, and a single tear made its way down his cheek.

"But what? Are you okay?" she asked. She'd never seen Neal cry before—not even when he'd told her about the horrible automobile accident that had killed both his parents and his two brothers years earlier. She had wept until there were no more tears while he consoled her and explained that he was glad they were taken quickly and hadn't suffered.

"Just my pride is hurting." The tremble in his voice matched the horrible look on his face. "I had saved a hundred thousand dollars to use for a down payment on one of the houses we're looking to buy as a surprise wedding gift for you, but some of the guys here at the conference invited me to a high-stakes poker game."

"That's illegal, isn't it?" Macy asked.

"It is, but I thought if I could turn my cash into enough to buy the house outright, then I could surprise you with it on our wedding day," he said after a long sigh. "I got in over my head, and now the people want their money today—right now. I could lose my job over this. There's no way we can get married if I'm unemployed. I would never feel right if you were the only one bringing in the bacon."

"How much do you need?" she asked.

"Just a quarter million. All you have to do is give me your bank numbers, and I'll take care of it from here. We're going to join our accounts on Monday, anyway, so this is just a couple of days early." Neal finally looked up and almost smiled. "I'm so, so sorry about all this, darlin'. I promise to never play poker again."

Macy's engagement ring caught the sunlight and sent a ray of light across her phone screen. She held it up and wondered for the first time if the diamond was even real. Neal couldn't be poor if he could buy her such a lovely ring.

"What are you looking at so seriously?" Neal asked.

"My gorgeous ring," Macy said, with a smile that she hoped he couldn't tell was fake.

"You will help me, won't you?" Neal's chin quivered.

"Of course, darlin', but I can never remember the numbers for the savings account where I have that kind of money," Macy told him with a twinge of guilt. "I'll have to go up to the house and find them in the file cabinet, then call the bank to transfer that much into your account. I will probably even have to drive into town to verify everything. I don't think they'll take care of it with just a phone call."

"But . . ." Neal looked genuinely puzzled. "I love you so much, Macy—but you told me you had full access to your money, didn't you?"

"I do, and there's about that much in my savings account, but the rest of what I have is invested with a company, and it would take a week or more to get all the paperwork done to liquidate all that. I'll text you the numbers as soon as I get all this straightened out," she said.

"That will have to do until Monday, when we really get to start sharing our lives," he said. "And, darlin', thank you so much for getting me out of this trouble." He finally smiled fully. "I promise this will be the last time I ever ask you for anything."

Red flags went up. Everything that she had been told played on a constant reel in her mind. "I should be going, if you need the money today."

"Yes, ma'am," he said with another sigh. "I will make all this up to you, I promise."

She heard voices behind him that sounded like children playing. "Who's there with you?"

"I'm in the lobby with one of the guys I owe money to. He brought his wife and kids to the conference. I'll be looking for that text—and, darlin', I can't wait to see you. Thank you so much for doing this for us."

"I'd do anything for you, Neal," she told him. The first lie she'd told in years. Guilt lay on her shoulders like hot coals.

"Hugs and kisses." He blew her a kiss.

"See you soon. Hugs and kisses." She blew a kiss back, and then she really started to mourn for what could have been.

Macy removed her engagement ring and held it up to the light. "Please be real," she whispered as she pressed it against the glass display case and tried to make a long scratch.

"What are you doing?" Sarah asked, coming out of the kitchen. "That case would cost hundreds to replace."

Macy's hands shook as she threw her ring across the dining area and then slumped down on the floor. "It's not real. It's fake. I'd bet dollars to cow patties that Darla Jo's is real."

Sarah crossed the room and picked up the ring. "What made you test it? What did Darla Jo say to you when she was here?"

"That she and Edward are leaving today for their island," Macy sobbed.

Sarah sat down beside her and draped an arm around her shoulders. "Why would that make you test this thing?" She held up the ring and eyed it carefully.

"What's going on in here?" Grace asked.

Sarah handed the ring off to her. "This isn't real. It won't scratch glass. And Edward and Darla Jo are leaving town today."

"Does that mean that Neal is in the clear?" Grace asked.

Macy took the ring from Grace and put it back on her finger. "It means I need y'all to go with me to Darla Jo's house right now. We'll talk on the way about why. My heart wants me to be wrong, but my mind tells me that I'm right. If Neal and Edward are the same person, I will never trust another man as long as I live."

Grace locked the front door and came back to extend a hand to Macy. "Let's go take care of this once and for all."

Macy put her hand in Grace's and stood up. Her heart was doing double time, and her head was beginning to ache, but she still held out hope that her Neal and Darla Jo's Edward were two different men. Her phone pinged. She checked it to see a message from Neal: Haven't gotten those numbers. Did you send them?

She sent one back: Working on it right now.

Sarah stood right beside her and read over her shoulder. "Working on what?"

"Long story, but here goes," Macy answered, and told them what had happened as they left the shop, got into Sarah's truck, and drove north toward the ranch that Henry had left Darla Jo when he died. Talk around town was that its sale was being finalized for a cool five million.

She ended the story with testing the diamond in her ring, but part of her was still holding on to hope that there was an explanation as they drove through town. Grace reached up from the back seat and laid a hand on her shoulder. "I'm so sorry—but, honey, it's over. Neal is not in San Diego. He's at Darla Jo's, and they are about to leave. Getting his hands on what you have is their final play."

"Why would he even want what I have in savings when it wouldn't be but a drop in the bucket compared to what Darla Jo has gotten from Henry's and Wesley's estates?" To keep from crying, Macy looked out the passenger-side window of Sarah's truck. Everything looked different than it had a week ago. Even the lovely signs of spring that sped past the windows were as dull as the ache in her heart.

"He thought he was going to get everything," Sarah said. "You didn't tell him that most of your money is tied up in investments, did you?"

Macy shook her head. "Not until today. I just told him what it all amounted to."

Sarah drove past the sign that said "Devine, Texas: Small Town. Big Heart. Great Future."

"Yeah, right," Macy muttered. "*Small town* is right, but it should say only fools have big hearts and think they have a great future."

"At least the first one is right," Sarah said.

"But that last one is probably going to break my heart." Macy tried to keep the tears at bay, but it was impossible. How could she have been so blind?

Sarah made a sharp left turn into the lane leading back to a long, low sprawling ranch house—and right there, in front of Macy's eyes, was Neal's bright red SUV. Macy straightened her back, set her jaw, and got ready for the battle. She had always been slow to anger, but seeing Neal's car parked there caused wrath to rise to a peak she didn't know she even had in her. She didn't have anything that faintly resembled a weapon, which was a good thing, but then she didn't need one.

Vengeance is mine, the annoying voice in her head said.

"Today, God needs a little help," she muttered.

Two little boys ran out of the house and got into the back seat of the SUV. Macy thought of the two boys that she and Neal had talked about having—Teddy for his grandfather, Elijah for hers. Had his parents really even been killed in a car wreck, or were they alive and well somewhere? Had he learned the art of conning from them, or had he and Darla Jo come up with that all on their own?

Macy's phone pinged. She checked it and found another message from Neal: They're getting really impatient, and I'm getting pretty scared right now. Need those numbers. Love you.

Darla Jo was so preoccupied with her blue purse, a small pink suitcase, and the yellow box of doughnuts that it took a moment for her to realize Sarah had parked right behind Neal's SUV.

"He's texting me about the numbers right now, and he's walking out the door to run away with Darla Jo," Macy growled.

"Oh. My. God!" Sarah said.

"He's really doing that," Grace gasped. "Let's go . . ." She swung open the truck door.

The little boys hopped out of the car and ran back into the house. The older one yelled, "We forgot to get the charge cords for our tablets."

Darla Jo raised her voice. "Well, hurry up!"

"This is my fight," Macy said through clenched teeth as she got out of the truck. "You can stop me from killing him outright, but other than that, I'll take care of it. I'm not planning on being in jail when Raelene graduates or when Audrey inherits the shop."

Darla Jo's face went blank when she saw Macy storming across the lawn. She dropped the suitcase, the doughnuts, and her purse, then turned around, screamed, "Edward!" and took off in a dead run toward the porch.

Macy ran faster in sneakers than Darla Jo could in three-inch high heels, so she beat the woman to the porch, jerked the phone out of Neal's hand, and threw it at the SUV. It hit just right, sending a nice big crack in the windshield. Darla Jo made it to the porch about the same time Macy drew back her fist and popped Neal—or Edward, or whatever the devil his name was—right between the eyes. Blood immediately ran from his nose and down over his lips, which didn't look so kissable right then.

She was about to hit him again when Darla Jo tackled her, and they both tumbled down the steps and out into the yard. Macy's redhaired temper became an uncontrollable force. She saw Grace and Sarah get out of the truck, but she held up her palm.

"Stay back," she yelled as she pulled Darla Jo up by a fistful of hair and dragged her to the SUV. "You can have him. I don't want him, but this is between me and Neal, Edward, or whoever he is."

Neal was suddenly beside her, with one hand trying to catch the blood flowing from his nose and the other attempting to free Darla Jo's hair from Macy's hand.

"Darla Jo, darlin'," he gasped, "I'm so sorry."

"You should be apologizing to me, not her," Macy growled and pushed his hand away from hers.

"Get my purse and suitcase," Darla Jo screeched, "and let's get out of here."

Neal ran back to pick up her things and, as the boys started to come back out of the house, immediately yelled at his sons, "You guys go back in and find my flip-flops. I just remembered I forgot to pack them." He grabbed the sack and tossed everything into the back of the SUV.

Who knew the creep had a true caring bone in his body? They're definitely not going to want to see this, Macy thought.

By then, Macy had pushed Darla Jo into the passenger seat with enough force that she was slammed up against the console. Then she went at Neal, using the kickboxing she'd learned at a defense class the church had sponsored a few years back. The first strike landed in his groin. He hit the dirt, rolled up in a fetal position, and moaned. She heard a rib crack when she landed the second one, and she had brought her foot back for another kick by the time Grace and Sarah pulled her away.

He was still rolling around in the grass and getting stains on his white slacks when she freed herself from her cousins and put a foot on his chest. Then she removed her fake engagement ring and threw it at him. "You almost made it, Neal—or Edward, or whatever your name is. I believed every word you told me. But in every bad experience, there's a good lesson to be learned. I guess now you'll have to live on what you and Darla Jo have swindled out of folks for the past ten years. Be careful—you might just die in your sleep like they did."

Darla Jo had gotten out of the SUV and was trying to get past Sarah and Grace. "Are you crazy? I'm calling the police right now!" she screamed as she fell onto the ground beside him and gathered him up in her arms.

"If you really want them, I'll call them myself and tell them what's been going on here," Macy said through clenched teeth.

"Just get out of here," Neal gasped.

"Let's go," Grace said.

"Nope, I want to tell the police about attempted fraud and see what they have to say about it," Macy said. "Maybe he can spend a night or two in county lockup while we straighten all this out. Plane tickets sure are expensive these days."

"Noooo," he said.

"Cut your losses and be glad that they aren't worse," Sarah said as she took Macy by the arm and led her back to the truck.

"Edward is really the love of my life. I would never hurt a hair on his head!" Darla Jo screamed at her.

Vengeance . . . the voice in Macy's head started.

"Save it," she barked at both the voice and Darla Jo.

"Daddy, we can't find them," one of the boys yelled from the front door.

"Look out by the swimming pool," Edward managed to get out.

Macy broke free from Sarah and went back to stand over the lot of them. "How many others were there before me?"

Darla Jo laughed. "That's classified, but you weren't the first."

"Will I be the last?" Macy asked.

"Maybe," Darla Jo answered. "The boys are getting older, and they need stability in their lives."

"You will pay for this," Macy whispered as Darla Jo got to her feet. "Somewhere down the road, you will pay dearly for what you have done and the hearts you have broken." She gave Darla Jo a hard push, and the woman landed on top of Neal.

"Maybe so"—Neal rolled over and wrapped Darla Jo up in his arms—"but we'll have fun on the journey to that place in the road. In another life, Macy, we might have made a good couple."

"In another life, you wouldn't have even looked at someone like her." Darla Jo managed to get into a seated position. "Now I have to change clothes. I can't travel like this, and you need to clean up. You can't go anywhere with dried blood on your face. Thank God the boys were in the house."

Macy got into the truck, took a deep breath, and let it out slowly. "My whole body is trembling with anger, and my ears are buzzing like a whole hive of bees have taken up residence there. Thank God y'all pulled me off him. I've never been so mad. The Jesus I thought I had in me was tested, and I failed."

"He's a con man, and that's a first cousin to the devil," Grace said. "Jesus would have kicked him a few times if he'd been here."

Sarah slapped the steering wheel. "I'm not moving. He's good at manipulation—let him work that vehicle around to get out of here. I hope they miss their plane."

"Looks like that witch decided to travel in her dirty dress and her messy hair after all." Macy pointed at the SUV; Darla Jo was already inside, and Neal was limping toward the driver's side.

"I bet they're not even going to an island." Grace frowned. "They're probably off to another town to swindle someone else."

"Maybe so," Macy whispered, "but at least they didn't take us to the cleaners on the way. I can't believe I was that gullible. From now on, if I even *look* at another man, you two have permission to put *me* in a convent."

"Our faith doesn't have convents," Grace reminded her.

"Then I'll use my money to start a monastery for sorry suckers like Neal—or Edward, or whatever the reincarnated devil is calling himself. So they can't hurt anyone else." Macy watched Neal expertly get the SUV out of the tight spot. Darla Jo blew her a kiss as they drove away. "That witch! I'd like to slap that smile right off her face. Why did she come into the shop today, anyway?"

"It was all part of the con," Grace said. "Edward was leaving with her. Neal was in trouble and needed a lot of money. You would panic to get him out of a bind and give him your bank numbers so he could wipe you out as they drove out of town."

"And they would laugh and laugh about it all the way to the airport," Macy said. "I need ice cream, and I need to settle down before I die of a heart attack at thirty-two years old. Take me home. I'll call Beezy, and she can meet us there."

"Are you going to weep and wail and lay around in your pajamas for weeks?" Grace asked.

"No, I'm going to call the sheriff and see if there's anything that can be done," Macy answered. "But if folks ask what happened, please back me up when I tell them that I broke up with Neal because he was seeing another woman. That's the truth—at least, part of it."

Grace patted her again. "No one needs to know any more than that, but I don't think there's a thing that can be done without solid evidence. Still, if Sheriff Mason knows about it, he might be able to put out an alert of some kind to keep them from conning someone else in the future."

Macy held her head high and kept a stiff upper lip, but inside, her heart felt as if it had been shattered into a thousand pieces.

Chapter Seven

All those old feelings of betrayal and hopelessness that she had experienced when Justin left her swept over Grace again on the way home that day. Macy's pain, her anger, her attempt to deal with it and still keep working with the public, the betrayal and guilt that Sarah felt . . . Grace understood all of it.

"I guess we can all three sympathize with each other," she whispered.

"One of our hymns says something about wanting to feel the pain my neighbors feel so I can sympathize with them," Macy said.

Sarah made the left-hand turn into the doughnut shop's parking lot and then followed the path back to the house. "Not me. I don't hear a hymn in my head right now. What I hear is that Miranda Lambert song about kerosene, where the lyrics say that she's been burned for the last time."

"This is my first, last, and never-again burning time," Macy said as she called Beezy. "We need you to come to the house, Beezy. Don't drive fast, but it's an emergency."

"Are we going to tell the girls?" Grace asked.

Macy dropped her phone in her purse and opened the truck door. "Yes, we're going to tell them. They are old enough to learn that not everyone can be trusted."

"Especially Audrey," Grace agreed. The way her daughter trusted those two friends of hers was downright scary.

Sarah led the way from the truck to the house. Audrey looked up from the sofa where she and Raelene were working on algebra, caught her mother's eye, and then saw Macy. She jumped up like she'd sat on an electric wire.

"What happened to you? Did y'all have a wreck or . . ." Audrey ran across the room and draped an arm around Macy's shoulders.

"I'll tell you all about it as soon as Beezy gets here," Macy answered.

"Just answer one question." Raelene laid the laptop on the coffee table. "Do we need to take you to the emergency room?"

"Lord have mercy!" Macy snapped. "Do I look that bad?"

Audrey turned Macy around so she could see her reflection in the mirror in the small foyer. "You tell us."

"Sweet Lord!" Macy shook off Audrey's arm and began picking blades of grass and leaves from her hair.

"You should see Darla Jo and Neal," Grace said. "They both look and feel a lot worse—and believe me, I didn't know Macy had it in her."

"You've been in a fight?" Raelene's eyes widened as big as saucers.

Macy gave up on her hair and headed to the kitchen. "I have, and I won, but I don't feel like I did."

Grace went straight to the freezer for a half-gallon container of rocky road ice cream. "We can start on this while we wait on Beezy."

"Hey, I'm sorry I'm late to the party," Beezy said, coming through the back door. "I drove as fast as I could—speed limit signs are just a suggestion when you get to be my age. What's going on?"

Raelene stood up and went to the counter for another spoon. She handed it to Beezy and pulled out the last chair for her.

"Ice cream?" Beezy sat down and dug into the container. "So it's true, is it? Neal left town this morning with Darla Jo, and those two boys she's got belong to him. I knew all along that she was up to something with those poor gentlemen, but I liked Neal. We're lucky that they're both gone. Devine doesn't need people like them."

Macy groaned. "I'd hoped that I could save a little bit of face."

"Bless your heart," Beezy said, "and I mean that in a good way. This is not your fault."

Macy took a deep breath, let it out slowly, and told Beezy and the girls what had happened that day, starting with Darla Jo coming into the shop and ending with details of the fight. "Yes, it is my fault for trusting too easily, but it won't ever happen again."

"That man is a . . . ," Beezy stammered. "If I hadn't promised God that I would clean up my language, I would . . ." She set her mouth in a firm line and rolled her eyes toward the ceiling. "Lord, forgive me for breaking my promise, but he *is* a son of a bitch."

"That means I've lost my substitute babysitting job, and I don't get to be a bridesmaid, either. But I would have loved to have seen that fight. I didn't know you took kickboxing lessons. Will you teach me how to do that?" Audrey asked but didn't wait for an answer. "I liked Neal. Why would he do this to us?"

Grace wondered why her daughter couldn't see that she was in the same kind of canoe that Macy had been paddling. Crystal and Kelsey were using her just like Neal had used Macy—maybe on a smaller level, but a con was a con, whether they were teenagers or grown men.

"Neal only liked himself. And he did it for money," Raelene answered. "My mama's boyfriend is like that in a way. He says his back is hurt and he can't work, so Mama supports him. He's just a lower form of a swindler than Neal, but they've both got black hearts."

"Vengeance belongs to the Lord," Macy said, repeating the words that had come to her mind more than once that day.

"But sometimes even God needs help," Audrey said.

Raelene nodded. "God couldn't build an ark, so he had Noah do it."

"You got that right." Audrey raised her hand for a high five.

Grace was shocked that the girls were united in any way, but it gave her a glimmer of hope that her daughter would open her eyes to what was really going on with her new friends.

Raelene slapped Audrey's hand and dug out another spoonful of ice cream. "Do you really think men like him will get their comeuppance, Macy?"

"I do, and when it happens, they'll remember how many . . ." Macy stuck her spoon back in the container, covered her face with her hands, and began to cry.

"I think God knows that Neal is an SOB," Audrey declared and glanced over at her mother. "I didn't use bad language. I spelled it out—and besides, it's the truth. So anyway, God will give us both a pass today, Beezy."

"That's good." Beezy had barely gotten the words out when her phone rang. She fetched it out of her skirt pocket. "I need to get this. It's my sister, but I'll make it quick." She slid her finger across the screen and said, "Hello, Mavis. I've got you on speaker with the Dalton family."

"Good!" a woman with a thin, high-pitched voice said. "Macy, I'm so sorry that Neal turned out to be a swindler. All of us at the church thought he was a good man, what with showing up to sit with you and being so kind to us old ladies. We almost feel as betrayed as you must, but we just want you to know we'll be praying for you."

"Thank you," Macy said.

"Beezy, I'm just reminding you that we're on for a game of poker this evening," Mavis said. "Now, get on back to your visit."

"I'll be there," Beezy said, then ended the call. "Now, where were we? So did Neal get any money?"

"No," Macy groaned. "Gossip sure travels fast."

"Granny used to say that it went even faster than the speed of sound," Raelene said.

"I believe it," Grace agreed. A picture of Travis flashed through her mind. What would he make of this kind of trouble, and would he still push to purchase the business and land?

"Me too," Sarah said with a nod.

"Thank God you have a bull-crap radar," Beezy said. "But rest assured, nothing like this has ever happened in Devine. People will be talking about it for weeks. I imagine that y'all better double the number of doughnuts you usually make for a few days."

Audrey scraped the bottom of the ice cream container clean, then picked up all the spoons and took them to the sink. "Why would they need to make more doughnuts?"

"The best place to get the good gossip is at the source," Grace answered. "Folks will be dropping by to buy doughnuts in hopes that they can get Macy to tell them more about Neal."

"I'm staying in the kitchen for the next month," Macy declared.

Grace had no trouble relating to Macy on that issue. She had refused to wait on customers when Justin left town and had spent weeks in the kitchen, making doughnuts and icing them. She and Justin had been high school sweethearts. She'd had no doubt that they would get married and grow old together. Then she had gotten pregnant, and he hadn't been ready to be a father. He had taken the coward's way out and left a note on the windshield of her car that said he just couldn't see a life of working, coming home, and raising a baby.

Beezy bumped shoulders with Grace. "What are you thinking about? That you'd like to strangle three men until their faces turn blue?"

"Three?" Audrey asked. "Is there more than Neal and Joel?"

"I'll provide the rope for the strangling business for Joel," Sarah offered.

"And since the girls have reminded me that sometimes God needs human hands to carry out His vengeance," Macy said, "I will gladly give you whatever you need to take care of Neal, or Edward, or whoever he is."

"Who's the third one?" Raelene asked.

Audrey glanced down the table at her mother. "That would be Justin, right? Mama, I don't need a father. I've got all of you to boss me around."

Grace gave her a thumbs-up. "But it would have been nice for him to stick around and see what an amazing daughter he helped to create."

Audrey gave her a crooked little smile. "But now you get to take all the credit if I turn out good."

"Or all the credit if you turn out to be a delinquent," Sarah reminded her.

"Enough about me." Audrey shot a dirty look toward her aunt. "Macy is the one we're here to support today."

Grace couldn't believe that Audrey had just diverted attention away from herself. Usually, like with most teenage girls, everything was about Audrey. If it rained, it was just so that her hair would frizz. If the power went out, she whined that God hated her because she couldn't blow-dry her hair.

"You're off in la-la land again," Beezy whispered just for Grace's ears.

"Yep, I am," she said with a nod. "To some degree, I've been where every one of you except Raelene have been, and I have the battle scars to prove it. I feel what each of you are going through and want you to know that I'm here to listen when you need to talk—and that goes for all of you."

"Except Raelene? What does that mean? That she can't come talk to you? Is that fair?" Audrey frowned.

"I've never been without a home or a place to stay, and my mother put me on the payroll at the doughnut shop when I was sixteen, so I've always had a job," Grace explained. "That's what I meant, and Raelene is always welcome to come talk to me anytime she wants."

"Girl, we were being paid to do odd jobs at the shop when we were thirteen," Sarah reminded her.

"But we didn't get to be on payroll and get a weekly check until we were sixteen," Macy said. "I remember feeling like a queen when I opened my first checking account."

"And how did you feel when you were twenty-five?" Beezy asked.

"When I found out how much money was in my trust fund, I *was* the queen." Macy smiled for the first time that day. "And to think I almost threw it all away on a con man."

"But you didn't, so take comfort in that," Beezy told her. "You girls would make your mothers proud. And someday when this young'un grows up"—she pointed at Audrey—"she's going to make y'all just as proud."

Audrey filled the electric teakettle with water and plugged it in to make hot tea. "I'm not sure I'm ever going to get married. If I want kids, I'll pick out a sperm donor that's tall, dark, and handsome and a genius who knows algebra, so my kids won't struggle with it."

"Why?" Beezy asked.

"Because of what's happening right now, today," Audrey declared with a wave of her hand. "Men can't be trusted."

"And girls who make you do mean things can?" Grace asked.

"I don't want to talk about that," Audrey answered. "But I do want to live in a town where I can sneeze and nobody calls my mama to see if I've got the flu. Maybe in a big city where nobody knew my grandmother—and I sure don't want to pour coffee and make doughnuts for a living."

Grace remembered saying the same thing to her mother when she was about Audrey's age. She'd had to eat those words, and they had been bittersweet. People had talked about her, and some had even said she was the reason her mother had died. According to them, she couldn't bear the fact that Grace was pregnant—the first in the long line of good Christian Dalton women who had taken the wrong path.

"If I didn't have a scholarship, I would beg for a job in the shop," Raelene whispered. "Living here and working for y'all is the best thing that's happened to me since my Granny passed away."

Macy reached over and laid a hand on Raelene's shoulder. "You can always come back on holidays and stay with us. This is your home now, girl, and we're glad you are here with us. You are family. Heck, I need this family, too—thank you all for being here for me today, and for helping me start to get through this. I'm still half expecting someone to wake me up any minute from this nightmare."

"Just keep telling yourself that you are strong and that when the time is right, a man will come into your life that will love you for yourself and not for your money," Beezy told her.

"Right now, I don't want to meet another man for a long, long time," Macy answered.

"Me either," Grace and Sarah said at the same time.

Chapter Eight

Happy first day of spring," Claud called out as he pushed open the door to the doughnut shop that morning. "March came in like a lamb, which means in a little more than a week, it'll be going out like a lion. But last evening the sky was red, and the old saying goes 'Red sky at night, sailor's delight.' I'm not a sailor, but I do like to fish, so I'm going to take that as a sign."

"We'll gladly take the month going out like a lamb instead of the lion." Grace filled three mugs with coffee and carried them to their regular table. "I've dealt with enough lions these past few days."

"We've still got time for a tornado or two by the end of the month," Ira warned.

Grace set a mug in front of each of the men. "Maybe I'll have a few days of peace between now and then. What can I get you guys today?"

"Just mix up a dozen and set them in the middle of the table. I'll treat these two old codgers today and take what we don't eat home with me," Frankie answered. "But be sure to put three of those with maple icing on them in the box, or we'll fight over them. And Grace, darlin', we've been downwind from all the rumors. The waters could get rough, if you know what I mean."

"I do, and we're ready for whatever life—or the universe, as the kids call it today—throws at us," Grace assured them.

"How's Macy holding up?" Ira asked. "That sweet lady didn't deserve all this."

"She's tough on the outside," Grace said in a low voice, "but this hasn't been easy on her. Neal— or whoever he is—really pulled the wool over her eyes."

"It's a good thing he and that woman left town, or the three of us might have been tempted to tar and feather them and ride them out on a rail," Frankie said.

Claud shook his head slowly. "Makes a body wonder what kind of heart is in a person that would make them hurt other folks. If there's anything at all we can do to help, just name it."

"Thank you for that," Grace said with a smile.

"We mean it," Ira said. "Just give us a holler if we can do anything."

"Will do." Grace had started back toward the counter when the shop bell let her know someone else was out and about at five o'clock in the morning. She turned to see Travis coming through the door. Today she took a long look at him. He was over six feet tall and had dark hair perfectly feathered back and brown eyes behind black-rimmed glasses. The cut of his trousers and buttoned-up shirt left no doubt that they were tailor-made to fit his frame. No wonder she was attracted to him—most women probably gave him a second look.

Travis caught her eye and nodded toward her. "Good mornin', Miz Dalton. Would you please bring me a cup of coffee and put whatever those guys ordered on my ticket this morning?"

"I sure can." She turned and rounded the end of the counter. The sparks that bounced around between them annoyed her. This was the wrong time to get involved in any capacity with anyone—and besides, he was only there to try to talk them into selling the business, not for any physical attraction.

She poured his coffee and carried it across the room. Her reflection in the glass door as she passed by it almost made her giggle. Those little vibes were just the result of having been alone for so many years. Travis might be rich, but she and her sister and cousin were very comfortable financially, so she dang sure didn't need to sell her shop and land.

She set his coffee in front of him. "There you go. Enjoy your breakfast."

"I heard what happened with Neal, and I feel that I owe you and your family an apology," Travis said in a low voice only for her ears. "I vetted him, but evidently he's quite the con artist. However, I am still interested in talking to you about this shop, or maybe about putting in a mass-production bakery."

"Still not for sale, and I wouldn't know anything about a factory," Grace said and walked away.

"Good morning, Grace," Lisa said as she and Carlita pushed their way into the shop and quickly claimed a table. "Bring us two decaf coffees and a dozen glazed doughnuts."

The twinge Grace had felt when she saw Travis and now the aggravation of having to deal with those two women sure didn't sit well with her this morning. She would have far rather kicked them out the door than wait on them, but she poured two mugs of coffee and filled a box with doughnuts.

"Enjoy," she said when she set their order on the table.

"How is Macy doing?" Lisa asked before Grace could get away.

"The poor darling. I can't even begin to imagine what she's going through." Carlita's expression was sincere, but it didn't fool Grace.

You would get some firsthand experience about what she's going through if you kept better tabs on your husband, Grace thought, *but you've got your head in the sand and your skinny butt stuck straight up in the air.*

"She is doing very well," Grace said and clamped her mouth shut to keep from saying what was on her mind.

"Well, well, well!" Sarah brought out another tray of doughnuts and slid them into the case. "I thought you two weren't ever coming back in this shop again. Have you changed your minds about your daughters keeping company with my niece?"

"We have not," Carlita said, "but we're just concerned for Macy."

"She is just fine," Sarah said. "Macy is tougher than you might think."

"How's it working out with Raelene living with y'all?" Carlita asked. "I heard that she's . . ."—she lowered her voice—"kind of weird and that Audrey is mortified."

"What was it that wise person said about not believing anything you hear and only half of what you see?" Grace asked.

"Poor little Raelene." Lisa sighed. "She didn't have much of a chance with a mother like Geneva. We were discussing her sad situation and thought we'd offer to help out by sending her over to the group home in San Antonio. We would feel so much better if she wasn't around our girls, even at school—and certainly not in our church."

Sarah crossed the room in a few strides. "She's just fine where she is, and we love having her as part of our family. I'm thinking of adopting her."

"I heard you are going to sell your shop and recipe and part of your land. Are you thinking of moving from Devine?" Lisa asked. "You know that my husband, Kenneth, is in the real estate business, and I'm sure he could get you a better deal for all this than you could get selling it on your own."

Grace whipped around and took a couple of steps back toward the table. "One more time: We. Are. Not. Selling!"

Carlita stirred four containers of cream and six sugar packets into her coffee. "It might be best for Audrey if you did move."

"I will miss these doughnuts when you leave," Lisa said and then lowered her voice when she nodded toward the other end of the dining area. "Is that the man thinking of putting in a mass-production bakery right here in Devine? Travis Butler? God knows we could use the jobs that a big factory would bring in."

Carlita giggled under her breath. "I bet you're just stringing him along to get at that Butler money. You'd be a fool not to, girl—and that would mean Audrey would go to school next year in San Antonio. All problems would be solved."

"One more time: We are not moving anywhere. And I'm not dating anyone." Grace went right back to the kitchen. "Lisa and Carlita are out there." She held her hands out, wrists together. "Handcuff me so I don't go back and pour a pot of hot coffee on their heads."

"I vote that we whip up some special chocolate doughnuts tonight," Sarah suggested. "We can dose them with laxative."

"I bet we could find some of that funny oregano somewhere in town to add to them." Macy wiped her hands on her apron. "But rather than make them sick, I'll take care of them. Enough is enough. I'm not hiding out anymore." She stormed out of the kitchen like she was heading for another bout of kickboxing.

"Mercy!" Grace said. "Her temper is risin', again. Haven't seen her like this in . . . ever."

"'Bout time," Sarah replied.

Macy marched out into the dining area, picked up a full coffeepot, and headed toward the end of the room where the guys were still talking. "How are y'all this mornin'?" she said cheerfully. "Need a warm-up?"

"Yes, ma'am," Claud said, "and we'd like to introduce you to our friend Travis Butler. He's thinking of putting in a big business right here in Devine. It would bring in lots of jobs that would revive the economy in this little town."

"Nice to meet you, Mr. Butler," Macy said as she refilled the mugs. "Good luck with your business."

"My pleasure," Travis said with a nod, "and I'm hoping that things work out."

She moved on over to the table where a couple of elderly ladies from church were wiping the sugar from their hands. "You girls need a refill?"

"You bet we do," Dotty said and then lowered her voice. "We're sorry about Neal, but we heard that you took care of it."

"I did, but it wasn't very Christian-like," Macy admitted.

"Jesus threw the money changers out of the temple for being dishonest," Dotty reminded her. "I heard that you might be selling this place. I'd sure hate to see that. It's been here my whole life. Your grandmother and mother both were my friends."

"There are days when I'd sell it, but I'm only half owner of this place. What I say is important, but what Grace says has always been the law, and nobody messes with her. If Neal had done her like he did me, he would have never fathered another child," Macy said loud enough that Lisa and Carlita could hear it like a crack of thunder.

"Amen to that," Dotty said. "But your mama would sure be disappointed if you girls sold the place. It's been here almost as long as Devine has been a town. And, honey, I hear that after the kickin' you gave him, he might not be thinkin' of fatherin' a child for a while anyway."

"You should never believe everything you hear," Macy said and then moved on toward the table where Lisa and Carlita were seated. "Y'all need a warm-up?"

Lisa nodded and held up her cup. "It's good to see you feeling better. I've been worried that maybe all this misfortune and then having Raelene living with you might be causing your headaches. Lisa and I were just telling Grace that we've got some connections with a group home up in San Antonio that we could call in a favor and get her into."

"Raelene pulls her own weight at our house, and she's a blessing to have around." Macy's tone seemed to lower the temperature twenty degrees, but she didn't care if these two never came back into the shop. "She actually helps heal my headaches with her oils."

Carlita's nose twitched in half a snarl. "Well, I suppose that you all would take in Geneva's kid. Birds of a feather, and all that—"

Macy cut her off before she could say another word. "If I could ever be as gracious and as kindhearted as Raelene Andrews, then I would feel like I had accomplished something with my life." She set the pot on the table, pulled out a chair, and sat down. "And if y'all don't stop spreading gossip about me, my family, or Raelene, we're going to take a little trip out back of this shop, and I'm going to kick your asses."

"If that's the way you feel, I don't imagine we'll be coming back anymore," Lisa said.

"You've promised that before," Macy said. "I'll believe it when I see it, and I don't think that losing your business will cause us to weep and moan and gnash our teeth."

Dotty gave her a thumbs-up sign, and Claud winked from the other end of the room. Macy didn't even bother cleaning up the table but headed right back to the kitchen. She slid down the back of the door and sat on the floor with her arms wrapped around her knees.

"My Jesus spirit got tested again, and I failed again," she said through clenched teeth.

Sarah sat down on one side of her and Grace on the other.

"Want to talk about it?" Sarah asked.

"I threatened to take Lisa and Carlita out behind the shop and whoop their asses if they didn't stop spreading rumors about me and Raelene," she answered.

"Well, halle-dang-lujah." Sarah hugged her tightly.

"As mad as I am, I know I could take on both of them with one hand tied behind my back and blindfolded. How dare they want to send Raelene to a group home and to suggest that she's the cause of my headaches?" Macy snapped.

"I'll gladly help if you ever really take on that business of whooping them." Grace made it a three-way hug.

"And like I said, I'm not hiding out anymore." Macy stood up and marched right back out into the dining room.

Grace hoped that Macy used up the last bit of her anger to wipe the floor with Lisa and Carlita. If that happened, Grace would volunteer to clean up the blood herself. She didn't even care if Macy kicked them through the glass windows.

Lisa raised her voice. "Macy, are you over your snit?"

Macy marched over to their table, placed her palms on the edge of the table, and leaned down and whispered, "No, I came back for a second round to tell you that if Audrey isn't good enough to be friends with your daughters, then you aren't welcome here as of this moment."

"Well!" Lisa huffed.

Macy leaned across the table until she was nose-to-nose with Lisa. "And besides, Audrey was most likely covering for Crystal and Kelsey when they found that contraband in her purse. We all know who the bad kids are."

Carlita jumped up so fast that her chair fell backward, sounding like a shotgun blast when it hit the tiled floor. "My daughter goes to church on Sunday, and she doesn't smoke or drink."

"Neither does Crystal," Lisa hissed.

Macy straightened up. "You poor things. You've got your heads even farther in the sand when it comes to your kids than I did with Neal. I will pray for you."

"They need more than prayers." Grace rolled her eyes toward the ceiling.

Macy stormed across the room and went back to the kitchen again. "We all need a vacation. Not just a trip to the lake for a picnic." She paced the floor. "We need to get away from this place for a week or two and catch our breath, or I'm liable to snatch those two out there plumb bald-headed."

"We'll get serious about taking the girls to the beach after Raelene graduates. There's no way we can take them out of school," Grace said.

"Serious about what?" Sarah said as she came through the door. "What were y'all whispering about out there when Carlita tried to break the floor tiles with her chair?"

Macy told the story as she continued to pace. "I was just telling Grace how much we all need some time away from Devine."

"I'm ready when y'all are," Sarah said. "Soon as the girls are out of school, let's really do that trip to Florida instead of just talking about it. On another note, who was that man over at the table with Claud and the others? The dining room is empty now, but they all four had their heads together like they were plotting something before they left. And the man paid the bill for all of them, so he must be a friend."

"Travis Butler. I forgot that you hadn't met him when he came in here before. He's the one who wants to buy our property and the recipe," Grace answered.

Sarah asked, "Is Travis the one that owns Butler Enterprises? I've heard of him and his big business."

"Probably so."

"Well, that will definitely set everyone in town on their ear trying to figure out the juiciest gossip," Sarah said. "Macy, honey, you may have to take a back seat."

"Just show me the way to the chair," Macy grumbled.

The bell above the front door dinged, and Grace went to wait on whoever was there. She frowned when she saw Carlita coming in with a smug look on her face.

"I forgot to get a dozen doughnuts to take home," she said. "Crystal is coming over to the house so she and Kelsey can work on their English today. They get so hungry after about an hour in Kelsey's room."

I wonder why? Grace thought as she boxed up the order.

Carlita pulled out a credit card and snapped it down on the counter. "Since you've only got a few left in the display case, I'll take all of those, too. I should get a discount for buying everything so you can close up shop for the day."

"It doesn't work that way," Grace said as she boxed up the last dozen assorted doughnuts in a second box, rang up the sale, and handed the slip to Carlita to sign. There wasn't a single doubt in Grace's mind that Carlita had come back to subtly put Grace in her place. Grace was the person who had to wait on Carlita, and that made her feel superior and maybe even a little self-righteous.

Sarah came from the back and began to set the chairs up on the tables so she could mop the floors. "For someone who wasn't ever going to come back in here, you sure are spending a lot of money on doughnuts."

"You really should get out more, Sarah," Carlita said with a sniff, "other than in bars on Saturday nights. You might even find a decent man who would have you."

Grace's hands knotted into fists, and her blood pressure shot up as high as the fluffy white clouds in the sky. Baiting Sarah like that made her want to throw punches.

"Or better yet, a man might come along that *I* would have," Sarah said. "One that will be faithful to me."

Carlita had picked up the two boxes but jerked to a halt. "What is that supposed to mean?"

"You figure it out for yourself," Grace answered. "We don't spread rumors. But take a long, hard look at your life and your family. You might realize that your kid is downright mean—and while you are facing reality, take a long look at your marriage."

Carlita got in the last words as she left the shop. "You are throwing mud at me that should be on you."

"What a bitch!" Sarah said, locking the door behind Carlita.

Grace followed her sister to the kitchen and could have sworn that she saw smoke coming out of Sarah's ears.

"Are you all right?" Macy asked.

Sarah gritted her teeth. "Nope."

"What happened?" Macy asked. "Sarah looks like she's ready to explode, and you don't look much better."

"Reckon you could do some of that fancy kickboxing on Carlita and Lisa?" Grace asked.

"I would be glad to," Macy said with a smile. "But that would spread even more rumors—and I, for one, am sick of them."

Chapter Nine

A knock on his office door brought Travis back to the busy present and away from thoughts about Grace Dalton. Without waiting for an invitation, Calvin poked his head inside. "Mornin'. You ready to get this day on the road? We're burnin' daylight. Delores is on her way."

"I'm ready," Travis said with a smile.

"What's going on?" Calvin asked.

"You've met my grandpa's friends. Claud, Ira, and Frankie have been trying to get me to put in a business in Devine, Texas, for a long time, and now they've come up with this idea of putting in a mass-production bakery. And I promised my grandpa back before he passed away that someday I would do something to help the little town of Devine. His mama's folks came from there way back when."

"A bakery?" Calvin's eyes widened. "Are you serious? We deal in land, developments, mineral rights, and that kind of thing, not cooking classes. Have you talked to the think tank about this?"

"Not yet," Travis answered. "They are working on an assessment for putting in a housing development down there. Devine is only thirty minutes from San Antonio, and as commutes go, that's not bad at all."

"Well, that sure sounds like something more down our alley than a bakery," Calvin told him.

Delores didn't even knock when she pushed open the door. She was really the COO of the company but hadn't wanted the title, so she just opted for supervisor. In reality, she knew more about Butler Enterprises than anyone.

"What's so important that you took me away from a meeting with the think-tank kids?" she asked.

"Travis wants to open a bakery," Calvin spit out.

"A bakery that sells doughnuts," Travis said.

He removed his glasses, cleaned them, and put them back on. "I forgot my briefcase this morning with some figures I've come up with on the bakery. I'll be right back."

He walked across the hallway to the elevator. The doors opened immediately, and he pushed the button to the seventh floor, where his apartment was located. His briefcase was sitting on his desk, right where he'd left it. He picked it up, went out into the hallway, and got back into the elevator. The seventh floor had a couple of smaller apartments that were used for business associates when they needed to stay in San Antonio. There were also two large conference rooms and a kitchen for a chef that came in when Travis needed her. For the most part, the whole floor was quiet, and Travis liked it that way.

The doors made very little noise as they closed. Travis studied his reflection in the mirrored walls and thought about Grace Dalton. From what Claud had told him, she was the one he would have to sweet-talk out of the recipe for those doughnuts. Her sister, Sarah, and cousin Macy usually followed her lead.

I can do that, Travis thought. *She might say the place isn't for sale, but everything has a price. But maybe I should wait a few days or even weeks to bring up the subject again. With all the turmoil going on in that family, they will not want to make any decisions now.*

The elevator opened without so much as a whisper, and Travis stepped out into a wide hallway with doors on either side. All the sixth-floor offices belonged to him and his staff. The fifth floor was occupied by his oil-business crews. The fourth belonged to a geological team that worked with the folks on the floor above them to scout out new land and territory for whatever purpose they'd need it. Third was the corporate legal team, second was the technological team, and first was the folks whom he called his think tank. They were employees who were always on the lookout for new businesses opportunities and who drew up the stats listing pros and cons for venturing out into those places. Then there was the lobby, which was set up with sofas, tables, chairs, and a kitchen for folks who wanted to relax during break or lunch times.

Delores knew everyone in the company, but he and Calvin worked mostly with the folks on the first floor.

He opened the door and walked into the office that had been passed down to him—the next Butler generation—and handed Calvin and Delores each a set of papers from his briefcase. Then he went over to the glass wall at the end of the room.

The view of the Riverwalk below him was spectacular, with its brightly colored umbrellas shading the tables for folks to sit at while they ate burgers or tacos. Small boats carried passengers up and down the river, and it didn't take a lot to imagine that they were laughing and talking, enjoying a vacation or just a day out with their families.

Travis sighed. A family was what he'd always wanted, but Erica hadn't been ready to be a mother; now he was past forty, divorced, and basically remarried to a huge corporation. "When would I have time for a wife and a child now?" he muttered.

"What was that?" Calvin asked. Travis's CEO and best friend had a full head of dark hair with lots of gray beginning to show through, brown eyes, and thirty pounds he'd gained since he married Maggie—mostly right around his middle.

"Nothing," Travis answered. "What's your first thoughts on the idea of building a pastry factory?"

He and Calvin had grown up together in this same building. Calvin's dad had been the CEO when they were kids. Looking back, Travis could see that they had been groomed from the time they were toddlers to take over the jobs they had right now. They'd gone to the same private schools and then on to the same university. When they'd graduated, they had come back to San Antonio and gone to work for Butler Enterprises.

"I don't think it's worth looking into," he replied.

"I'm not going to venture an opinion until we turn the think tank loose on it. It's pretty far-fetched for what we do, but if the first-floor kids think it's a viable endeavor, and you are serious about it . . ." Delores paused. "Why would you want to do this?"

"There's this little bakery down in Devine that makes the best doughnuts I've ever eaten. They'd have to sell me the recipe before I would put in a factory, though, and the owners keep telling me that it's not for sale," Travis answered. He went on to tell them about having breakfast with his granddad's friends. "I thought we could send out some of the think-tank folks to every bakery in San Antonio and have them buy a dozen doughnuts tomorrow. While they do that, I'll drive down to Devine and pick up a couple of every kind they make there. Then our first-floor crew can do a taste test and give us their opinion. The folks down there are having some family issues right now, so I'll be careful about approaching them for a few days, but I want to be ready when the time comes."

Calvin made a pot of coffee and poured three cups; then he added cream and sugar to his, cream to Delores's, and left Travis's black. He set them on a small table for four that overlooked the view of the Riverwalk and sat down in one of the chairs.

"You're going to get out of the building two days in a row. Those must be some very good doughnuts," Delores said.

"I thought we were researching a couple of hundred acres for a housing development in that area," Calvin said. "Are we really looking into both?"

"One or the other," Travis answered and sat in one of the three remaining chairs. He took a sip from his cup of coffee—the first of what would be many. He shut his eyes for a moment and got a visual of Grace bringing a tray with a yellow box in the middle over to his table. *Do I really want a bakery, or do I just want to spend time with her?* he wondered. She was the first woman whom he'd felt any kind of vibe with since Erica left him almost ten years before.

"Well, I think it's a crazy idea—but then, it might prove to be lucrative. This is really thinking outside the box," Calvin said.

"We pay a whole floor of people to do our thinking for us on new ideas, so let's do that taste-test thing in the morning and see what they think," Delores answered and slipped her phone out from her jacket pocket. "I'll call down to Lucy and tell her what we need. Shall we set up conference room two for the taste test? I'll tell my intern to bring in milk and juice and make a pot of coffee."

"Whichever room you think is best." Travis took another sip of his coffee.

"I'll whip up some forms to track the taste test, too. And one more question: What will we do with all the leftovers?" Calvin asked.

"Put them in the lobby kitchen for the rest of the employees. They'll enjoy having doughnuts to snack on all day," Travis said as he pushed back his chair and stood up.

"Hey," Calvin called out as Travis headed for the door. "Before we get started with business and I get into trouble at home, Maggie wants you to come to dinner Friday night. She's invited a friend over, and she doesn't want her to feel like a third wheel. I'll grill some steaks, and we'll play cards after dinner."

Travis chuckled. "Tell Maggie I love her, but no thanks. I can see right through what she's doing, and I'm not ready to date."

His grandfather's voice popped into his head: *Not even this Grace lady that you keep thinking about? Admit it, you are attracted to her.*

"Ready or not, she's pretty persistent." Calvin laughed with him. "You could just come by some evening. The girls miss their Uncle Travis."

"I'll keep that in mind," Travis said.

"I understand they're both driving now. Does that make you feel old?" Delores teased.

"Yep, it does," Calvin admitted. "Maggie is happy that they're both driving so she doesn't have to be constantly taking them to classes. When we were kids, Travis and I just ran all over our grandparents' ranches and made our own fun. Nowadays, kids have to take piano lessons, dance lessons, tennis lessons, and God only knows what else to fill up every minute of their time."

"Statistics say that keeps them out of trouble," Delores said. "Or so my granddaughter tells me when I fuss about all the classes that she has her two kids enrolled in."

Calvin shook his head slowly. "*Kids* is spelled *T-R-O-U-B-L-E*. Trouble finds them, and they welcome it with open arms."

"You wouldn't take anything for those girls," Travis told him. "But if they're that much trouble, then why are you trying to talk me into a relationship that would lead to kids?"

"You are right. I wouldn't take a million bucks for each of them, but I wouldn't give a plug nickel for two more just like 'em. And maybe I want my partner to have the same problems I do," Calvin answered.

Travis had trouble sleeping that night. He kept trying to figure out whether he really wanted to go ahead with the bakery idea or if he just wanted to see Grace again. Maybe he wanted to prove to himself that everything and everyone had a price, and she was no different.

Walking six flights down would be a good morning workout that would justify a couple of Grace Dalton's doughnuts on the drive back to

San Antonio, he reasoned with himself. He whistled on the way down to the underground parking garage and used his key fob to unlock his SUV.

His grandfather's voice popped into his head again as he slid in behind the wheel and started the engine. *Why are you going after this? Grace told you no. Is it the challenge, or do you really want to own a commercial bakery?*

"I have struggled with those questions all night and still don't have an answer, but something tells me that I need to pursue this," he answered as he drove out of the garage and onto the highway.

I'm glad that you are taking your promise serious about helping the town of Devine, but what I want to know today is if she is pretty.

"She's short, has mossy green eyes; blonde hair that was up in a net but looked like it might hang to her shoulders; curvy figure," Travis answered.

What if she doubles down again on not selling her place, no matter what you offer? Are you going to admit that you just want to get to know her better? his grandfather asked.

"It's not a romantic thing," Travis protested, and then wondered if he was fooling himself. Was that little zing he'd felt when her hand brushed against his a real attraction?

His mind drifted back to his first impression of Grace. If his ability to judge a character hadn't failed him, he would say that she was sure of herself, determined, a hard worker, and she didn't take sass from anyone. A lot like Erica, only not as edgy as his ex-wife had been just before she decided that she didn't love him anymore. He didn't know if she'd changed in the past ten years or not. Maybe she had lost that sharp tongue since she married Ronald.

He and Erica had grown apart during their ten-year marriage, and he had attributed that to the fact that they had both been working hard and spending far too little time together. Then she had met Ronald, the CEO of a marketing firm based in London, at an oil conference she had attended for the corporation that she worked for. Ronald had offered her one of those jobs that meant twice as much money, but she had to move to London. She didn't think twice about taking the job—or about discussing it with Travis before she did. She had been sure that they could manage a long-distance relationship, but she had been dead wrong. Three months later, her lawyer had served him with divorce papers.

"I guess three months is the limit for a long-distance relationship," he said as he drove into Devine. "But she got the surprise."

Erica had thought she'd get a chunk of Butler Enterprises as well as half the house they had bought together. But things had been set up so that Travis wouldn't actually own anything until after his father passed on or handed the reins over to him.

"Served her right," he said. A picture of Erica on the day they decided to get married at a chapel in Las Vegas flashed into his mind. On the way to the place, she had stepped in a puddle of water, so she had taken her sandals off and gotten married in her bare feet.

"That was the Erica I loved," he said. "That was the love of my life, not the one who hired a team of lawyers to get a big divorce settlement." He remembered those first days and their little apartment, where they had been happy—but then Erica had started climbing the corporate ladder, and before long, her job in the equities business meant more than spending time with him. They had already drifted apart when she took the job in London.

The Devine Doughnut Shop's gravel parking lot right off Highway 173 was crowded, but he snagged a place not far from the door. Through the windows, he could see that all four tables were full. Hopefully, there was—at least—one of each kind of doughnut still left in the display cases.

He opened the door to find two other people in line ahead of him, which gave him plenty of time to study Grace for a few minutes. When the customers asked about the stories going around town that someone was going to buy the Double D, she replied that the rumors were just gossip. She had no intentions of giving up the family business, she told them with such conviction that Travis almost called off the great doughnut run going on in San Antonio.

Maybe an offer that will make your head swim might change your mind, Travis thought.

When he finally stepped up to the counter, Grace looked at him with a smile. "Good morning. You've missed Claud, Ira, and Frankie. They've been gone for about an hour."

"I want two doughnuts of every kind in the case," he said and then blurted out, "and I'd like to ask you to go to dinner with me Friday evening." If she said yes, he could figure out if the feeling he had was true attraction or just admiration for a determined woman.

"I can do the doughnuts, but right now there's too much on my plate for dating," she said as she filled one box and started on a second one. "I appreciate the invitation, though."

"How about lunch in my office just to talk?" he pressed.

"Why, and talk about what?" She set the boxes on the counter and rang up the sale.

He handed her several bills. Another spark passed between them when she laid the change in the palm of his hand—just like the one that he'd felt when he saw her the last time.

"Even if you won't sell me this shop, I'm still thinking of putting in a mass-production pastry shop, and I'd like to pick your brain," he answered.

The whole place had gone so quiet that the whir of the ceiling fans sounded as loud as helicopter blades.

"I could do that, *Mr.* Butler, but I don't know what I can help you with," she told him.

He raised an eyebrow. "I'll pick you up at one o'clock, then, on Friday, and we'll discuss it then, if that's all right?"

"This is not a date," she assured him. "I'll drive myself to your office, if you'll just give me the address. My family, as you know, was almost betrayed. We came back stronger. But right now, I need to be here for them."

Travis fished a card from his pocket and laid it on the counter. He was disappointed, but he appreciated Grace for standing up for her family. "I understand, and I'll be expecting you. Do you like pizza?"

"I love it, and I'll bring a dozen doughnuts for dessert," she answered and then looked past him at the next customer.

He ate a glazed doughnut and one maple-iced on the way back to the office, then licked his fingers and wiped the sticky steering wheel with a wet wipe he pulled out of a container in the back seat. By the time he made it to the sixth floor with the boxes of doughnuts, the kids from the first floor were all reading through the forms that Calvin had printed up.

Kids? he thought and smiled. Every one of them had a master's degree, and more than half of them had a doctorate. Some of them had IQs that were off the charts, and they were all grounded in the ability to find new and innovative ways to do business.

Calvin tapped a fork on a coffee cup to get everyone's attention. "Okay, Travis has an idea . . ." He went on to tell them about the bakery, then: "We're going to cut each of the doughnuts that he's brought back from the bakery into fourths. What we want you to do is taste one of the ones that he brought and then one of the same kind from a bakery or even two here in town, and then give us your opinion on which one you think is best. There's no passing or failing the taste test. Judge them on the forms you've got."

"I like this kind of test," one girl said.

"So do I," Calvin said with a big smile, and then moved over to stand beside Travis while Delores laid each of the Devine Doughnut Shop's pastries on a disposable plate and cut them into four pieces.

"Don't tell Maggie about this test. She's got me on a low-carb diet. It's not my fault that I've gotten fat in the last fifteen years. She's a great cook, but when I went for my checkup last week, the doctor said I needed to lose thirty pounds to bring my A1c and my cholesterol down. Maggie will flip out if she finds out I've eaten half a dozen doughnuts."

Travis sat down in a chair. "Why didn't you tell me that you were having health issues?"

"Didn't want you to worry. Too bad I can't eat like you do and never gain a pound—but then, it's always been that way, even when we were kids," Calvin said after a long sigh. "I could look at a candy bar and gain five pounds. You could eat three of those big ones and never tip the scales an inch."

Travis made a motion like he was zipping his mouth shut. "My lips are sealed, but I'm getting you into a gym with a personal trainer before the week is out."

Calvin sucked in air and let it out in a whoosh. "I knew I shouldn't have told you. I hate sweating—and dieting."

"And I can't run this company without you," Travis said. "We'll both go to the gym. You've been fussing at me to get out more."

"I'd rather go for drinks after work—or even down to that doughnut shop *before* work," Calvin huffed.

"You're my best friend, Calvin, and company and work aside, I don't want to lose you," Travis told him, and a cold shiver chased down his spine at just the thought of not having Calvin around.

The moment that Travis was outside, the buzz of whispers and conversations sounded like a hive of bees. There was no doubt in Grace's mind that everyone in the shop had heard Travis ask her out for a date and then to his office to discuss a pastry shop once she'd turned him down.

She hoped that they had also heard her tell him that she was not putting the Double D on the market.

Sarah brought the final tray of doughnuts out to the display case and wiped her forehead on a napkin she pulled from a dispenser. "We've made twice our normal amount all three days this week and sold out before noon," she said and then lowered her voice. "We're going to have to hire more help or else think about—"

"We need to talk," Grace whispered and led the way back to the kitchen. As soon as the door was closed behind them, she shook her finger at her sister. "Don't say a word about selling where anyone can hear you." She paced the floor as she told Sarah and Macy about Travis Butler buying so many doughnuts.

"He must be having a brunch, or else he's planning to eat a lot of doughnuts," Sarah said.

"I bet he's seeing if all the varieties are as good as what he had earlier when he was in here with Claud and the guys. I don't like the idea of him testing our product—or maybe even giving it over to a bunch of food chemists to try to reverse engineer the recipe." Macy stuck all the dirty trays in the sink and began to rinse them. "Grace, what do *you* think he's doing with them?"

"I have no idea, but there's more," Grace said. "He asked me for a date."

The bell on the door let them know that either someone was leaving or arriving. Grace went back out into the shop with Sarah and Macy right behind her.

"You don't get to drop that bombshell on us and then leave," Macy whispered to her back so customers wouldn't hear.

The group of women sitting at the table to the right had left, but Lisa and Carlita came in right behind them and settled down at the only clean table in the shop. Macy rolled her eyes toward the ceiling but called out, "Good morning. What can we get you?"

"Hot tea and half a dozen doughnuts with chocolate icing," Lisa said.

Grace nodded, filled two mugs with hot water, and added a tea bag to each one. She rounded the end of the counter, wishing the whole time that she had made chocolate icing with an unhealthy dose of laxative in it. "Might as well get this over with."

"I heard that Travis Butler was in here this morning and asked you out on a date. You need to be careful. He might be playing you just like Neal did with Macy," Lisa said. "He's probably nice to you just to get you to sell him this shop, and like I told you before, our husbands"—she glanced over at Carlita—"could get you a better deal than you can get selling on your own."

"And faster," Carlita said. "You might even be able to move before the end of the school year."

"When I want your advice, I promise I'll ask for it," Grace said.

"I suppose it would be a good thing for jobs, but I like our little town just the way it is," Carlita said with a sigh. "Just think of all the riffraff a factory would bring in. Trailer parks would probably pop up everywhere, and our girls would be going to school with . . ."

"With kids like Audrey, who isn't good enough to be friends with your daughters?" Grace fought the urge to spit in their mugs and set them down on the table.

"You're unusually rude this morning," Lisa snapped. "I don't know why we even try to visit with you."

"Because you want to see if we'll spill the tea on the latest gossip," Sarah answered from behind the counter. "We're all out of chocolate doughnuts. What else can I get you?"

"Glazed is fine," Carlita said.

"Coming right up." Sarah put six in a box and took it over to them, then grabbed a broom to sweep up the floors for the third time that morning.

Lisa pointed across the narrow room toward Macy. "Grace says she won't sell this place. What about you? It's evident that you aren't a very good judge of character, but would you go against your cousin?"

"Are you just trying to stir up trouble?" Macy asked. "What we decide or don't decide with this place is a family matter that we will never discuss with anyone. But you can go out there and tell all your nosy friends that we aren't selling the business or our recipe. As far as my character judgment—you better be careful not to throw stones from inside your glass houses."

From Lisa's expression, it was obvious that Macy's comments about their husbands had not landed. "If that's the case, why is Grace going to have lunch with Travis Butler?"

"Again, none of your business." Grace tried to keep calm, but even she could hear the edge in her voice.

Grace turned and headed toward the kitchen. She sent up a silent prayer: *Lord, please send some more customers in here. If there's a lot of people, then maybe those two won't be so brazen and nosy.*

"He's not as sexy as Justin was, but he's not bad," Carlita said.

"Whew!" Lisa fanned herself dramatically with her hand. "I still get hives when I think about Justin."

"Why's that?" Grace stopped at the end of the display case.

"Honey, you have to know that several of us spent a little time with him before he took off," Carlita answered.

"You were both already married before he left town, so you know what that makes you. And you have the audacity to say what you did about Audrey," Grace growled. "And FYI, I'm not the marryin' type—and if I was, it wouldn't be for money."

"And that's why you're still stuck in a joint like this," Lisa said. "You're not old yet, but you will be someday, and what will your prospects be then?"

Grace turned back and snapped, "Maybe I'll come up with a new topping for doughnuts when I get really old. Something that old folks will love, but it will choke all gossiping hussies to death."

Finally, Lisa and Carlita left, tossing their hair in one last insulting flounce, and even though there were a dozen doughnuts of various varieties still in the case, Grace locked the door. "We'll take what's left home. The girls will enjoy having some for their after-school snacks. I sure wish those two would realize they aren't welcome here."

"They think they're on a pedestal, and we're just here to wait on them," Sarah told her.

"Amen!" Macy said with a nod. "I sure wanted to kick the legs out from under Carlita's chair, so it's a good thing we are closing." She got three bottles of sweet tea from the refrigerator and led the way to the cleanest of the four tables. She sat down and propped her feet up on an empty chair. "Now, let's talk about Travis—or better yet, let's talk about Justin. Do you believe what those two hateful women said about him?"

Grace sat down, propped her feet on the same chair as Macy, and told them about her plans to have pizza with Travis. "I wouldn't have believed anything those women said a few years ago." She twisted the top off one of the bottles and took a long drink. "But right now, nothing would shock me. It just makes me more determined to shun relationships."

"Let's see." Sarah used the final few inches of the chair for her feet. "A couple of weeks ago, you said that you couldn't date now because any man would run if you introduced him to Audrey."

"And now"—Macy opened her bottle and downed a fourth of it before coming up for air—"you roll over and agree to meet a man for pizza when he asks with a lame excuse about picking your brain. Girl, Travis is just like Justin and Neal, only he's got a little different angle. He's trying to woo you into selling him our shop."

"He can 'woo' away," Grace said. "And for your information, I only said I'd meet with him to shut him up. It's going to be a one-and-done deal. And I also wanted to give Lisa and Carlita something to talk about other than you and Neal. I'm killing two birds with one stone."

"You are one devious woman," Macy said and threw up her hand for a high five. Grace slapped it and took another drink of her tea. "They keep promising they won't come back in here, but we see them almost every day."

Sarah pushed Macy's feet to the side. "You're taking all the room."

"Am not." Macy pushed back. "And, honey, they couldn't resist returning to the place that's got the best gossip in town right now. Rumors are like air and water to them: if they don't get a good portion of both every day, they'll wither up and die."

"Think we'll get the blame if Mr. Money Pants doesn't put in a factory?" Sarah asked.

"Probably," Grace replied, and shrugged. "We might even go back to only making half as many doughnuts as we've had to do since all this started. Please keep this Friday thing under your hats. I don't want Audrey to know about it. She gets so dramatic about every little thing."

"Amen to that," Macy agreed.

"Yep." Sarah finished her tea, stood up, and began cleaning. "Our worlds have sure changed in the past few weeks."

"Mama used to say that change was good for us," Grace reminded them. "She said it kept life from getting boring."

"I'd take a little dose of boring right now," Macy said. "Do y'all realize that for us—mentally speaking—March came in like a lamb? I was getting married. Even though we didn't know it, Sarah was falling in love at the time. Audrey hadn't gotten caught with contraband at school yet. Is it going to go out like a lion—creating more havoc in our lives?"

"Good Lord, I hope not!" Grace shuddered as she stood up and tossed her empty bottle into the trash and then dragged the can over to the far end, where Sarah was cleaning up a mess. Crumbs were all over the table, the four chairs, and the floor. "How could anything be worse than this month has already been?"

"That other-shoe business could happen," Sarah reminded her.

Grace shook her finger at her sister. "We're not going to let any more shoes drop. We've had enough." But down deep inside, she didn't believe a word of what she said.

Chapter Ten

ever had a project like this, but I'm not complaining," Lucy said as she and the other ten members of the think tank set about comparing the doughnuts. "I can already tell you after the first bite that the Devine pastries beat these two, but Calvin said the owner isn't ready to sell."

Lucy was one of those medium-height, brown-haired, green-eyed women who would blend so well into a crowd, no one would ever notice her. She wore glasses, with lenses almost as thick as Travis's, and had a gravelly voice like a longtime smoker. She was the first one he had hired when he decided to incorporate a think-tank crew, and she'd told him in her interview that she had never smoked or done drugs. "I love my mama, my boyfriend, and Jesus—but I do drink a little," she'd said. He had hired her on the spot, and now she was the supervisor on the first floor, answering only to Delores, Calvin, and Travis.

"I've never known you to test out a business like this before making an offer on it, but I guess you have your reasons," Lucy said.

His grandfather was back in his head. *And what are those reasons? Be honest with yourself.*

Travis thought of the way the vibes danced around him when he was in the doughnut shop and wondered if Grace felt the same. Was this cat and mouse game she played for real, or was she trying to tease him into a higher price for her company? Or was she sincere in her refusal, and there was electricity between them both?

"What is it about the dough that's so different?" he asked to get his mind off the other questions. "I can't put my finger on it. I need help figuring out if I'm right or not. I would imagine most places have a standard recipe, but my friends down in that area tell me the Devine Doughnut Shop makes the dough in small batches by an old family recipe."

Calvin reached into one of the Devine boxes and picked up a whole doughnut with frosting and sprinkles.

Delores slapped his hand. "Not a one of us need to eat whole doughnuts."

"You've been talking to Maggie," Calvin moaned.

Travis chuckled under his breath and then picked up a fourth of a glazed doughnut from one of the local pastry shops and ate it. He took several sips of hot coffee and then ate a piece of one of the same type from Devine. "There is definitely a difference. The one from Devine is a little lighter, a little sweeter, and the dough itself isn't quite as stark white."

Delores ate a piece of one with chocolate icing from a different local shop and then a little bit of one from the yellow box. "You're right. What makes the difference is the bread recipe. Should we send some of these"—she pointed toward the yellow boxes—"off to be analyzed?"

"No, I'm not ready for that step in this process just yet," Travis answered. "Grace told me that the shop isn't for sale, but we all know that everything has a price."

Audrey seemed to float into the house that Wednesday afternoon. Her face was all aglow with a brilliant smile, and she danced around the living room to music that was only in her own head.

Grace looked up from one of her mother's old cookbooks. "What's got you so happy?"

"Did a good-lookin' boy ask you to the prom?" Sarah asked.

"Not yet, but a couple have been flirting. I can't wait until next year, when . . ." Audrey stopped midsentence.

"In my day the boys asked the girls," Grace said, remembering how Justin took her to both her junior and senior proms. She didn't even have to close her eyes to visualize the dresses that she had worn to each.

"Y'all are all old." Audrey kept dancing. "I'm happy because I don't have to sell the shop when I inherit it. Talk at school is that we'll be moving to Europe in the summer because you are finally letting someone buy the place and are dating a very rich man. Next year, I can either shop in Paris for my junior prom dress or maybe I'll have a designer make it for me. We won't have to buy off the rack. Crystal and Kelsey have already been asked by two of the most popular boys in school, and their mamas are taking them to a designer in San Antonio to have their dresses made."

"Sorry to burst your bubble, darlin'," Grace said. "We are not selling anything, and I'm not dating a rich man. He asked me to dinner, but I said no."

Audrey stopped in the middle of a spin, threw herself onto the sofa, and laid her hand across her forehead in a dramatic gesture that would have made Scarlett O'Hara proud. Raelene came into the house, saw her lying there, and rushed across the room.

"Are you all right? Do you need a cold cloth?" she asked.

"My world has fallen apart," Audrey groaned. "Why do things like this happen to me? I've had nothing but bad luck for weeks now. Crystal and Kelsey said they can only be my friends at school."

Raelene took a couple of steps back, dropped her backpack, and slumped into a chair. "I guess the rumors aren't true?"

"What rumors?" Macy covered a yawn with her hand as she entered the room.

Grace shrugged. "Rumors have made a mountain out of a molehill. Do you girls remember that old game of Telephone, where someone would whisper something to the person sitting next to them, and then that person whispers it to the next and so on, all the way around the room? The last person says what he heard?"

"No," Audrey whispered, as dramatically as if it might be her last word.

"Me neither," Raelene said.

Macy sat down in a rocking chair near the cold fireplace. "The game starts out by someone writing down a sentence on a piece of paper; then he or she starts it like Grace said, and the final person either writes down what they heard or else just says it out loud, and then the first one reads what was really said at the beginning of the game. That's kind of like what happened today, and the rumor that reached the end is a far cry from the first sentence that was said."

"Yep," Sarah agreed with a nod.

"What was the original sentence?" Raelene asked.

"That I'm going to have lunch in Travis's office and give him pointers on a factory that will turn out doughnuts," Grace answered. "What is the final one?"

"That you and Travis Butler have been secretly dating for months," Raelene answered, "and you're getting married this summer, and Audrey is going to have her prom dress made by a French designer next year."

"Oh. My. Goodness!" Macy giggled. "And you believed all that, Audrey?"

"Don't be giving me grief," Audrey smarted off. "You believed Neal."

"That's coming close to sassing, and there is a penalty for that—like maybe you get to work in the shop on Saturday," Grace said in a low voice.

Macy's face turned beet red, and it was not a blush. "And, girl, we are trying to protect you from people just like Neal. Your new friends are worse than he ever was."

"Sorry!" Audrey grumbled. "And they are not."

"Yes, they are," Raelene said.

Audrey popped up to a sitting position, tucked her blonde hair behind her ears, and glared at Raelene. "And just what is that supposed to mean?"

Raelene raised a shoulder in half a shrug. "Crystal and your other best friend, Kelsey, were whispering about punking you while I was having lunch in the library. Their mamas told them about Travis Butler when they came to the school to bring their lunches. That gave them the idea, and they just ran with it. Crystal said they could tell you anything and you'd believe it, and Kelsey mentioned that you'd covered for them with the cigarettes and liquor, so you thought they were really your friends."

Audrey's lower lip quivered. "That's not true. They *are* my friends, and they wouldn't *do* that to me."

Grace moved over to the sofa and draped an arm around Audrey's shoulders. "I'm so sorry, darlin'."

"But, Mama"—tears began to flow down Audrey's cheeks—"it can't be true. I gave up all my other friends that I've had since kindergarten because Crystal and Kelsey want us to be *exclusive*."

Grace pulled a tissue from a box on the end table and wiped her daughter's tears away. "It's a tough lesson, but one that I hope you only have to learn just this one time."

Audrey buried her face in Grace's shoulder. "I just can't believe they would do that to me when I've been so good to them."

Grace remembered saying the same thing to her mother when Justin had left the note on her car. She caught Macy's eye and knew, without a doubt, that her thoughts were going in the same direction—how could Neal do that to her when she had been so good to him? Then she shifted her gaze over to Sarah, and the expression on her sister's face said the same thing—how could Joel treat her like he did?

Thank God we've had each other to get through the tough times, Grace thought, then turned her attention back to Audrey. "You will make other friends—and maybe this time, you'll think more about real friendship than popularity."

"But, Mama, I want to be popular," Audrey moaned.

"Then you have to pay the price for it, and it's high dollar," Raelene told her.

Audrey raised her head and shot Raelene a dirty look. "What do you know about it?"

"I've never been popular. Don't want to be," Raelene answered. "So I don't know much about it, but I sure don't want to be if I have to sell my soul to be in with that crowd. If you would have been sitting with me on the bus, I would have told you what they said before now."

Grace had had a few close friends as a child and up into junior high school, but when Justin came into her life, she'd done the same thing that Audrey had—spent less and less time with them and devoted more and more to Justin. Then he left, and her old buddies moved on, and she had no one except Sarah and Macy.

Sarah spoke up. "Friends can be and often are fickle . . . but, honey, family is forever."

"And sometimes family is just as fickle as friends," Raelene whispered.

Audrey set her jaw and narrowed her eyes. "I'll get even. Maybe not tomorrow or even next week, but they will pay for pulling this mean prank on me."

"The best way to get even is to ignore them. Just pretend that they don't exist," Macy advised. "Don't let them bait you into an argument. Ignoring them gives you power over them and takes away all the power they have built up over you this year."

Audrey nodded, but the look in her eyes said that she would take care of it in her own way. Grace had seen the same determination in Sarah's eyes more than once when they were teenagers, and it never involved ignoring someone who had been hateful. One time when she and her sister had been in junior high school came to her mind as clearly as if it had happened just yesterday.

"You are thinking about . . . ," Sarah whispered and poked her in the arm.

"Yes, I am—and thank you again." Grace grinned.

"What?" Audrey sat up straight and raised an eyebrow.

131

Carolyn Brown

"A girl was spreading rumors about me when I was a freshman. Sarah was in seventh grade, and she took up for me," Grace explained.

Audrey stood up and began to pace the floor. "I wish I had a sister. What did you do, Sarah?"

"I took care of the problem, and then I was suspended for a week for fighting and had a devil of a time getting my grades back up to passing since I had to take a zero on every assignment that week," Sarah answered. "Then Mama made me work at the shop all week. I had to get up and be there by three in the morning. She told me I needed to learn to use my brains instead of my fists, to think about that every morning when my alarm went off while it was still dark outside."

Audrey stopped in front of the fireplace and popped her hands on her hips. "Raelene, if you hear anything else, will you tell me?"

"Depends," Raelene answered with a shrug.

"On what?" Audrey asked.

"On whether you are my friend or not?" Raelene asked. "At home, you treat me like maybe I'm one, but you still think you're better than me. Around your so-called school friends, you treat me like they do. I don't want a half-time friend, Audrey, and I don't want to feel like I'm someone you wipe your feet on, either. It's either all in or all out."

Grace could almost see the wheels in Audrey's head spinning. Evidently, Raelene did, too, because she stood up and went nose-to-nose with Audrey. That reminded Grace of the times when she'd done the same thing with Sarah, back when they were both about the same age as these two girls.

Finally, Raelene shrugged and stepped back. "It's a simple question, but I can't think of a better way to get back at Crystal and Kelsey than to ignore them and be friends with me. You don't have to make up your mind right now, but could we please go have some cookies and milk in the kitchen? I miss the days when y'all brought home leftover doughnuts from the shop."

"So do I," Grace said as she stood up, "but we've still got some of those really good peanut butter cookies you made, so I'm not complaining too much."

Raelene led the way to the kitchen. "I love to cook. Granny let me stand on a chair and help her when I was little." She took a gallon of milk out of the refrigerator and set it in the middle of the table. "Y'all just go on and sit down. You've served people all morning. Let me take care of this."

"I'll get the glasses while you get the cookies," Audrey said.

Grace could hardly believe that her daughter was offering to help do anything. Usually, she had to be told—sometimes half a dozen times, and then results came only after an argument about how she was treated like hired help. Maybe the days of Crystal and Kelsey using her were coming to an end.

"This is really nice, girls," Macy said as she pulled out a chair and sat down. "It's not often that we get to be the ones who are waited on."

"You are welcome, but it's the least I can do," Raelene said.

Audrey sucked in a lungful of air and let it out in a whoosh as she set five glasses on the table, then added a fistful of paper napkins. Grace had seen that gesture many times and knew that what followed it wasn't always pleasant.

"Raelene, why did you even tell us what Crystal and Kelsey did?" Audrey asked. "You could have kept quiet about it and let me make a bigger fool of myself."

Raelene set a plate of cookies on the table and took a chair. "Several reasons. One is because you need to know before they embarrass you even more by spreading around to the rest of the school that you're an easy mark who will do anything to stay in their mean-girl group. They have a private little message group among the two of them and a few more girls where they gossip about everyone. The second reason is that family takes care of family, whether they're related by blood or by heart. And three is that those two girls have picked on me since we were in elementary school, and I don't owe them anything like keeping my mouth shut." She filled her glass with milk and passed the jug over to Macy, then stacked three cookies on a napkin.

"Thank you," Audrey muttered. "How do you know about the message group?"

"Are you a part of that?" Grace asked.

"Not yet, but Crystal said if I pass a year's initiation, then I could be," Audrey answered.

"No, you won't," Raelene told her. "Crystal's and Kelsey's mamas are on the judging panel for the cheerleader tryouts next year, and you know what they've said about you." She raised her glass of milk and took a long drink. "And those two are just mean and hateful. They'll use you and then dump you and find someone else to be their little patsy. They came by the library table where I was having a sandwich and studying. They made a big show of coughing all over my food, and Kelsey even managed to sneeze on it. I threw it in the trash."

Audrey was about to bite off a piece of cookie, but she put it down. "Why didn't you do something about it?"

"What would I do?" Raelene asked. "If I tattle on them to the principal, they'll deny it—and who's got the power, them or me? Both of their fathers are on the school board. If I start a fight, *I* would get expelled, which would probably mess up my scholarship. It's only two months and a few days until graduation, and then it will be over. I've put up with their hatefulness for all these years, so I can endure it for a little longer. But just in case I ever need to prove something, I keep a journal with dates, times, and locations about all the ugly things they've done."

Audrey just nodded and set about having her after-school snack, but Grace could see the wheels turning in her head again, and Lord only knew where they would land when they stopped moving—or what would happen in the next few days.

"I *am* your friend," Audrey finally said. "And thank you."

Dark clouds covered the moon when the three women set out for the doughnut shop on Friday morning. The heaviness in the air testified that rain was on the way. A streak of lightning lit up the nearly black sky for a moment, and thunder rolled right afterward.

Macy used her key to open the kitchen door and stood to the side to let the other two enter first. "I love rainy days but not stormy ones. Should we still make a double batch this morning? This storm will keep a lot of people inside."

"Not when there's gossip as juicy as what's going on now," Sarah answered and flipped on the lights. She had always dreaded when there was juicy gossip to be told over doughnuts and coffee, but even more so these days, when the gossip had to do with her family. That hadn't happened very often, but the past few weeks had sure made up for lost time.

She'd been raised in this little shop, and everything from the rack of metal trays to the huge bins of flour and sugar was familiar to her. What her mother had said about change being good flashed through her mind.

"Change is scary, isn't it?" she muttered as she got out the big bowls to mix the dough in and set them on the counter.

"Mama said it was good for us, but she didn't say it was easy," Grace reminded her.

"She also said that sometimes we have to step out of the forest to see the trees," Macy added. "All these trees are going to smother me before the end of May, when we take our first-ever real vacation."

Sarah gave her a quick hug. "Hang on, darlin'. Together, we'll get through one day at a time until we can leave the forest for a little while."

Grace sang a line from a hymn: "One day at a time, sweet Jesus . . ."

"Amen!" Macy said. "Remember what your mama told all three of us? A three-corded rope is hard to break. We are strong. We can endure this until May. Y'all keep telling me that and maybe I'll make it until then. Now, what if we mixed up two batches in each bowl instead of one?"

"Then the dough would spill out over the top when it rises, and Mama said that the secret in our doughnuts is that we make them in small batches," Sarah answered.

Macy poured warm water into three bowls and added two table-spoons of yeast and half a cup of sugar to each one. "I guess in that instance, change would not be good."

Sarah stirred what was in the bowl in front of her. "We can't sell the recipe, but we can sell the property and the store. It's set up to make pastries, but it could so easily be turned into a small bistro or burger kind of café. We're living in a rut—get up and be here by three so that we can have doughnuts ready at five when we open the doors. Go home after we clean up and close up to take a nap, have supper, go to bed by nine so we can be ready to go again the next day."

"What are you suggesting?" Grace asked.

"That, like Mama said, change is good for us," Sarah said. "What if we get out a map, blindfold Audrey or Raelene, and play Pin the Tail on the Donkey? Only instead of a donkey, wherever they put a tack is where we move and start over."

"What would we do?" Macy asked. "This is our life."

"Maybe we could live in Paris for a couple of years and fulfill Audrey's dream to live in France, or we could go live in a place near the water. I could *so* be a beach bum." Sarah sifted flour into the foamy liquid. "Anything would be a change from what we're doing now."

"What if we ran into Darla Jo and Neal on the beach?" Macy asked.

Sarah shivered. "That would be our luck to run into them on what-ever island we decided to visit, now, wouldn't it? Or maybe Joel and his family."

"Good Lord!" Grace gasped. "That would be a disaster—and besides, I'm not sure that would be good for Audrey. She needs to learn that you don't fix problems by running from them like Justin did. And we've kind of adopted Raelene. She needs a stable home to come to on holidays and when she has a break from school." She kneaded the dough in her bowl a few times, then pushed it back and set up another one.

All three of them seemed to be thinking about making a change. The need for a change, even if it broke that three-corded rope, lay heavy on Sarah's heart. She felt that if she didn't do something soon, like in the next couple of years, the "trees"—as Macy called all the drama going on around them—were really going to smother her. "You're probably right, but a change looks good to me. I'm thirty-five years old, and if I'm ever going to have a family, time is running out. Most guys my age are either married and have a family started or are just out for a good time and want no commitments. Like some guys I could mention."

"My clock is ticking, too," Macy said with a sigh, "and I want a family so much it hurts, but I just can't imagine not doing what we are right now every day." A smile broke out across her face. "But I've got to admit, I could go for a beach bum if he was honest and treated me right. Not that beach bum getting married to Darla Jo, though."

"Maybe what we need to do is close shop as soon as school is out and take Raelene and Audrey to Florida like we've talked about. Make it a reality instead of an idea," Grace said. "It would be a test to see if we would even consider a drastic change or if we'd be homesick and wishing for our old routine after the first couple of days away from Devine."

Lightning flashed through the window, and thunder sounded as if someone had spilled a whole wagonload of potatoes on top of the shop. It startled Sarah so badly that she dropped the wooden spoon she was using to stir the dough.

"Dammit!" she swore under her breath. "That scared the bejesus out of me. I love the sound of rain, but I've always hated thunder and lightning."

"Probably because Mama used to talk about lightning coming down through the rafters in church and striking someone who had been gossiping or who had done wrong things," Grace said with a giggle.

"Is that an omen? Is it telling us that we should all walk away from this business or that we shouldn't close up shop for two weeks?" Macy asked. "It came when we were talking about both."

"I'm not sure, but whichever it is, it has got my attention." Sarah wiped up the mess on the floor and got a clean spoon from a drawer. "I like the idea of closing up shop and taking a family vacation. We could call it Raelene's graduation present from us."

The rain began in a downpour, with a hard wind that slammed a spray of water against the windows so hard that Sarah thought they might crack and break any minute. "If the windows break, then I think it's a sign that we need to move away from Devine. Let's plan on heading to Florida first. I hear the beaches are white and that this is a lovely time of year to visit."

"If they break," Grace said with a nervous laugh, "we will put both girls on homeschooling and be gone tomorrow. That way, I don't have to deal with Travis Butler."

At five o'clock, the display case and the parking lot were both full. The rain had slowed to a drizzle, and the lightning had stopped flashing. Sarah slid in the last tray of doughnuts and opened the front door. In just a few minutes, the tables were all taken and there was a line at the counter. Umbrellas dripped on the floor, and the whole place buzzed with conversations.

"Neither rain, nor wind, nor fear of tornadoes shall keep folks—whether we like them or not—away from doughnuts and gossip," Sarah said with a long sigh and headed to the cash register to ring up sales.

"Amen!" Grace nodded toward Carlita and Lisa coming through the door. She grabbed a tray, put three cups and a coffeepot on it, and headed over to the table where Claud and his two buddies were sitting.

"We were surprised to hear that Audrey is back in school. We really thought it would be best if that girl was homeschooled," Carlita said.

"Maybe you should do that with your kids," Sarah said.

"Don't you get sassy with us," Lisa said. "We'll boycott this business."

138

"Please do," Sarah snapped.

"I heard that Grace is getting married and leaving Devine," Carlita said and laid a ten-dollar bill on the counter. "We'll take a dozen assorted to go this morning. Are you and Macy going to be able to keep this place going without her?"

Sarah made change and leaned as far over the counter as she possibly could to mutter, "Who told you that?"

"We have our sources," Carlita said with a smug grin.

Lisa stepped around from behind Carlita, clearly eager to amplify any mean gossip. "Audrey must be all excited about moving to Europe. Who would have thought that Grace would snag a man like Travis Butler?"

"It's a mystery, for sure, but from what we know, your two daughters started that rumor just to mess with Audrey. Enjoy your doughnuts and coffee," Sarah said and dismissed them by looking past them to the next customer.

Carlita grabbed the bag and the change that Sarah had laid on the counter, and they left in a huff, like usual.

The rain had almost stopped when Audrey and Raelene arrived thirty minutes before the school bus was scheduled to run that morning. The windows were all intact, so Sarah figured that she couldn't tell them they would be doing their homework on the beach after all.

"Did you girls have breakfast, or do you want to choose something from what's left in the case?" she asked.

Audrey set her backpack on an empty chair and stood her umbrella beside Raelene's just inside the door. "I want doughnuts and milk. I need lots of energy for today."

"Girl, don't do anything stupid," Sarah warned.

Audrey just smiled and rounded the end of the display case. "What kind do you want, Raelene? Get us a table before the next wave of customers come in here and take them all."

"Chocolate, maple, and sprinkles," Raelene answered, and looped the straps of her backpack over a chair.

A cold chill danced down Sarah's spine. Sarah had always felt like Audrey was as much her child as Grace's. She had walked the floor with her when she had colic as a baby, had read hundreds of books to her when she had chicken pox at three years old, and had cried with Grace the first day that Audrey went to kindergarten. "You are being too nice today, girl. I really hope you aren't about to do something you'll regret."

Audrey flipped her blonde hair over her shoulder. "Whatever I do, I dang sure won't regret it. White or chocolate milk, Raelene?"

"Chocolate," Raelene called back.

Another rush of people came inside out of the rain. Grace waited on the ones who claimed the tables while Sarah filled the orders of those who were lined up, and Macy ran the cash register. Sarah didn't even realize that Raelene and Audrey were gone until she heard the school bus rattle to a stop at the edge of the parking lot.

"Grace," she whispered when her sister passed by on her way to get a coffeepot, "you might as well get ready for a storm bigger than the one that just hit us. Audrey was nice to Raelene, and she's up to something that she said she would not regret—her words, not mine."

"Sweet Jesus!" Grace groaned. "How was she nice?"

"She waited on Raelene," Sarah answered. "There's a storm coming, and it's going to make a tornado look like a gentle breeze."

"Sweet Jesus!" Grace groaned a second time. "Maybe we should go get her at school and make a run for Florida right now."

Sarah nodded. "Might be a good idea."

Chapter Eleven

ater that day, Grace made sure that Travis didn't think this was a date in any form or fashion by wearing the kind of clothes she wore at the shop every day. She went straight from work in her jeans and T-shirt with the Devine Doughnut logo on the front. She was familiar with San Antonio, but when the lady's voice on her GPS said, "You have arrived," and she had parked right outside the tall office building, she wished she'd taken a little more time with her appearance.

"They probably won't even let me into Butler Enterprises looking like this," she muttered. She dug around in her purse for lipstick and a hairbrush, tilted the rearview mirror down, and pulled her blonde hair out of its ponytail. She rolled her eyes toward heaven and gave thanks for the wet wipe—left over from when she and Audrey had eaten at a rib joint—she found in the console and used to remove the pink icing from the toe of her sneaker.

"What was I thinking?" she asked herself on the way to the glass entry doors, which were etched with "Butler Enterprises" in large block letters. "Here I am, carrying a box of doughnuts. The people in this place will think I'm a delivery person."

You were thinking that his office would be a lot smaller than this? The voice in her head that sounded a lot like her mother's broke out in laughter. *You should have done your homework on this man, my child.*

Cool air rushed out when the doors opened automatically into a huge fancy lobby. Grace squared her shoulders and determined that neither Travis Butler nor any of his employees would intimidate her. She marched up to the reception desk located in the middle of the lobby and was about to tell the smartly dressed woman why she was there when Travis waved from a nearby elevator and motioned for her to join him.

She bypassed the desk but caught the look of surprise on the woman's face when Travis met her halfway across the lobby.

"I'm so glad you could make it," Travis said and ushered Grace into the elevator with a hand on the small of her back. "Pizza awaits us in my office."

Grace held up the yellow box she was carrying. "And these are for dessert."

Travis flashed a bright smile. "I've been looking forward to those all morning."

His hand was so warm on Grace's back that she was sure, if she pulled up her shirt and looked in a mirror, the print would be there in bright red. No man's touch, not even Justin's, had ever made her lose her ability to speak like Travis's did on the elevator ride up to the sixth floor. In just a few seconds—which seemed like six months—the doors opened into a hallway with paintings of San Antonio on the walls. They were all signed by different artists, and all of them looked very expensive.

"Lovely art," she said.

"My dad loved this city and commissioned several artists to paint it. I've always loved the way most of them saw the different places with a unique eye." He opened the door to an office, and his hand went to her back again. "Come right in. This is where I spend nearly all of my daylight hours and a good percentage of my night ones, too."

"Oh. My. Goodness." Grace saw the buffet table, with its crisp white cloth and food laid out, and the small round table covered with a red-and-white-checkered cloth and set up for two people—but she ignored all that. She headed straight for the expansive glass wall over-looking the Riverwalk. "This is amazing."

"I inherited this office when my dad retired five years ago. I've always loved that view. It makes me feel like I'm not cooped up in an office at all."

"I could understand how it would," she whispered. If she had a view like this back home, she might never want to leave the doughnut shop.

"I thought we could do buffet-style and take our plates to the table and enjoy the view while we visit. What would you like to drink? I like a cold beer with my meal, but since you'll be driving home . . ." He let the sentence dangle.

She set her box of doughnuts on the end of the table. "Sweet tea would be great. Thank you."

Travis crossed to a bar on the far side of the room and brought back a bottle of cold sweet tea and set it on the table. "Please, help yourself to the buffet. I wasn't sure what you would like, so I just had my chef set it all up like a pizza bar."

Grace picked up a bowl and made herself a salad, topped it off with French dressing, and carried it to the table. Then she went back for breadsticks and two slices of pepperoni pizza. Food usually took care of all her problems—anxiety, joy, sorrow, anger. That afternoon, she fully well expected it to take care of all the emotional upheaval of the past few weeks, plus sitting down to eat with Travis. His smile was genuine, and his slow Texas drawl was soothing to her ears; plus, his eyes sparkled with life and excitement.

The bowls and plates were fine china with the Butler Enterprises monogram in gold. The stemmed glass full of ice that Travis brought to the table along with her bottle of sweet tea was etched with the same. With all the fanciness and the view, she felt as if she were eating at a five-star restaurant, not in an office.

Travis brought a salad and then a plate piled high with pizza and breadsticks and a small bowl of marinara to the table. "I love pizza, but

I love your doughnuts even more. We've done some research this week, and the consensus here at Butler Enterprises is that the ones you make are the best in this part of Texas."

"How did you decide that?" Grace asked, suspecting she knew the answer.

"Remember when I came into your place and bought doughnuts of every kind a few days ago? We had a taste test. We cut each one into four pieces and then asked my employees from the think tank to taste test them against several bakeries here in town. Hands down, Devine Doughnuts won," he answered.

"Thank you," she said, then frowned. "'Think tank'?"

"The first floor is devoted to my younger business-development people," he said.

"You've got lettuce in your teeth," she said and immediately wished she could shove the words back into her mouth.

He removed the bit of lettuce with a napkin, then smiled again. "Is it gone?"

"Yes, and I apologize." Grace fought back a bit of heat in her cheeks. "I'm used to living with two teenage girls, my sister, and my cousin, who is like a younger sister. We say what we think too often."

"I like honesty, and there's no need to apologize," Travis told her.

"So, one whole floor is a think tank?" Grace asked. "Is this whole building just for your business?"

"We have a big corporation here, and we're growing every year," he said between bites. "You are aware that Claud and his cronies would like to see your doughnuts sold all over the United States, and so would I. I'd be willing to buy the recipe and let you continue to use it in your shop for the next say"—he frowned—"twenty-five years. That way, your lifestyle could continue as it is, but I could—"

Grace held up a palm. "Stop right there."

"Is there a loophole where you wouldn't sell me the recipe?" he asked. He went on before she could assure him again that she was *not*

144

selling: "Maybe instead of getting money, you would own a nice big chunk of stock in the bakery, and I could hire you to show my staff how to make the doughnuts in small batches. We could only make a certain amount to ship out each day. Law of supply and demand would work."

Grace was getting a little annoyed at his constant asking and trying to figure out ways to get her to agree to his plans. It was very evident that he was only talking to her because of the deal, and that was a waste of her time. "Like I said the first time you asked about buying my recipe: even if I could, I wouldn't. And I'm not interested in owning shares of a mass-production bakery. Even doing what you suggested would put the recipe in the hands of other people, who might take it home with them and put it on the internet. So the answer is and will always be no. But thank you for the offer."

"That just burst my bubble," Travis said with a long sigh. "I guess I can be thankful that Devine is only half an hour away and I can either drive down there or send someone to get pastries for me anytime I want."

"You better buy extra on Saturday," Grace said with a smile. "We aren't open on Sunday."

Travis bit into a slice of pizza. "I'll remember that." He chewed quickly and swallowed. "Would you consider selling me the acreage around your business so I can put in a housing development?"

Grace shook her head. If awards were given for persistence, he would have a blue ribbon. "That land belongs to all three of us, so I couldn't make that decision," she answered. "My first notion on the idea is to turn the offer down. That would put a housing addition right next to our shop."

"Which," Travis said with a smile, "would be amazing for business. Every one of those people would figure out how good your doughnuts are and buy them on their way to work each morning."

"And it would give us close neighbors," she countered. "I'm not so sure we're ready for that, but I will ask my partners for their opinion.

Isn't there other property near Devine that you could buy? I've seen signs that say 'acreage for sale' between Devine and San Antonio."

"Probably. But to help the town financially, I should think about building within the city limits, right?" he asked.

Grace kept eating but nodded and wondered what Sarah and Macy would have to say about selling their land. The property, like the shop, had been in the family for so long that she couldn't imagine selling it, or having anyone live close to them.

"You're frowning," Travis said.

"Am I?" She raised an eyebrow. "I can't imagine that Macy or Sarah will want to sell the land, but I will ask them."

"Will you let me know what your partners say about your land sometime next week?" Travis asked. "I'd like to give Claud and the guys some good news before the bad. They were all pumped up about a factory in Devine."

"I can do that," she agreed.

"How about I pick you up for dinner on Wednesday, and we can talk about it more then? How many acres do you have?" he asked.

"We own half a section, which is three hundred and twenty acres. We have three hundred leased to a rancher, who runs cattle on it right now. The lease is up on May 1, but he has always renewed it," she answered.

"Wow!" Travis exclaimed. "If I sold it in three-acre lots and advertised it as rustic life out of the city, we could sell a hundred homes down there; most likely, they'd be under contract to buy as fast as we could get them built."

Grace wanted to ask just who *we* would be. Did he have investors outside this huge building with one floor devoted to a group who did nothing but think? Or was he so rich, he could jump into a project like that without anyone having a say-so? But she just finished her last few bites, pushed back her chair, and brought the doughnuts to the table.

"Now for the best part of the meal." Travis opened the box and took out one with sprinkles.

"Same," Grace agreed as she picked up her favorite—one with maple icing. "What are you going to do with all the leftover pizza and breadsticks?"

"I'll have Calvin and Delores box it all up and take it all down to the kitchen for everyone to snack on all afternoon," he answered. "That's what we did with all the leftover doughnuts from the taste test, and there wasn't a single one left at the end of the day." He lowered his voice and leaned over the table. "But the first-floor kids insisted on taking those from your shop right to their floor. They don't play well with others," he said with a deep chuckle.

"Who are Calvin and Delores?" she asked.

"Calvin is my CEO, but he's also my best friend and has been since we were babies. We grew up in this building, went to the same schools, and came back here to work after we graduated college. Delores is the woman behind the scenes for Butler Enterprises. She's actually the COO, though she doesn't like titles. She knows everything about everything. She began working here before I was even born. She's probably seventy-four years old, and I hope she lives to be a hundred—not only for what she does for the company but because I love her that much," he explained.

Not many men would use those words to describe an employee, even their CEO and COO, Grace thought. They also wouldn't have that look of happiness on their faces when they talked about a friend. Or, for that matter, they wouldn't have been so gracious about lettuce in their teeth, either.

"And your parents now?" Grace asked.

"They have several homes, and right now they're in London," he answered. "They get back to the States a couple of times a year—usually around Christmas and sometime in the summer."

For her second doughnut, Grace opted for one with chocolate icing. "That sounds like a very good retirement. Please don't advertise the offer to buy our land until it is a done deal," she continued, "because I don't think we'll be interested in selling, and it will just stir up more drama and rumors in Devine."

"I won't, but you didn't answer me about dinner on Wednesday evening," he said with another smile.

The way he paid attention to her and respected her rejection made Grace like him—especially when she remembered how his hand had felt on her back. She shouldn't accept his invitation. She'd turned him down for a dinner date once, and after the way Neal had pulled the wool over Macy's eyes, she wasn't sure she should trust any man—especially one who had his mind set on buying her business and land.

"Well?" he asked.

She meant to tell him no, like she did the first time—she really did—but when she opened her mouth, she said, "Yes, I'll go to dinner with you, but it has to be on my terms. We aren't going to discuss business, and it can't be at a fancy place. Maybe just a burger and fries—but not in Devine. There's enough talk going around down there without me fanning the fires."

There, she thought. *That should make him back down for sure.*

"Sounds good." He flashed another one of his brilliant smiles. "We'll go to the Dairy Queen down on the Riverwalk. No talk of business. I promise."

"I'll meet you there," she said and pushed back her chair. "I should be going. You'll need to get back to work."

"Why?" he asked. "I'd planned a two-hour lunch. We've still got an hour left, unless you have plans and need to get home."

"Nope, I don't have plans," Grace answered and pulled her chair back up to the table.

He chose another doughnut from the box—a strawberry-filled one.

"Did you ever want to be anything other than a baker?" he asked. "Not that I'm complaining. These doughnuts are really good."

"Nope. How about you?"

"I thought I'd like to be a rancher like my grandpa," Travis answered. "Sometimes, I still do. I loved running wild on the ranch as a child, and helping my grandpa with the cattle and the chores, but I'm an only child, and the business needed me. I was groomed from a young age to take the reins, and by the time it was my turn, I had learned to love this as much as ranching."

Silence settled around them, but it wasn't uncomfortable. Grace didn't feel like she needed to fill the emptiness with words, so she finished her doughnut and refilled her glass with the last of the tea in the bottle.

"My biggest regret is that my folks haven't gotten to enjoy grandchildren," Travis finally said. "I always thought I'd get around to having a family, but . . . I'm in my forties. I wonder if that ship has sailed."

Grace hoped she didn't have chocolate on her teeth when she smiled. "Don't you know that forty is the new thirty? You're still young enough to start a family if you don't linger much longer. And now, I thank you for the lunch. It was amazing, but I should be going." She pushed back her chair and stood up. She had learned enough from Macy's mistake to know that a man could worm his way into a woman's heart by telling her about his hopes and dreams—and maybe not just Macy's but her own experience with Justin and Sarah's with Joel. Then, when he had her hooked, he would get what he wanted and leave her high and dry.

"I'll walk you out to your car," Travis said. "After that meal, I should walk around the block a few times, but I've got a meeting scheduled for three."

He ushered her into the elevator with his hand on her back again, and tiny bursts of heat did their little dance up and down her spine.

Grace was not a poor person, despite her appearance that day, but why would Travis be interested in her?

Stop it! her mother's voice scolded. *You are not the first woman to have a child without the benefit of a marriage license, and you won't be the last. Get off the guilt wagon and quit being ashamed of your past. It is what it is, and there's no changing it. You've been a good mother, and this man would be lucky to even be allowed to buy you a burger.*

"Thanks, Mama," she whispered.

And don't let that man buy my recipe, your land, or your soul, her mother's voice said loud enough in her head that she could hear it above the sirens only a few blocks away.

She reached into her pocket, brought out her car keys, and unlocked her vehicle when she was a few feet away. Travis walked her all the way to the driver's-side door and opened it for her.

"Thank you for lunch," she said. "I enjoyed it."

"Me too, and thank you for the dessert," he said. "I'll see you on Wednesday. Seven in front of the Dairy Queen work for you?"

"That sounds good." She fastened her seat belt and looked up to see Travis standing on the sidewalk, waving at her.

"Well, Mama, what do you think of that?" she whispered.

She didn't get an answer, so she waved back and drove away.

Macy brought out two bottles of water and set them on the front porch. Then she eased down on the top step and watched Sarah plant flowers in the bed that reached all the way across the front of the house. "I'd help you, but if I touched them, they would die, and if I touched the dirt, it would be poisoned for at least a hundred years."

Sarah dug a hole and slipped a lantana plant out of a pot. "Why do you say that? My mama didn't have a green thumb, either, but your mama sure did. When I was a little girl, I loved working in the flower beds with her. You just didn't want to. I wonder how Grace is doing."

"Probably taking things very serious, like she has her whole life," Macy answered. "She's always felt like she had to protect me and you, and then be a perfect mother to Audrey when she was born. She needs to let go and enjoy herself." Macy twisted the top off a bottle of water and handed it to Sarah. "I'm not wondering about that. I can't wait until she gets home and tells us if he asked her out on a real date, and not just a slice of pizza in his office."

"How can you even let those thoughts in your head after what we both just went through?" Sarah took a long drink of water, wiped the sweat from her forehead on her shirtsleeve, pulled off her gloves, and sat down on the bottom step. "Travis is probably just being nice to get what he wants. In this case, it would be the recipe or the shop. He might even try to find a *loophole*"—she threw up air quotes—"so that we could sell our business to him and still keep the shop. I wonder if he really wants it or if he just keeps asking so he can see Grace."

Macy's thoughts about not having the shop went two ways: One part of her wanted to have a reason to leave Devine and never look back. Another part was fine with staying right there in her comfortable little rut and never getting away from it—gossip, early rising, all of it. She saw Grace coming up the drive and went inside the house, got another bottle of water, and brought it out to the porch.

"It's a beautiful day," Macy said when Grace got out of the vehicle and sat down on the top step beside her. "Have some water. Sit down and tell us all about your slice of pizza and if we need to dig the bridal magazines out of the trash bin."

Grace opened the bottle and took a long drink. "Well, it was a little more than a slice that we just took from a box . . ." She went on to tell them everything she could remember. "I don't know if he's playing me to get what he wants—we're all three very familiar with men like that—or if this dinner date on Wednesday night is because he wants to get to know *me*. Whatever. I didn't expect him to agree to it."

"Maybe he's as confused as you are." Macy turned up her bottle of water and took a long drink. "He wants our shop and our land, but it could be that he's not used to being told no on anything, and you intrigue him because you won't let him have what he wants."

Sarah shook her head. "As much as recent events have made me need to get away from Devine for a while, I don't want to sell our land, and I sure don't want to live next to a gated community of million-dollar homes."

"We would begin to feel like the poor relations up next to those big fancy places, and I kind of like not having neighbors," Macy said. "I don't know why I ever thought I wanted to live in the city. We have to deal with people in the shop, so it's kind of nice to come home to nothing but the sounds of birds and a few cows mooing off in the distance."

"It's the chance of a lifetime," Grace said, "but I agree with y'all. The only way I'd think about selling our land is if we closed shop and moved away from Devine. I don't want to live cramped up by that many neighbors, either."

An image of a moving van flashed through Macy's mind, and it didn't make her sad. Quite the contrary. She was happy as she imagined herself getting into her car and following the truck out to the highway and heading south right behind it. Then she thought of the day when she had confronted Neal and watched him leave Devine. Tears welled up in her eyes at just the idea of leaving her family behind if Sarah and Grace went a different way.

"I may cancel," Grace said. "We've made up our minds about the land. I can tell him that over the phone. Besides"—she nodded toward Audrey and Raelene coming up the path—"that way, I don't even have to mention it to them. Audrey would sell the blue streak in her hair to get out of Devine, and she would drive us to drinking something stronger than sweet tea with her pouting if we didn't move away."

"And if she thinks you're going out with Travis, she'll have you married by the weekend," Sarah said.

"How was school?" Macy asked when the girls reached the porch.

"All right," Raelene answered and headed on into the house. "I'll get the dusting done right after I grab a snack."

"I'll be in and help you in a few," Audrey said.

Macy gasped and shook her head. "What did you say?"

Audrey slumped down in the swing and set it in motion with her foot. "I owe Raelene."

"How's that?" Sarah asked.

"She helped me with my algebra at noon today, and I made a ninety on the test this afternoon. And I'm out of real money until I get my allowance. I told her we were friends, and I've been steering clear of Crystal and Kelsey. But she doesn't really believe me yet, so I have to help dust to pay for her lessons."

When Raelene had moved into the house, Macy had worried that Audrey might push her around. She was glad to see that she had been wrong. "Sounds like a good deal to me, if you got that high of a grade."

"Before I go do a job I don't like to do—how did your lunch go with Mr. Rich Britches? Any chance I've got to deal with a stepdad in the future? If that's the case, I need to meet him in the first stages of this romance. I'm not real interested in his money, but I want to know if he's got a 'love 'em and leave 'em' attitude like my biological father had. And I don't have to remind any of y'all about men right now. None of y'all have been real good at figuring that out, so I'm sure you'll need my unbiased help."

"Lunch went fine. I told Travis we aren't selling the shop and that we aren't interested in selling our land," Grace answered. "And how did you know about that?"

"Mama!" Audrey rolled her eyes. "The gossip at school is just as hot as it is anywhere else. Crystal's mama found out about y'all's little visit and called her when we were on the bus. I guess they think they can get information out of me, but that ship has sailed."

"I told you we should take her to school instead of letting her ride the bus." Macy groaned. "I remember what went on when I rode the bus, and that was before we all had a cell phone. We heard more gossip on the ride home than some folks got on their landlines or over the backyard fences."

Audrey removed her hoodie and tossed it over to the other end of the swing. "I'm going to grow old and die right here in this house, aren't I? I'll make ten dozen doughnuts one morning, sell them all, and come home to drop down dead with a heart attack."

"I hope not," Macy said. "I hope you find somebody to love and spend the rest of your life with, and you die of old age with a smile on your face."

Audrey sucked in a lungful of air and let it all out in a whoosh. "I can't sell the recipe for our doughnuts, but I can sell our land, our home, and the shop building. Is that right?"

"If I live to be seventy, you will be almost fifty. I suppose if I turn it over to you then, you can do whatever you want with it," Grace answered.

"That gives me a long time to think about it. If I keep the shop, I can always put rat poison in Crystal and Kelsey's doughnuts. Right now, I'm going to go get a snack and help Raelene. Dusting, as bad as I hate it, is better than thinking about being old," Audrey said with a long sigh before disappearing into the house.

Macy tipped up her water bottle and drank what was left. She remembered being young and thinking about what it would be like to be fifty years old and wanting to live anywhere but Devine, Texas.

"Yep," Grace said.

"What are you agreeing with?" Sarah asked.

"I'm sure we're all thinking the same thing," Grace answered. "That when we were all about Audrey's age, fifty was old, and we dreaded the idea of spending the rest of our lives in the shop."

Macy nodded. "You nailed it—but little did we know that our friendship would help us get through good times and bad. I feel sorry for Audrey because she doesn't have a sister. No offense, Grace."

"We can adopt Raelene," Sarah suggested.

A wide grin spread over Macy's face. "I kind of like that idea."

"Why don't we take Audrey not having a sister as a sign that we are the last generation of sisters and cousins who will keep the shop open?" Grace said.

"That's too sad to think about," Macy said and headed in the house. "I'd rather help the girls dust than think about that, and I'm not real fond of that job, either."

Sarah pulled on her gloves and went back to her flower beds. "I went to town today to buy plants for this little job, and I caught a glimpse of a man outside the drugstore that reminded me of Justin. Have you ever thought about what you would do if he showed back up here and wanted to be a part of Audrey's life?"

"What on earth brought that to your mind?" Grace asked.

"Just thinking of the three men who've done us dirty," Sarah answered.

"I hope he doesn't ever come back to town—but if he does, I pray that it's not until Audrey is a lot older. She is dealing with enough right now without all the emotional upheaval of him trying to wiggle his way into her life."

"You are dealing with trying to raise a teenage daughter on your own and a man who you can't be sure if he's trying to con you out of your business or if he likes you." Sarah kept an eye on her sister as she worked.

"I'm not doing any of that on my own," Grace answered. "I've always had you and Macy. And even Raelene and Audrey are being a support in their own way. Who would have thought that my daughter would say that she wasn't interested in the Butler money but she wanted to meet him to be sure he wasn't trying to trick me into that."

Sarah remembered the picture of Joel's family and wondered if it was better to have a father who cheated and lied or to have no father at all. "Do you regret not having a father around when we were growing up?"

Grace handed her a marigold plant from the box on the porch. "Never thought about it much. Daddy died when we were so young, and Mama stepped right up to be both parents to us; then Macy's dad passed away, and Aunt Molly came to live in the house with us. Mama has been my role model for a single mother, even if I didn't realize it until right now. Do you wish we would have had a traditional family?"

Macy came back outside and sat down on the porch. "What are y'all talking about?"

Sarah packed the loose dirt around the plant and dug another hole. "How I might have turned out different if we'd had the heavy hand of a father, but who knows? I rebelled against discipline, so I might have been worse. How about you, Macy?"

"Never thought about it at all," Macy said. "Mama taught me to trust that God is planning for us and to trust in that. I've tried to—even at times like these, when I can't imagine why He would send someone like Neal into my life."

"Maybe it's so that you won't ever let all that sweet talk fool you into trusting the wrong person." Sarah slipped a flower into the hole and straightened to a standing position.

Grace picked up a pot of petunias and handed it to her sister. "We'll never know what kind of path we would have taken if we could go back and undo the past, will we?"

"No, but I can tell you a little about the future," Sarah said with half a giggle as she toed the dirt that had brought the giggle up. "I will be very careful about who I trust—and I will probably never like to dust. I'd rather dig in the dirt."

"What's so funny?" Grace asked.

"I guess Macy and I were digging in the dirt, so to speak, when we let those scumbags Joel and Neal into our lives," Sarah said.

Grace's frown deepened the few crow's-feet around her eyes.

"You'd have to be in my warped state of mind to understand all of what I said." Sarah wiped her eyes on the sleeve of her shirt and then dropped back to her knees. "But, like you said a few days ago, we are going to check any man out thoroughly before we fall in love. And that means Travis Butler. Now, on to another subject: Can you believe that Audrey is in there helping Raelene? I figured there would be an ice storm in hades before she ever became Raelene's friend, especially after that first day when I brought her to the house."

"That's easier than visualizing the two of them sitting together in the library and Audrey asking Raelene to help her," Grace said. "You remember how gossipy girls were in school. Technology has changed the world, but human nature and teenage girls are the same. By the end of the school day, all of Audrey's friends had probably realized that she has been hanging out with Raelene for the past couple of days. It's not a matter of whether the nuclear fallout will hit. It's more a matter of when, because Audrey is baiting a bear. I just hope that she's really becoming friends with Raelene and not just using her to get back at those other two."

Sarah slipped the last petunia plant into the flower bed and sat down beside Grace on the porch step. "Think Audrey will do something stupid?"

"You can bet the shop on it," Grace said with a nod.

Chapter Twelve

G race was in that state between being almost awake and not yet fully asleep on Friday evening when her phone pinged. She fumbled around on the nightstand and read the text message with one eye open: Had a wonderful time at lunch. Looking forward to next Wednesday.

"Uh-huh," she muttered and tossed the phone on the end of the bed. She closed her eyes, but she couldn't go back to sleep. Her thoughts went from worrying about Audrey's temper when she was pushed too far and Raelene putting up with bullying to keep her scholarship to what she was going to do about Travis and the date on Wednesday. Somewhere in the middle of all the flipping from one side to the other, fluffing up her pillow half a dozen times, and cussing Travis for waking her up with a text, she realized that some folks didn't go to bed as early as she did. But then, they didn't have to be at work at three in the morning, either. That should be an omen that she didn't need Travis in her life—not even their sleeping schedules matched.

Morning came way too soon. She'd only had a few hours of sleep, and she'd dreamed about Travis the whole time and woke up cranky. She dressed in her usual jeans and T-shirt with the Devine Doughnut logo on the back. As she brushed her blonde locks up into a ponytail, she noticed a gray hair and groaned.

Stop feeling sorry for yourself. Gray hair is earned, so own it and be proud of it, the voice in her head that sounded so much like her mother said.

"I'm entitled to whine a little. I have a teenage daughter," she muttered.

She heard both Macy's and Sarah's bedroom doors open and close as she walked out into the hallway.

"Mornin'," Sarah muttered and covered a yawn with her hand.

Macy agreed with one word: "Yep."

"Sounds like y'all didn't sleep any better than I did," Grace said and followed them through the living room and then outside. The moon and stars usually brightened the path to the shop, but that morning, another round of dark clouds covered the sky. The air felt heavy, as if rain were on the way, and way off in the distance, Grace heard a faint rumble of thunder.

Sarah opened the back door into the shop. "If you tossed and turned half the night, then you're right, where I'm concerned. I kept thinking about Audrey."

Macy followed her inside and turned on the lights. "If she will take punishment for her friends like she did with the cigarettes and booze, then what will happen if those mean girls bully Raelene in front of her at school?"

"It won't even be as pretty as when you tried to kick Neal into a bloody mess," Grace answered. "Remember when she made a believer out of that kid in kindergarten for putting dirt on her new shoes?"

Macy set the usual large bowls up on the counter. "She was the smallest kid in the classroom, and that boy was the biggest, but she didn't think twice about tying into him."

"Yep, the storm isn't just coming from the sky," Grace said. "She's always been quick to sass yet fairly slow to anger. But when the pot boils, it comes right out over the top and spreads everywhere."

Macy added warm water to three bowls and commented, "Just like Sarah."

"Hey, now!" Sarah objected as she added yeast and sugar to each bowl. "Grace is just as bad—and you're one to talk after what we saw you do to Darla Jo and Neal."

"I'm quick to anger and, most of the time, quick to cool down. You two . . ." Grace paused. "Are the ones that let something fester until it explodes. Which reminds me, what would each of you do different about Joel and Neal now that time has passed?"

"The Bible warns us against killing," Macy answered.

"Forget the Bible," Sarah said. "I would have wrapped Joel up in that bedsheet and worked him over with whatever I could find in the hotel room. The ice bucket comes to mind. I just realized that both of those two sumbitches had names with four letters and that ended with an *L*."

Grace thought about Travis—five letters, and no *L* in his first name. Should the one in *Butler* be cause for alarm?

Macy hadn't spent nearly enough time on the Sunday school lesson, so she headed off to church earlier than usual. Finding the room clean and in order just like she'd left it the week before, she sat down behind the desk and opened the lesson book and tried to get some ideas about how to bring the story of Noah down to today's teenagers. Her mind drifted off to Audrey and Raelene, and suddenly, an idea popped into her head. She would discuss how the attitudes of the animals had to change while they were in the ark together or else there would have been chaos.

She was still making notes when Grace and the two girls arrived with several other teenagers right behind them. Grace came right over to sit behind the desk with Macy, but Audrey looped her arm through

Raelene's and ushered her over to the chair at the end of the semicircle and then sat down beside her.

"Talk about an attitude change," Macy whispered.

"What was that?" Grace asked.

"Just something I was thinking about for today's lesson," Macy answered.

Crystal and Kelsey came in together and gave Audrey and Raelene dirty looks. They took their seats, glared at Macy and Grace for a second or two as well; then Crystal pulled a can of soda from her backpack. Grace wagged a finger at her. Crystal huffed in annoyance, but she returned the drink to her backpack. Kelsey nudged her and slipped her a piece of chocolate. Grace picked up the trash can and crossed the room with it.

"You girls know the rules—and if you continue to break them, then you'll face the consequences." Grace held out the trash can. "Put your candy in here. And if any of you want to test me, then next week, you will be leaving your backpacks on the front pew in the sanctuary. And that's where you will sit during services."

Macy wished she had the courage and power that Grace had, but she was simply too easygoing to even *threaten* a child with that punishment, much less carry through with it. "Thank you, Grace," she said, then continued, "We all need discipline in our lives, and I appreciate you taking care of that for us. Now, let's talk about our lesson for today. How many of you have read it?"

Audrey and Raelene raised their hands and got more hateful looks from Crystal and Kelsey.

"Thank you," Macy said with a nod and a smile. "For the rest of you, the study today is about Noah and the fact that he had so many animals on the ark—some of them were friends in nature, but a lot of them were enemies. How do you think they survived all those weeks in that big boat without the lions killing the zebras?"

"Because while they were locked up, they had to change their attitudes in order to survive. A lot like we have to in school every day, with kids who really don't like others," Audrey answered.

"Or we don't change our attitudes"—Crystal crossed her arms over her chest—"and the weak ones . . ."

"The weak ones are eaten by the strong ones," Kelsey butted in. She shot a smug look toward Raelene.

"Not in the ark," Raelene spoke up. "They all got along until Noah opened the doors and let them out."

"That's just a fairy tale," Crystal countered. "I'm not sure I even believe in the Bible."

"It's probably just a work of fiction," Kelsey added.

Audrey stood up so fast that her chair hit the tile floor with a loud noise. "Come on, Raelene, we need to go sit beside my mama and aunt. Lightning is liable to come down through the roof and zap Crystal and Kelsey for talking like that in church."

As if on cue, thunder rolled in the distance, and a bolt of lightning struck a tree not far from the window.

Audrey picked up her chair and Raelene's and carried both to the front of the room. "That was God's warning shot. Raelene and I will feel a little safer up here."

Macy bit back a smile when the thunder behind the lightning rolled so close to the roof of the church that several of the kids cringed. "That's what Noah and his family probably heard just before the rain started. What were all the people who had been making fun of Noah feeling about then, do you suppose?"

Audrey made a show of sitting down in her chair. "If it had been me, I would have been wishing I hadn't asked my friend to cover for me when they did a locker check at school."

"Well, our so-called friend shouldn't have been stupid enough to shove our contraband down into her purse instead of sneaking it into her locker, which had already been checked," Kelsey smarted off.

Raelene held up her hand. "I would have been thinking that maybe I should have taken swimming lessons or learned to love sushi."

One of the other teenagers frowned. "Why sushi?"

"Think about it," Raelene said. "If you're treading water, you'll have to catch a lot of fish with your bare hands and eat it raw if you expect to survive."

Macy nodded toward Raelene. "I wonder how many thought about how mean they had been to Noah and his family while he was building the ark."

"I would imagine most of them," Audrey answered, but she stared right at Crystal and Kelsey.

A cold chill started at the top of Macy's spine and wiggled all the way down to her toes. She'd seen that glare before, and it told her the ice that Audrey's former friends were standing on was beginning to crack.

Despite the third day of rain and thunderstorms, Grace hardly had time to keep the coffeepots going and customers taken care of on Monday morning. Even with all the hustle and bustle, answering questions about whether she was selling the shop, and others about whether she had been dating Travis Butler for several months, every time the phone rang, she jumped.

At noon, she locked the front door, put the last three doughnuts on a plate, and took them to the only clean table in the place. "Macy, please get us some tea or coffee or even milk, if there's any left; we'll have a moment of peace before we clean up."

"I'll bring what's left of the gallon of milk to the table and a couple of bottles of tea. The coffeepots are empty," Macy said from behind the counter. "My feet are killing me. Neal did give the best foot massages. I miss that."

"Joel did, too, but when I saw that picture of him and his wife, I wondered if he gave her massages, too." Sarah joined Grace. "Do you think that there's a good man out there who isn't married or a con artist?"

Grace thought of Travis. "Maybe. But so far, we seem to be cursed. Do you think it's because we've eaten too many doughnuts in our lifetimes?"

"If it is, I might stop eating them." Macy brought the milk and tea to the table and took a chair. "But I think me and Sarah have the mommy itch. We both want a family so bad that we trusted too easily in the relationship."

"Sometimes kids aren't . . . ," Grace started but then her phone rang. She slipped it out of her hip pocket and groaned. "It's the school."

She pushed the speaker button and laid the phone on the table. "Hello, this is Grace Dalton."

"Ms. Dalton, this is Jane Wilson, the secretary at your daughter's school. How quickly can you get down here? We have a problem." Her tone sounded frantic.

Grace was already on her feet. "I can be there in five minutes. Is Audrey okay?"

"I just need for you to get here," Jane said. "There's been an altercation, and we need your help."

"I'm on my way," Grace said as she grabbed her phone and headed for the door. "I knew this was coming. The other shoe has dropped."

"Yep," Macy said. "Want us to go with you?"

"I'll call if I need you," Grace threw over her shoulder as she cleared the door.

"Call no matter what!" Sarah yelled.

A hundred scenarios ran through Grace's mind as she drove to the school and parked as close to the front door as she could. She jogged from her vehicle to the principal's office, where four girls sat in folding chairs: Audrey and Raelene on one side of the room, Crystal and Kelsey on the other. Grace could almost feel the temperature in the room rising by the second from the heat flowing from one set of girls to the other. Lisa and her husband were standing behind Crystal, and Kelsey's parents were behind her. The odds—four against one—didn't seem quite fair, but Grace was ready to go to battle for her girls.

This is one time when I wish Justin was here to help with whatever has happened, she thought as she took her place behind Raelene and Audrey. The second thought that surfaced was how she'd feel with Travis beside her. He was a solid guy—stalwart and fair. What would he do if he were right there?

Carlita's sneer made Grace want to finish the fight that the girls had started. Then Lisa pointed at Grace and said, "Trashy people raise trashy kids."

Grace looked down and saw blood on Audrey's arm. That's when she figured she could take them all on with one hand tied behind her back.

"It would be best if you stayed out of my shop and kept your opinions to yourself," Grace said, glaring at the whole bunch of them.

All four girls looked like they had barely survived a tornado. Their hair was a mess, their makeup had smeared, and black streaks ran down their faces from tears flowing through mascara. Crystal was sporting a busted lip, and a nice purple bruise was already forming under Kelsey's eye. Grace caught Raelene's eye and realized that her arm was bloody, too.

"This all happened because you took that kid into your house," Lisa shouted at Grace, pointing at Raelene.

"No, this happened because your daughter and her friend are bullies," Grace said in a normal tone. She wasn't going to lower herself and get involved in a shouting match, but her hands doubled up into fists. If push came to shove, she was ready.

Mr. Barstow looked up from the other side of his desk. "These girls were fighting in the library. I've listened to each of them and have learned that Crystal and Kelsey have been bullying Raelene for quite some time. She has given me a documented account of all they have done to harass her through just this year, and she assures me that she has more journals at home."

"The manual says that she is supposed to report that . . . if it's true," Carlita said through gritted teeth. "You can't punish my child for something that happened in kindergarten." She patted Kelsey on the shoulder.

"She was afraid if she reported the abuse and harassment that it would get worse," Grace said and nodded toward Kenneth and Walter, the two fathers. "Your daughters tell around school that since you are on the school board, they can do anything they want and get away with it—up to and including not doing their homework. Raelene was afraid if she took up for herself, she would lose her scholarship for college."

"You've said what?" Walter demanded of his daughter, Kelsey.

Before she could answer, Grace asked her daughter, "What happened, Audrey?"

"Crystal and Kelsey came into the library, where we were working on my algebra. I had just finished the assignment, and now I'll have to do it all over again," Audrey said.

"Kelsey grabbed the papers and tore them up, then Crystal threw our lunch on the floor and stomped on it," Raelene added.

Audrey raised her hand. "I'll admit I threw the first punch, because when they do that to Raelene, the librarian makes *her* scrub it all up, and that's not fair."

"In her defense, she doesn't see what they do because they are so sneaky," Raelene said and pointed at Kelsey. "After they destroyed Audrey's lesson, Kelsey whipped out a pocketknife and began slashing at us." Raelene held up her arm. "I got away, but they grabbed Audrey. Crystal held her arms from behind."

"Kelsey said that she would cut up my face so bad that no one would ever want to be my friend, not even Raelene," Audrey said. "And she would have, but Raelene jumped on her back, and she dropped the knife. Then the librarian came, and here we are."

166

"Is there any truth in this?" Crystal's father had a horrified expression on his face.

"Of course not," his wife answered. "Crystal is a good girl, and these two are lying riffraff. Look at her face. Not even makeup is going to cover that."

Kenneth glared at his wife. "She's a spoiled-rotten brat, and you've made her that way!"

Good for you, Grace thought.

"Before we move on, maybe you should all just watch this." The principal turned his computer monitor around to face them and hit a button. "We have cameras all over the school. This one is from the library at noon today, and we can verify Raelene's accusations about harassment. Audrey and Raelene are telling the truth about what happened."

Grace set her jaw, clenched her teeth, and sent a look meant to fry Lisa and Carlita where they stood. Those two women should be punished as much as—or more than—their daughters.

Crystal pouted. "We were just taking up for ourselves. Audrey started it when she—"

"When she what?" Kenneth asked.

"When she left us to be friends with *that*." Crystal pointed at Raelene. "She's trashy and . . ."

"Everyone is laughing at us because we got thrown over for *her*." Kelsey's tone was as cold as her eyes were hot when she shot a dirty look toward Raelene.

"That's enough," Kenneth said and turned to the principal. "What's the punishment for this?"

"They will all be put on distance learning for ten days while the parents file a form. Since Raelene's parent is out of town, I suppose—"

"Raelene is already eighteen and can take care of legal matters on her own, but I'll support her in this. She lives with us and is part of our family now. Just give us the forms and let me take these girls to the hospital to see if they need stitches," Grace said through gritted teeth. The other shoe that had dropped that morning wasn't the size of a flip-flop; it was more like a combat boot filled with concrete.

"Following the investigation, we will decide if the four of them can come back to school this year—all but Kelsey. She will be on distance learning until next fall for bringing a weapon to school," the principal said. "Neither of the girls who were bullying Raelene or who were intent on cutting Audrey will be allowed to attend any school functions."

Gold bracelets sounded like wind chimes when Carlita popped her hands on her hips. "Kelsey won't ever come back to this school. I'll be putting her in a private school after this, so I don't even need those forms."

"Oh, yes we will!" Kelsey's father disagreed loudly. "You have let our daughter run wild far too long. This time, she is going to be held accountable for what she's done. I apologize to you girls—and to Grace—for this."

"Noooo!" Crystal moaned. "That means we can't go to the prom, and we've both got dates already."

Kelsey turned around and pointed her finger at her father. "I will run away if you—"

Walter gave her a look that caused her to drop her hand. "Today, I'm confiscating your bullying costume, girl, and I'm resigning from the school board. I'm ashamed that you have been using my position to try to get your way. This is inexcusable."

The principal raised up to his full height—which had to be every bit of six feet, four inches—and clapped his hands. "That's enough out of all of you. Miz Dalton, you can take Audrey and Raelene to the hospital now. I'm sorry that Raelene has been the subject of harassment, and I hate to send her and Audrey home for fighting. Even if the decision is made to put all four of them on distance learning until next fall, she can come back and graduate, and even deliver the valedictory speech. You can pick up the forms on your way out."

"What about my scholarship?" Raelene's chin quivered.

"That's between you and the school, but this could have a bearing on it," the principal said. "We will have answers for all of you within two or three weeks. If you want to hire lawyers, that's up to you."

"Crystal, you can begin by apologizing to these girls," Kenneth said.

"I will not," his daughter said.

"Then that car you want for your birthday next month is off the table," he said.

"I'll walk before I tell either one of them that I'm sorry," Crystal hissed.

"Who's going to hide your cigarettes?" Audrey asked as she stared Crystal right in the eye and then shifted her gaze over to Kelsey. "And who's going to hide your whiskey now that the two of you won't have me to take the fall for you anymore?"

"Is that true also?" Kenneth asked.

Crystal hung her head and refused to answer.

"She's lying again!" Lisa shouted.

"Then I guess you are grounded until this is all taken care of, young lady," Kenneth told his daughter.

"And you, young lady." Walter tapped Kelsey on the shoulder. "What were you thinking? I hope you will enjoy boot camp this whole summer, because that's where I'm thinking you should go."

Grace's blood pressure was so high, she could hear a whooshing noise in her ears when she walked the girls down the hallway and out to the vehicle. "How bad are those cuts?"

Raelene pulled up her sleeve. "It's just a scratch, honest. I don't have insurance, and I haven't saved enough money for a doctor's visit."

"It's gaping open," Audrey said, "and so is mine, Mama. Why did I ever think of them as my friends?"

"Because you wanted to be popular," Grace said. "But you've learned a lesson, so that's a good thing. Neither of you need to worry about the cost of getting you stitched up."

"Thank you," Audrey said. "It's not a long cut, so maybe they can just put butterflies on them."

Grace handed Audrey her phone. "Call Sarah and Macy and tell them what happened. They're probably already worried to death."

Grace listened to her daughter and Raelene tell the story, sometimes even finishing each other's sentences, and by the time they reached the emergency room, the noise in her ears had settled down.

They had barely gotten into the lobby and told the lady behind the desk why they were there when Crystal and Kelsey and their parents arrived.

"What are *you* doing here?" Audrey snapped.

"We're here to offer to pay for any medical bills and for my daughter to apologize. Kelsey? Do you have something to say?" her father asked.

"Nope. Put me anyplace you want, but I'm not apologizing," she said.

"When we get home," Walter said with a sigh, "I plan to take the door off your room, and you will do your homework at the dining room table. Your privacy is gone, and it's going to take you a long time to earn my trust again."

"Come on, Kelsey," Carlita begged. "Just say you're sorry, and this can all go away."

"No, it won't," Walter said, "but it will be a start."

"I won't," Kelsey said. "And, Mama, you won't let him do that, will you?"

"I'm afraid it's not up to me this time," Carlita answered with a long sigh.

"One more chance, Crystal," Kenneth said. "What Kelsey's dad says is just the beginning. You have lost your phone and your laptop, except for schoolwork. I can't believe you've used my place on the school board to bully other kids, for God's sake."

"Then you should take up for me and fire Mr. Barstow for expelling me," Kelsey said to her father. "Crystal should be the one seeing a doctor. Raelene busted her lip when I was holding Audrey down. She should go to jail."

"I'll resign my position when I take the forms back for their investigation," Walter said.

"So will I," Kenneth agreed with a nod toward Audrey and Raelene, then shifted his eyes over to the woman behind the desk. "Send the bill for whatever these girls need to me. I will pay it."

"Why are you doing this?" Raelene asked.

"Because you *could* go to the police and file a lawsuit against our daughters for assault and battery—and probably *should* since you've been wronged all these years," Kelsey's dad said. "I will be glad to pay the bill, but I'm begging you not to ruin their lives with a police record."

"They already are ruining my life." Kelsey whirled around and stomped her foot, but her sneakers didn't make a sound on the tiled floor. "Prom is in a few weeks, and I've been invited, and Mama said we could have my dress made special."

Grace was reminded of that quote about sound and fury meaning nothing, but in her boiling anger, she couldn't remember the whole thing.

"Sue me," Crystal spat out. "Prison would be better than what I'll have to do."

"Thank you for the offer, but I will take care of my own," Grace said. "Just keep those two away from me, my shop, and my kids."

"Again, I'm sorry," Kenneth said as they left the ER lobby.

"Audrey and Raelene," a nurse called out and took the girls right back to a cubicle, where she cleaned and examined their wounds. "Looks to me like butterflies might be all you need, but I'll let the doctor make that decision. I'm pretty sure you'll both need tetanus shots since you never know where a pocketknife has been." She disappeared behind the curtain.

"Why did you take up for Raelene?" Grace asked.

"Because she's my real friend," Audrey said. "She helps me and doesn't demand things from me, like making me hide contraband—or taking whatever I'm wearing, like my favorite bracelet or necklace. 'If you're going to be our friend, then you have to share,' is what Crystal or Kelsey would say, only they never shared back with me."

Grace felt a ray of hope—almost like a rainbow at the end of a fierce storm—at Audrey's answer, but that didn't keep her blood pressure from shooting up again. "That's bullying. Why didn't you tell me?"

"Because I wanted to be popular like they are, and they said I had to do whatever they told me, or I couldn't be their friend," Audrey said. "They said it was like being in a college sorority."

A female police officer poked her head around the curtain and asked, "Are you Audrey and Raelene? Could we ask you a few questions?"

"Of course." Grace motioned her inside.

A male officer followed her, crowding the small cubicle. "We understand that you girls got into a fight at school and a knife was involved. Is that right?"

"Yes, sir, but we are not pressing charges," Audrey said.

"Doesn't matter if you do or don't; we have to investigate." The lady, who had a tag on her uniform that said *Bradford*, pulled out a notepad.

"Raelene has been bullied for years by two girls that I thought were my friends. They came in the library, where we were working on lessons, and started bullying her again. They ripped up my algebra paper and threw it on the floor, so I got mad and threw a punch. Kelsey pulled out a knife"—Audrey held up her arm to show the officer the cut—"and Crystal grabbed me and held me while she sliced my arm. Raelene pulled her away and gave her a black eye but got her arm cut while she was doing it. End of story."

Grace almost smiled. That version was so much shorter than the one that they had told Sarah and Macy on the way to the hospital, but at that moment, she couldn't have been prouder of her daughter.

"Okay, then," the male officer said. "We'll file this report, but if you change your minds . . ."

Raelene looked him in the eye. "We won't."

"If you do, give us a call." Officer Bradford put her pad away, and they disappeared.

Grace turned to Raelene. "Why did you help Audrey when she'd been mean to you all year and you could lose that scholarship for college?"

"She's my only friend . . ." She paused. "And because family is more important than a scholarship."

Chapter Thirteen

The weather had finally cleared up and the sun was out, so Grace expected Sarah and Macy to be on the front porch when she got home with the girls, but they weren't. Sarah's truck and Macy's SUV were there, which meant they were either in the shop or taking a nap. Grace couldn't believe either of them could sleep at a time like this. Her own nerves were frayed at the edges, and all she wanted to do was get back in her vehicle and leave. The gossip vine was probably already smoking and would burst into flames any minute.

"Do you think Crystal and Kelsey's daddies will really make them do what they threatened to do?" Raelene whispered.

"I hope so, but I wouldn't count on it," Grace answered from the front seat of her vehicle. "They should be held accountable for what they've done, but Lisa and Carlita will probably sneak around and let them do whatever they want to do."

"Get ready to start getting up before the crack of dawn." Audrey sighed. "We'll both be working in the shop as punishment for basically getting expelled from school."

Raelene opened the door. "Whatever your mama decides, it was worth it."

Audrey's giggle sounded more like a snort. "Yep, it was."

The two girls got out of the car and walked up to the porch together. But Grace sat there behind the wheel for several minutes, her mind going in circles. She had wanted Audrey to have a good friend, one who didn't ask her to do unthinkable things, but she sure didn't expect for her prayers to be answered by her daughter and Raelene getting into a fight.

Her hands began to shake so badly that she couldn't hold on to the door handle. She'd never been much of a drinker, but right then, a good strong double shot of Jack Daniel's sounded perfect. She finally laid her arms across the steering wheel, rested her forehead on them, and took several deep breaths. She'd always been a rock until the dust settled, and then she'd fall to pieces. Tears welled up in her eyes and the dam broke and sent them flowing down her cheeks to leave wet spots on her Devine Doughnut T-shirt.

Her precious daughter, whom she'd birthed after all those hours of labor, and then the one whom they'd taken into their home could have bled out right there on the library floor. Would the librarian have expected them to rise up from the dead and clean that up, too?

Don't blame that person, her mother's voice whispered. *Raelene didn't report that she was being harassed, so it looked like she was being messy on purpose.*

Before Grace could argue, the back door of her SUV slid open, and Sarah and Macy got inside. She quickly raised her head and wiped her face on the sleeve of her T-shirt. "What a day," she muttered.

"How are you holding up?" Sarah asked.

"Not worth a damn," Grace admitted. "It broke my heart to see . . ." She burst into sobs.

Sarah patted her sister on the shoulder from the back seat.

"Where did y'all come from?" Grace did her best to get control of her emotions, but it wasn't happening. She was the strong one—the oldest one—and she shouldn't fall apart in front of the others.

"We waited until the girls were inside before we came out here," Macy answered. "Is the story they told us all true? They both look like they've fought with a Weed Eater, and it won."

175

"Is it too soon to ask what the other two looked like?" Sarah asked.

"One had a busted lip and the other one a black eye, but our girls were cut. I'm glad they were able to close the wounds with butterflies, but the girls had to have tetanus shots. The police came to the hospital. I'm so proud of Audrey that I could . . ." Grace took a deep breath, closed her eyes, and held back more tears. "I shouldn't be proud of her for fighting."

"Yes, you should," Macy disagreed. "You should be proud of her for standing up for herself and her friend."

"Amen," Sarah added. "Those girls are young, and they'll get over this—but what about you?"

"I want to start the engine of this car and leave," Grace admitted. "All the drama of not selling our shop, the land, and the stuff with Joel and with Neal . . ."

"Thank God no one knew about Joel," Sarah said.

"And now this." Macy shook her head. "I'd like to take off, too—so fast that the dust would still be settling when I hit the highway."

"Then let's do it," Sarah whispered. She pulled out her phone, looked something up, and then put it back in her pocket.

"Since we talked about a trip for Raelene's graduation, I've been doing some research," Macy said. "There's this cute little motel on the west end of Panama City Beach. Sarah can get the plane tickets and the rental car arranged, and I'll take care of rooms."

"If we can get to San Antonio by four o'clock," Sarah said, "we all can catch a five-thirty flight to Pensacola, Florida; be there by ten tonight; and get a rental car."

"That's only two hours from right now." Grace gasped. "We've never closed the shop before, except on Sundays. All these years, folks could depend on us being open at five in the morning. We should think about this for a day or two, and maybe even put a little ad in the newspaper saying we won't be open," she argued, but at the same time, just the thought of warm sand beneath her feet calmed her nerves a little.

If you agree with them, you won't have to deal with the drama this situation is bound to create, the voice in her head reminded her.

"The girls can make a sign and tape it to the inside of the door," Macy suggested. "Are you in or out? We need to know right now."

Grace's mind whirled around like one of those whirligigs that kids hang out a car window. "I'm in," she whispered. "We won't know anything about the investigation for a while, anyway, and it can be a test as to whether we really want to sell our land and shop, even if we can't let go of the recipe."

"Great! Then we've got some work to get done." Macy hopped out of the vehicle and jogged to the house.

"Don't pack a lot," Sarah said as she crawled out of the back seat. "There's a couple of beach-type stores that sell bathing suits and all kinds of clothing near the place."

"What have I agreed to?" Grace whispered.

"Our first vacation ever." Sarah sighed and opened the door for her sister. "Get a move on it. We're burnin' daylight, as John Wayne said."

"I don't even own a suitcase," Grace muttered as she got out of her SUV.

Sarah was already on her way to the house, but she stopped at the bottom of the porch steps and turned around. "Borrow one of Audrey's old backpacks. No suitcases means no waiting in line at the baggage claim."

"This is insane," Grace said. "I cannot believe I'm agreeing to this."

Sarah draped an arm around her sister's shoulders. "The timing is perfect, and God only knows how bad we all need to get out of town for a while. Go tell the girls to get hopping."

Grace glanced down at the newly planted flower beds. "What if there's no rain while we're gone?"

Sarah ushered Grace to the porch and opened the door. "If the flowers die, I'll just buy more when we get home. Do you realize that I'm thirty-five years old and have never flown anywhere?"

"Me either," Grace told her.

"First time for everything." Sarah disappeared down the hallway, leaving Grace in the living room with two wide-eyed girls.

"What are y'all talking about? Florida? Rain? Flying?" Audrey asked.

Grace sat down in a recliner across from them. "We are going to use this time you're out of school as a test for me and Sarah and Macy. I want you girls to make a sign that the doughnut shop will be closed for a while. We'll tape it to the inside of the door as we are leaving. After that, you need to pack for a trip to Florida. You will be responsible for keeping up your distance learning while we are there."

"Are . . . you . . ." Audrey sputtered. "We should be punished."

"Not rewarded," Raelene gasped.

"Sarah tells me that a backpack will do since we can shop for what we need when we get there. And, girls, you two shouldn't be punished for taking up for each other. That's what family does," Grace said.

When neither of them moved for what felt like a whole minute, Grace clapped her hands. "Get crackin'. This is my first vacation in my whole life, and I don't intend to miss the plane."

"It's my first one, too," Audrey chimed in. "When we did drive somewhere, we always had to be back in time to open the shop the next morning, or if we went on Saturday, we had to be back Sunday evening to get things ready for Monday. We can't miss the plane, Mama."

"But . . ." Raelene shook her head slowly. "I can stay here and keep up the house and flower beds and . . ."

"No!" Audrey raised her voice. "You have to go with us."

Grace pointed toward the door. "Family doesn't leave family behind."

Raelene blushed.

The girl was thinking about finances, for sure. "Don't worry about money. This is our graduation present to you, and we'll take care of everything. Audrey, please rustle up a backpack for me. Now, go!"

"Yes, ma'am." Audrey jumped up from the sofa and wrapped her arms around her mother. "Thank you, Mama."

With tears streaming down her face, Raelene made it a three-way hug. "I've never been anywhere farther than San Antonio on a school trip. I feel like I'm dreaming."

If Grace had had a single doubt in her mind, that brief moment erased it. For the first time in a year, her daughter had hugged her and said *thank you*.

Sarah led the way into the airport and up to the ticket counter, where she explained that they were all flying newbies and needed help. The woman at the counter pointed toward a kiosk and motioned for them to follow her. She showed them what to do and stayed with them until they all had tickets in their hands.

"Thank you," Sarah told the woman.

"I'm starving," Audrey said. "We didn't get any lunch, and we were too afraid of what kind of trouble we were in to even grab a snack."

"We should have time to grab something after we find our terminal," Grace said. "I'm hungry, too. I still can't believe we are doing this."

"Just think"—Sarah moved up to the front of the line—"we'll be breathing ocean air before we go to bed tonight."

"I've never seen anything bigger than Pilgrim Lake," Raelene said. "Granny taught me how to swim there one time when Mama let us borrow her car for the afternoon."

Grace patted her on the shoulder. "None of us have been very far, either. We all had a senior trip to Galveston, but I hear the beaches in Florida are much prettier."

"I'm scared," Audrey whispered.

Raelene looped her arm through Audrey's. "I want to see everything out the window. I don't want to miss one single thing."

"Thanks," Audrey said meekly. "I'll be glad when we get there, but until then I can't believe that I'm not dreaming."

"I guess you know if you've rebelled and gotten a secret belly ring, it will set off alarms," Grace teased as they lined up to go through TSA.

Audrey shook her head and removed her shoes. "Just my ears are pierced—and no tattoos. How about you, Raelene?"

"Neither one," Raelene answered.

"But you're already eighteen, right?" Audrey asked.

"As of February 1," Raelene answered. "And to be honest, I'm scared of needles more than I am of flying. I closed my eyes and held my breath until the nurse finished the shot at the hospital."

"I'll be seventeen June 1," Audrey said. "Mama, there's a place to buy sandwiches and drinks. Can we stop there? I can see our terminal from here."

"Sounds good to me," Grace answered.

"I kinda feel sorry for Crystal and Kelsey," Raelene said on the way to the small deli. "We're getting to go on an awesome vacation, and if their parents really meant what they said, they're having a rough time."

"I don't feel sorry," Audrey said. "They've been bullies too long, and I'm ashamed to admit it, but I helped them by letting them control me. I checked on the drive up here, and we either have to stay out of the water or put waterproof bandage things on our arms. That means even if the sun is hot enough for us to lay out and work on our tans, we can't because our arms will have a big splotch of white on them, and that's because Crystal and Kelsey tried to slice us to pieces. So I don't feel one bit sorry for them."

Sarah chuckled. "That's my girl!"

Chapter Fourteen

I guess the girls aren't going to waste a single minute," Sarah said as she slid the glass doors open and stepped out on the patio. "They're already headed toward the beach even though it's dark."

A crescent moon lit up the waves as they crashed against the white sand. The lights from the heated swimming pool on the other side of the railing from where Sarah stood illuminated two couples enjoying a midnight swim. Flashlights lit up little portions of the beach where folks were out looking for shells washed up from the surf.

Grace and Macy joined her, and all three took in several deep breaths of the salty air. No one said a word for several moments, and Sarah wondered if they were thinking the same thing she was.

"All that drama back in Devine seems to be far away," Sarah finally said.

"How can anyone look at something this spectacular and even think about their troubles?" Macy whispered. "I'm going to join the girls. I'm not waiting until morning to get sand between my toes."

"I still can't believe we've done this, but I'm glad we did. That sand is so white that it glimmers in the moonlight. I can't wait to put my toes in the water." Grace sat down in one of the white plastic chairs and removed her shoes.

"I'm going, too," Sarah said and then covered a yawn with the back of her hand. "Y'all don't leave me on the beach if I fall asleep." She closed her eyes for just a minute and let the sound of the surf sink into her soul. When she opened them, she had a smile on her face; she knew beyond a shadow of a doubt that they had made the right decision to get away for a while.

"We might all sleep beneath the stars." Macy was already ahead of them and halfway around the pool area when they started that way.

"Welcome to our first vacation ever," Sarah said.

"If we never do anything but sit on the patio and listen to the ocean, it will be the *best* one ever." Grace looped her arm through Sarah's and gave her a quick sideways hug. "Thank you and Macy for doing this. If you would have given me a day or two to think about it—"

"We would have never done anything," Sarah butted in. "You've never been impulsive."

"We all three make a good crew: I'm grounded, you're impulsive, and Macy is the spiritual one of us," Grace said and stepped off the bottom of three steps right out onto the beach. "Like that rope Mama talked about, it takes all three of us to make a good strong unit. Oh! My! Goodness! This sand feels so good."

Sarah broke free from her sister and jogged across the beach to the edge of the water. She sat down and stretched her legs out far enough that the waves washed up over her feet and to the knees, soaking the legs of her jeans. The water felt like a cool seventy-five degrees, just like the research she'd done on the plane said it would be.

Macy sat down beside her, and then Grace joined them on the other side. After only a few minutes, Audrey plopped down beside her mother, and Raelene dropped beside Audrey. From where they were, the only sounds they could hear were those of the surf and a seagull off in the distance.

Raelene finally broke the silence. "There are no words," she said. "But I'm going to try to write my next English Comp II essay on the way I feel right now."

"Comp II?" Audrey asked.

Sarah listened to her niece and her friend talking plans for the future and wondered what her own tomorrows might hold. Would she ever find someone to love her and who wanted to start a family? That's what she wanted above all things, and yet it seemed far-fetched. But thinking about a baby of her own and a husband to share her life with put a smile on her face.

"I've been taking concurrent college classes since last year. When I start college—or maybe I should say, if I *get* to go—I'll already have twelve hours done with," Raelene explained. "I want to thank y'all for bringing me with you. If this night was all I got, and we had to go home tomorrow, it would be . . ." She hesitated.

"No words, right?" Audrey asked.

"Yes," Raelene answered. "'No words' is right."

"I understand just how you feel," Audrey agreed. "In less than twenty-four hours, we've been kicked out of school, had our first airplane ride, figured out how to rent a car and get here, and now all this." She took it all in with the wave of her hand. "Like Mama said, family don't leave family behind. Besides, I'm glad you are here. These old ladies couldn't keep up with me after the first day," she said with a giggle.

"Out of the mouths of babes," Sarah whispered. Someday, she was going to have a family, and she intended to bring them to the beach at least once a year. One thing she'd come to understand in the past twenty-four hours was that getting away wasn't just a luxury; it was a necessity. For the first time in weeks, peace washed over her—and she liked the feeling.

"'Old ladies'?" Grace nudged her daughter's shoulder.

"Yes, ma'am, all of y'all are old," Audrey answered and then jumped up and ran down the beach with Raelene right behind her. "Bet y'all can't run as far as we can."

"Of course not." Grace raised her voice. "We're old, remember?"

The girls' giggles faded, and soon they were just dots with a crescent moon and stars above them. Grace lay back in the sand and stared up at the sky. Sarah and Macy followed her lead.

"Remember when we used to lay on the grass and see what kind of animals or shapes the clouds were?" Grace asked.

"One of the first memories I have is of all three of us laying in the yard, just like we are now. Grace, then Sarah, and me," Macy said. "Y'all told me that the clouds looked like a teddy bear. I couldn't see it, but I believed you. I must've been about three years old. The next time I remember laying in the yard was when my mama died. We went to the backyard and laid down in the grass and looked up at the clouds that day, too." She wiped her eyes on the sleeve of her shirt. "These are tears of joy that remind me that we've always had each other's backs."

"Yes, we have. I remember us doing that when our mama passed away," Sarah said. "Grace was pregnant, I was home from my first year of college, and you had finished your sophomore year in high school. That's when we took over the business. We saw a big fluffy cloud in the shape of a heart that day."

Grace sat up, pulled her feet out of the water, and laced her arms around her knees. "We fell into a schedule that summer, and I felt so bad that you had to give up so much, Macy, to help us. Maybe this time away will help make up for that."

Macy stared up at the stars a little longer, then sat up. "I agree with what Raelene said. If tonight is all I ever got, seeing this and feeling the peace I've got in my heart right at this moment just sitting here and listening to the surf . . ." She paused and took a breath before she went on. "It would be worth every day I've worked at the shop. And FYI—as the girls say—I don't feel like I gave up anything at all. I've had the support and love of family all my life."

"We all have," Sarah said. "I don't know which is more impressive: the surf or the sky. We've got the same moon and the same stars at home, but somehow, they seem brighter here. If we ever decide to move from Devine, this is where I want to live. Think they'd sell us this hotel? We could pool our money and run a place like this rather than spend the rest of our lives making doughnuts. Or we might buy that vacant building across the street and make pastries."

"I'd rather just retire—" Grace was just about to finish that thought when her phone pinged.

She dug it out of her hip pocket to find a text from Travis: I hope I didn't wake you, but Claud called me. Are you really out of town? We have a date on Wednesday.

"Dammit!" she swore. "I forgot to call Travis and cancel our date."

She quickly typed out a message to send back that said the family had taken an impromptu two-week trip to Florida. "'So sorry,'" she said out loud as she tapped out the words.

In a few seconds, her phone rang. When she saw that it was from Travis, she stood up and walked away from her sister and cousin a bit for privacy. "Hello. You're up late."

"I had to go over an acquisition, but it's not unusual for me to work this late," he said. "Is everything all right with you? Claud called to see how the bakery business was coming along and told me that you had closed up shop for two weeks."

"It's a long story," Grace said.

"I'm not a stalker, I promise, and I respect your decision not to sell your business . . . but if I fly to Florida, is our date still on?" he asked.

"That . . ." Grace hesitated, not at all sure what to say.

"What?" Travis asked. "That it's too far? That you think I'm a stalker? That the answer is no?"

"Why would you fly all the way down here for one evening? For one date?" she asked.

"Calvin and Delores have been fussing at me for ten years to take a little time off for me, so I would be staying more than just one day," he said. "The company owns a beach house near Panama City Beach, and there's an airport not far from there. If you're anywhere close—"

"I am," she butted in, "but why do you own a house here if you haven't taken a vacation in ten years?" The thought of Travis flying that far just to take her to dinner and spending his first vacation in years with her was mind boggling.

"The company owns the house, and it's for all of our employees to use when they need a place to stay for a family vacation," Travis answered. "What do you say? Would it be okay for me to come down there?"

Travis Butler, owner of Butler Enterprises, was asking her, Grace Dalton, if it was all right for him to plan his vacation around her and her family? That blew her mind even more than him just being there for an evening. But it didn't mean that she was trusting him not to have an angle for the trip—such as sweet-talking her out of her business.

"Are you sure about this? I believe you were originally going to pick me up at seven on Wednesday."

"Why not make it Tuesday?" Travis asked.

Did she even have the right to subject all the women in her family to another person on their vacation?

"Unless you need it to be earlier or later," Travis answered.

"Seven is good. I'm in room 201 of the Sugar Sands," she told him, already worrying about how to tell the rest of the family the news.

"Great!" Travis sounded genuinely excited. "Invite the rest of your family to come along with us. Calvin has bragged about a restaurant there called the Perfect Pig for years. Maybe we'll go there. I haven't been down in that area in more than a decade, so I'm sure it's changed. We can discover and rediscover all the fun places together."

"In one night?" she asked.

"No, in one week," he chuckled. "See you later—and thank you, Grace."

One week? She started to say something, but he ended the call before she could get a word out.

"What was that all about?" Macy asked.

"Did I hear you make a date with Travis?" Sarah sputtered before Grace could open her mouth. "What's going on?"

"We *all* have a date tomorrow night, and we'll be going to a place called the Perfect Pig. Let's go get some sleep because in the morning, before we go shopping, we're going for doughnuts at Thomas's. We'll see if it can run us some competition." Grace stood up and extended a hand.

Macy put her hand in Grace's and allowed her to pull her up. "I'd bet that nobody in any state can make doughnuts better than we do."

Sarah got to her feet without any help. "I'll do some research on the doughnut place as well as the restaurant, but why do we *all* have a date?"

Grace looked up at the night sky one more time and saw a falling star as it zipped through the darkness and appeared to land in the water way out there on the far horizon. "I get to make a wish. I just saw a falling star."

"I'd say that's a good start to our vacation—but you didn't answer my question," Sarah said.

"Travis said to invite the whole family, and I need your support. I want y'all to give me your opinion just in case he asks me for a second date." Grace could hear her mother's voice again: *Grace Dalton, you don't need anyone's support or advice. You'll know if he's not worth a second date, and you're strong enough to tell him no about that just like you did on selling the business.*

Thanks for that vote of confidence, Mama, but I'm not bringing anyone into the family without their approval.

"We've got your back—and believe me, we will put him to the test. No more cons or sleazy men are going to sneak into our family," Macy said.

"And if we find out he's lied to you about anything, we will put an end to any more dates. There's plenty of fish in the sea around these parts," Sarah told her.

"I have a closet full of nice things at home," Macy groaned the next day when they went into the little pastry-and-burger shop a couple of miles down the road, "and I . . ." She stopped inside the door and took a deep breath. "This place smells amazing. Do you think this is what hits our customers' noses when they walk into our shop?"

"What has the smell of pastries got to do with whatever is in your closet?" Audrey asked.

"I'm old, remember? So my mind jumps from one subject to another," Macy said with a grin. "I was about to say that I wish I had brought more clothes with me so we wouldn't have to leave the beach and go shopping, but then I got a whiff of the doughnuts. Do y'all realize that we never get to eat pastries from another bakery?"

"I'm a thrifter," Raelene said, "and why would anyone eat dough-nuts from another place? That would be like choosing bologna over steak."

"That's a sweet thing to say," Macy told her.

One of Raelene's shoulders raised in half a shrug. "It's the truth."

"What's a thrifter?" Audrey asked.

"I like secondhand stores, thrift shops, and consignment places," Raelene answered with a slight blush.

The folks in front of them got their food and went outside to eat at one of the picnic tables, and then the girl behind the counter smiled at Macy. "Good morning. What can I get you today?"

"We'd like five bacon, egg, and cheese biscuits; half a dozen glazed doughnuts; three black coffees; and two chocolate milks," Macy answered and turned around to face the other four. "This morning, it's my treat, and I want to hear more about this thrift business. I've heard of those kind of stores, but we never have time to check them out."

The girl who had taken their order cocked her head to one side. "How did you know that I'm a thrifter?"

"I'm so sorry," Macy said and pointed to Raelene. "I was talking to her. She was about to tell us about shopping in thrift stores."

"Want a list of which ones are good and which ones to steer away from around here?" the girl asked.

"That would be great," Raelene answered. "Did you get that shirt at one?"

"Yep," she answered with a smile. "Everything in my closet comes from thrift stores. I love clothes, and I sure don't make enough to buy brand-new. I could text you the addresses of the good places."

"I don't have a phone," Raelene said.

"I do. Would you text me the list?" Audrey asked.

The girl slipped her phone out of her hip pocket, and Audrey added her phone number to the contacts.

The girl quickly sent the list. "Hope that helps. Your order will be ready in just a few."

"Thanks," Audrey said.

Macy led the way to a table near the back of the small dining area. "Now, tell me what this thrift stuff is about, Raelene."

"We've all helped organize donated clothing for the church closet a few times, but I figured that was freebies for the needy. I've never been in one for outfits." Sarah pulled out a chair and sat down. "Y'all remember that little antique lamp in my bedroom at home? I saw it in the window of a store in Hondo and bought it. But I didn't look around at anything else."

"We're always ready to just go home and rest up for the next day after we work from three in the morning until noon, so we don't get out to do much shopping," Grace added as she sat down beside Sarah. "Buying online has been my salvation."

"I can't wait to get my first car," Audrey said with a sigh. "Then I can go to the mall in San Antonio every Sunday afternoon. But now I'm ready to hear about this thrifting idea. I liked that shirt the girl that waited on us had on. Do you think her thrift store will have it in my size?"

"I doubt it," Raelene said with a soft giggle. "Thrift stores that sell donated or pre-owned things like clothing or shoes just have a single size or only a few. But there's purses and jewelry at a decent price—and also furniture, books, lamps, and lots of other things. Since Granny and I didn't have a car, I didn't get to go very often, but a few times, Mama drove us up to some places near San Antonio. I would save the money I earned waitressing in the summertime so we could go to the thrift stores for my school clothes."

"Macy," the girl behind the counter said, raising her voice, "your order is ready."

Raelene was up and out of her chair before anyone else could move. "I'll get it."

"What do y'all think?" Macy asked. "Shall we let Raelene take us thrifting? We could buy things we might only use for the beach for a lot less money."

"I wouldn't want to do it at home. What if someone at school donated something and I showed up with it? They would all know I was buying my things at a garage sale–type store," Audrey whispered. "But it might be fun here."

Raelene brought a tray with their food on it and set it in the middle of the table and turned around to go back to the counter. "Be right back with our drinks."

Audrey hopped up out of her chair. "I'll help you with those." Then she turned back and whispered to her mother, "But I'm not wearing used shoes—not even if they're giving them away free."

Raelene stopped, turned around, and nodded. "Me neither. It's not really a choice for me, though, because I wear a size five, and not many people wear shoes that small. So are we going to look through the thrift stores before we go to what Granny and I called the *hooty-tooty* places?"

"Sounds like an adventure to me," Sarah answered and reached for a biscuit. "I'm starving, so dig in. Audrey, you girls can navigate for us with the addresses on your phone. How many are there?"

"About a dozen, unless we go on into Panama City, and then it would be even more," Audrey replied and then bit into her biscuit. "I should have ordered two of these. I'm"—she smiled and looked across the table at her mother—"hungry to death."

Grace's brilliant smile lit up the whole room. "I thought being a teenager had made you forget all about the good times."

"That's one of my first memories," Audrey said between bites. "I'd wake up at the doughnut shop and smell them cooking and tell you that I was 'hungry to death.' You would let me choose which one I wanted for breakfast, pour me a glass of milk, and then put half a dozen doughnut holes on the plate with my choice of the day."

Raelene took a sip of her milk and pushed an errant strand of dark hair behind her ear. "You lucky dog. I ate oatmeal every morning until Granny passed away. And she put in raisins."

Audrey finished off her biscuit and bit into a doughnut. She slung an arm around the back of Raelene's chair. "Stick with me, and I promise you can have all the doughnuts for breakfast that you can eat for the rest of your life."

"I plan on living until I'm ninety, or maybe even a hundred," Raelene told her. "Are you still going to be running the shop then?"

"Yep, I am," Audrey said with a nod. "It's a legacy, don't you know? A family thing you'll probably be helping me with when you are a hundred."

Chapter Fifteen

"I'm in shock," Delores gasped. "Give me a minute, and I'll get all the arrangements made."

"I'm going home and back to bed," Calvin whispered. "I know I'm dreaming."

"Nope, you are not," Travis said as he signed the last of a stack of papers on his desk. "I'm really leaving for a week. I plan on taking Grace and her family to dinner tonight in Florida, and if things go well, I will ask her out again. If not, I'm going to relax on the beach and maybe even read a book for fun. I'll be staying at the company beach house. I've got a meeting with the think tank before I go, and that's all I'm doing for a whole week."

"Is this woman someone you could really get involved with?" Delores asked. "You do know that she's got a teenage daughter—and believe me, I know from experience that they can be horrible little creatures."

"I like Grace," Travis said. "She didn't try to impress me. She was totally herself and as honest as they come. I don't know about a relationship. I'd be willing to start off with a friendship and see where that goes."

"Well, she has to have magic powers." Delores opened her tablet and began to push buttons. "If she can get you out of Texas on a trip, then I already like her."

"And on short notice like this," Calvin agreed with a nod.

"I hate to tell you, but you aren't going in the company plane today," Delores said. "You promised the first-floor kids that they could use it this afternoon to fly to that conference in Vegas that kicks off tonight. How about leaving tomorrow morning?"

Travis was disappointed, but he didn't go back on his word, and it was too late to get all ten of that group on a commercial flight. He could possibly go commercial, but if there was a layover or a problem, he wouldn't get there by seven anyway.

His grandfather's voice was back in his head: *Ever think that this just might be an omen? Don't go flying off—quite literally—without figuring out why you are going.*

"See what kind of arrangements you can make for them, and I'll get in touch with Grace," Travis said. "I'll be down on the first floor if you need me."

"What kind of car do you want at the airport when you reach Florida? Limo? It's easier for me to do this right here than get your assistant," Delores said while still looking at her tablet.

"I don't need a limo," Travis replied. "I'm not trying to impress anyone. An SUV will be just fine." He remembered the way Grace had looked when she had come to the office to have lunch with him—jeans and her work T-shirt—and how at ease she had been eating pizza and doughnuts with her fingers. But most of all, she had held her ground for her little shop, and probably would for her land. Money didn't talk to Grace; family and her heritage did. That intrigued Travis more than anything had in a long time.

"I haven't seen that expression on your face in a long time," Calvin told him.

"I haven't been on a vacation in a long time," Travis said as he headed toward the door.

"Remember, we've got that big merger meeting first thing Wednesday morning, so you'll have to be home in a week," Delores reminded him.

Travis waved over his shoulder. "I'll be back on Tuesday evening."

He whistled all the way to the elevator and pushed the button for the first floor. When he stepped out, Lucy was exiting the one right next to him.

"Are y'all excited about this trip?" he asked.

"Oh, yeah!" she answered with a smile and a nod. "It's always good to network with other folks and companies to see what's new in their fields. I'm glad you came down here this morning. We're ready to sit down and talk to you about this bakery business."

"Then I'm glad I caught you before you left." He opened the door leading into the open space where their cubicles were located and stood to the side to let her enter first.

"Hey, everyone, gather around the table," Lucy called out.

Travis took his place at the head of the long table, and the rest of the group pulled chairs up on both sides. "Okay, what have you figured out about this factory business?"

Lucy sat down at the other end of the table and opened up a folder. "We've approached it from every angle—both putting one inside the city limits of Devine and also in other places—and every time, we came up with the same answer: that little bakery works because the small-batch idea and the method they use to bake is what makes them unique."

"Lucy has the figures for you, and it's just not a viable venture in our opinion," Barton, one of the other members, added.

"Trying to copy something like that would be like turning an oil well into a peach orchard. It simply will not work," Clara said. "I'm sorry that we have to be the bearers of bad news, because we all know that you kind of had your heart set on this. Unfortunately, that also is the situation with the piece of land just south of Devine you'd proposed for that housing development. Even if it was for sale—which, I under-stand at this time, it's not—it's not a good location."

"For one thing, it's another four miles out of the city, which makes for a bit of a longer commute, and the landscape isn't good; plus, there's a huge spring-fed pond at the backside of the land. That means the water table isn't far down, and the houses you would have built wouldn't be as stable as they should be," Devon said.

"I see," Travis said. "Yes, I was hoping for better news, but I pay you all to be honest with me, so we will withdraw any offers on these projects. When you return from your trip, I want you to dive into finding me about three hundred acres of viable land for a housing project that is within the Devine city limits."

"Will do." Lucy stood up and handed him the folder. "Here's the official findings on the bakery and the Dalton land. We've put it all on a digital file as well, but I know how you like hard copies."

"Thank you for doing all this"—Travis pushed his chair back—"even though it didn't turn out as I had hoped."

"That's what you pay us for," Lucy said.

Travis was glad to find his office empty when he got back up to his floor. He needed time to think and to go over the figures in the folder—but more than that, he wanted to be completely honest with himself about taking a trip to Florida. Had he been going to try to charm Grace into selling her properties to him, or was he really interested in her as a woman?

"This has been so much fun," Audrey said as she threw herself backward onto the sofa in the living room of the condo that her mother shared with Sarah and Macy. "I must have gotten a thousand dollars' worth of clothes for less than a hundred."

Raelene pulled her purchases out of her bags and laid them out on the kitchen counter. "And some of our stuff still have the tags on them, so you know they've never even been worn. This bathing suit is one of those, so I'm putting it on right now and going outside. I've never swam in a pool—always just the lake or a pond."

Audrey was on her feet and had dumped her bags on the sofa in a blur. "Me too. Mama, is it all right if we leave our stuff in here while we swim?"

"No problem," Grace said with a nod. "Go have fun. Just remember, we've got to be dressed and ready to go to dinner at seven."

"But . . . ," Audrey whined as she picked up a red-and-white polka-dotted bathing suit, "do Raelene and I have to go? We'd rather watch the sunset on the water."

"You'll be missing out. And how can you give me your opinion about Travis if you don't meet him?" Grace asked. "You can always watch all those hunky boys play volleyball tomorrow evening."

"I'm going to be brutally honest and tell you if I don't like him," Audrey declared, and Raelene burst out laughing, doubling over.

"And we did see some boys that took our eye," Raelene said, causing Audrey to laugh right along with her. "One even winked at me."

"I'm not surprised that the boys are looking at both of you. You are beautiful young ladies. And, honey, as far as being honest with me, I would expect nothing less from either of you," Grace told her. "Now, bandage up each other and go have fun. Be sure to slather on some of that sunscreen we bought. You both look like you've been soaked in buttermilk."

Audrey giggled and rushed into the bathroom to change. Grace got a visual of her as a toddler, running through the house strip-stark naked when she got finished with her bath.

"Free as a bird," she muttered.

Sarah and Macy were both dressed in new bathing suits when they came out of the bedroom. "That's the way I feel when I'm standing here in this open door, looking out and listening to the surf," Sarah said. "Are you coming with us, Grace?"

"I'll be along in a minute. My body hasn't caught up with that late night. I woke up at four this morning and thought I'd overslept, so I'm going to sit here for a minute or two and catch my breath."

"My internal clock doesn't know it's on vacation, so I was wide awake at three. I got up and sat out on the patio for a little while and told myself it was Sunday, even though it isn't; it must've worked, because I got sleepy," Macy said with a chuckle. "See you in a little bit down on the beach. I intend to soak up as much sun and get as much sand between my toes as possible every day we're here."

Grace waved at them, rested her head on the back of the sofa, and closed her eyes. She listened to the surf and the girls' voices as they played in the pool. In just a few hours, Travis would be in town for a week. On one end of the emotional stick, the idea made her nervous; on the other, she was excited about going to dinner with him and getting to know him better. From what she'd seen, he didn't act all entitled and like a rich man, and she liked that about him. But—and there always seemed to be a *but* when she even thought about dating—Grace was who she was and had a "take me as I am or leave me" attitude. He might not like that—or the fact that she had a daughter who could be, and most of the time *was*, a handful.

"Who knows? He might still be trying to get me to sell him our land and figuring out a loophole to get our recipe," she muttered.

She had only met him those times when he had come into the shop and when she had lunch with him, and only the good Lord knew how far her relationship radar was off these days. Just like Macy, she had thought that Neal was a good man with a kind and romantic heart. That idea could sure enough be hammered to the back door with a tenpenny nail as a reminder of her abilities to judge a man.

She had dozed off when her phone vibrated in her hip pocket and jarred her awake. She pulled it out, saw that it was Beezy, and answered on the second ring. "Hello, Beezy. I've been meaning to call you all morning, but these girls have kept me hopping since sunrise."

"What hotel are you in?" Beezy asked. "I've got my bags packed and my plane ticket bought. I'll get an Uber at the airport and be there by bedtime. There's no way you girls are going on your first vacation without me."

"We are at a place called the Sugar Sands. If you don't mind sleeping on a bunk bed, there's plenty of room in our motel for you," Grace answered, "and we'll love to have you for two whole weeks."

"Thank God!" Beezy said with a long sigh. "I can't even go to the post office or to the library without people swarming around me like ants and asking a million questions about all y'all. Honey, I'd take a trip to the desert with nothing but cactus and lizards just to get away from all this drama."

"Well, darlin', this is a very peaceful place, and we'll all be tickled to death to see you. Raelene has introduced us to thrifting, so keep some room in that packed suitcase."

"She's a smart girl, but I'm ready to walk out the door. I bought half a dozen of those embroidered dresses when we were on the cruise and have fallen in love with them. I feel like I'm wearing my nightgown when I put one on. Do they have those chairs and umbrellas for rent on the beach?" Beezy asked.

"Yes, ma'am, they do," Grace answered.

"Then I'm all set, but I will need to hit a bookstore. I only had room to bring the one I'm reading, so if you go thrifting again, I might go along to buy used books," Beezy said. "Or we could forget the books, and I'll teach the girls to play poker."

"Sweet Jesus!" Grace gasped.

"Hey, they need to learn," Beezy said, "or else when they go to college and the boys talk them into strip poker, they'll be in trouble."

Grace jumped to her feet and paced around the floor a couple of times. She had known that the day would come when Audrey would leave Devine and go to college and that Sarah had been a party girl in her university days. But she had never let things enter her mind about boys in the same dorms, strip poker, frat parties, and all that.

"Are you still there?" Beezy asked.

"I'm here," Grace answered and shook the ideas out of her mind. "What time does your plane land? We have an SUV rented, so I can drive over and get you."

"Oh, no you won't." Beezy's tone sounded just like Grace's mama's. "You've got to be exhausted. I'll handle any arrangements myself. I have a cell phone just like you do, young lady."

"Okay, then." Grace didn't even bother to argue. "But don't stop for vodka. There's a liquor store just down the strip. I'll make a run down there and get what we need."

"Deal!" Beezy said. "My sister is taking me to the airport, and she's not a happy camper. Nobody in town knows how long you plan to be away, so she's pitching a hissy fit because I won't be here to play poker with her and my Sunday school class after church on Sundays. And there she is now, honking the car horn. I swear to God, she's the most impatient woman the good Lord ever gave a soul to. I'll see you this evening."

"Lookin' forward to it," Grace said. "Have a safe journey."

"What you are supposed to say is 'have a fun trip.'" Beezy giggled. "Bye now."

The call ended and Grace slumped down in one of the two chairs at the end of the coffee table.

"Strip poker," she groaned. "Whatever Audrey is thinking shows in her expression, so she'll be the one with nothing but her underwear on at the end of the night."

Her mind was still staggering around that idea when her phone rang again. Figuring it was Beezy, she didn't even look at the name of the caller. "Hello?"

"With one word, you sound like you've got the weight of the world on your shoulders," Travis said.

Her breath caught in her chest. She wasn't sure if it was because of his slow Texas drawl or if it was because of the idea of Audrey having no restrictions when she went to college in a couple of years.

"Just dreading the future," she said and told him about Beezy's call and what she'd said about playing cards.

Travis chuckled. "Beezy's right."

"Are you speaking from experience?" Grace asked.

"Yep, I am—and yes, I lost," Travis admitted. "Audrey sounds like she'll be able to hold her own in any situation."

"Yes, she has been known to." Grace sat up straighter. "Are you on the way to the airport?"

"I can't get there until tomorrow," he said. "We had a flight problem with the company plane, but I'll be there in the early afternoon. Can we still plan on our date at seven tomorrow evening . . . please?"

Grace was actually glad for the news. "Of course. Seven?"

"That sounds great. I'll pick all y'all up at six thirty. I'm so looking forward to a vacation. I haven't had one in years," Travis said.

She stood up and walked over to the open patio doors and stepped outside. "We'll be ready. Have a good trip."

"I will. Goodbye, Grace," he said.

The call ended before she could even say goodbye. She took in the salt air with every breath and watched her girls argue over who had won a race from one end of the pool to the other. Finally, she laid the phone in her hand on the bar to her right, unlocked the gate out to the pool, and sat down on one of the many empty chaise longues.

Audrey swam over to the side of the pool. "Mama, we're glad you're here."

Raelene was right behind her. "We need a referee for our races, but you should go back inside and put on your suit. I wish I could call Granny and tell her about all this. She would be so excited that I'm getting to experience such an amazing trip."

"I wish I could call Crystal and Kelsey." Audrey frowned. "But then, I'm showing everyone on social media what a beautiful place this is. Since Crystal and Kelsey can't see it, then I'm not tormenting them—I'm doing what's right," she said with a smile and a shrug.

Grace thought of all the times her mother had to settle heated discussions among all three girls. "I came to tell you that we'll be having supper here. Travis can't come . . ."

"Oh my!" Audrey said with fake concern. "Did Mr. Rich Britches call it off because he can't really afford to take us all out to eat? I'm glad he's not coming after all. This is a family vacation, and he's not family."

"No, he did not," Grace snapped, "and don't butt in again. He had a conflict of schedule with his company plane."

All the color drained from Audrey's face. "He's got his own plane? I guess he *could* take us to a fancy place."

"I told Travis we would go to dinner with him tomorrow evening, but let's all of us girls have pizza delivered tonight. I'm going to make a run to town for some groceries before I go out to the beach. Anything you girls want?"

"Potato chips, root beer in bottles, and chocolate," Audrey answered. "And, Mama, I kind of have another confession. Since I'm being brutally honest with you about Travis, then I should probably tell you this, too. Crystal and Kelsey wanted me to call the school and say there was a bomb the day we went back to school after spring break."

"But she told me," Raelene said, "and we looked up what would happen if she got caught. I told her they were batshit crazy. Whoever does that can do some serious jail time because it's a felony."

"They said that I couldn't be a friend of theirs if I didn't do what they wanted and that they would get even with me. That's when I started to really realize that you were right about them, but I didn't want to admit it. That was probably the reason they were so ugly to me and Raelene on Monday," said Audrey.

"Good grief!" Grace hadn't realized what a blessing Raelene coming into their lives really was until that very moment.

"I know," Audrey said with a nod. "I was willing to take the blame for their stupid things, but that was going too far."

"Yes, it was." Grace's voice sounded hollow in her own ears. She needed to get away and think about things, so she stood up and took a step toward the condo. "I'm off to the store, and then I'm going to have a couple or three hours out on the beach. Raelene, is there anything you want?"

"I don't drink soda, so maybe some tea bags and sugar. Those individual bottles are so expensive. I'll be glad to make it by the pitcher. Other than that, I'll be happy with whatever you bring," she answered.

"She really likes salsa, chips, and cashews," Audrey said. "And we'll share whatever you buy—but could you get us some stuff for breakfast to have in our room, like those frozen bacon, egg, and cheese biscuits? Want me to call Sarah and Macy and tell them what's happened so they won't rush back to change for dinner?"

"I'll let them know, and I will make sure you girls have something to snack on in your room," Grace replied with a smile. "Oh, I forgot, Beezy is coming in tonight—and she's not family."

"Yes, she is, just like Raelene is. And I'm sorry that I said that about Travis, Mama," Audrey said and then pushed away from the side of the pool. "Beat you to the other end, Raelene."

"No, you won't!" Raelene yelled.

The lyrics from that old *Annie* song about tomorrow being only a day away played over and over in Grace's head as she picked up the keys to the rental SUV and headed outside.

Chapter Sixteen

*G*race got a call from Beezy when she landed and then another one when she was in the parking lot of the Sugar Sands. She rushed outside, waved at her, and gave her a hug. The Uber driver set her bags out of the back of the black SUV.

"Thanks for keeping me company from the airport to here," Beezy said to the driver. "And now, Grace, you can roll one of these suitcases to our room, and I'll take care of the other one. I love to fly, but this time, I got seated by an old woman who just wanted to talk about her illnesses. I pretended to fall asleep so I wouldn't have to listen to her talk about her gallbladder surgery. Poor old darlin' doesn't seem to have much of a life."

Grace opened the door to their unit and stepped back to let Beezy go inside ahead of her. "Welcome to Florida. Macy did good when she found this place."

"Well, butter my butt and call me a biscuit," Beezy said with a giggle. "This isn't a motel, kiddo. This is a condo. I could live here for months instead of days. It's a heck of a lot better than the room I had on the cruise ship." She parked her suitcase beside the bunk beds and headed to the doors that opened out to a view of the beach. "Where is everyone?"

"Down by the water, enjoying the surf and the sand. We even had supper down there, and I'm supposed to bring you to them as soon as you get here. We're all so excited that you flew out to be with us," Grace answered. "There's a slice or two of leftover pizza and a cold beer in the fridge. I've got what we need to make margaritas."

Beezy opened up a suitcase and peeled out of her slacks and shirt. She removed a long, flowy dress and slipped it over her head. "Beer and pizza is good. Let's take it to the beach. Y'all can take turns filling me in on what happened at the school. I know it's got something to do with Carlita and Lisa's girls, but for the first time in history, they aren't spreading gossip. The only thing they've said is that Audrey got them in trouble."

Grace looked down at Beezy's shoes. "You can't get sand between your toes in those."

Beezy sat down on the sofa and removed her sneakers. "I hope I won't need these the whole time I'm here."

"Maybe not for most of the time," Grace said with a smile.

"Get that pizza and beer and tell me what's going on that I have to wear shoes at all while we walk down to that lovely beach," Beezy said.

"Yes, ma'am," Grace said with a salute. She picked up a six-pack of beer with one hand and the pizza box with the other. Just having Beezy there seemed to add another layer to the happiness of their vacation.

"I earned the title of Bossy Beezy when I was a little girl, and I will exercise it whenever I want," she said with a giggle. "God, it's good to be here with y'all. This is my idea of a real vacation—and, honey, I love this place. Now, talk to me about the other times when shoes are necessary."

Grace led the way out to the patio, locked the sliding glass door behind them, and tucked the room key into her pocket. "We are all going to dinner at some place called the Perfect Pig tomorrow night for supper. Travis Butler will be picking all of us up at six thirty."

"The Travis Butler who wants to buy your shop and/or your land?" Beezy asked. "Won't he take no for an answer?"

"He's already taken a few noes, but he's coming down here to see me," Grace answered. "Maybe it's just to try to sweet-talk me into some kind of deal—and if it is, tomorrow night will be the only time I see him."

"I don't know anything about the man, but you be careful, girl. Remember what Sarah and Macy just went through," Beezy warned. "Ira, Claud, and Frankie aren't always the savviest fellers, God bless 'em."

"I will be careful," Grace said. "I'm glad we're all going to supper together. I want all of you to give me your first impressions of him. Especially before I go out with him alone—that's saying that he ever asks me out for a second date."

"Oh, honey, you know you'll get mine, and I will be honest. I don't ever want you to have to suffer again like you did when Justin broke your heart," Beezy said as she went down a couple of wooden steps and then out onto the sand. "This is as white and as fine as sugar. I guess that's where they get the name for the motel."

Before Grace could answer, Macy and Audrey raced across the beach to see who could reach Beezy first. Audrey won by several yards and wrapped Beezy up in a fierce hug, then took a step back for Macy to get her hug.

"I'm so glad you made it," Audrey said. "I know it's only been a few days since we've seen you, but it seems like forever. It's like time stands still in this place. I could stay right here forever."

"You're going to love it here, Beezy." Macy took Beezy by the hand and led her toward the rented chaise longues. "We've only been here one night, and we're already planning to come back during Raelene's Christmas break. We rented chaise longues for the whole time so we could have our chairs all close together, and we got you one as soon as we heard you were on the way. Sarah and Raelene should be back soon. They went for a jog down the beach."

Beezy eased down into one of the loungers. "Okay, Audrey, while I eat, you can give me the real story behind why y'all were able to get out of school and come here. All I've heard is that you got Carlita and

205

Lisa's daughters in trouble. Those two may explode because they can't spread gossip."

"If they did, folks would find out the truth about Crystal and Kelsey," Audrey told Beezy. "I was kind of an idiot, but Raelene helped me see what kind of mean girls I was running around with—and worse yet, letting control me." She went on to tell Beezy the whole story and ended with the fight in school. By the time she had finished, Raelene and Sarah had returned.

Sarah hugged Beezy, twisted the top off a beer, and took a long drink. "Add all that to the mess Macy and I've been through, and you can understand why we all needed this time away."

"I'm glad that y'all were able to leave for a while. I need to get away from Devine right now, too." Beezy finished off a slice of pizza and opened a beer for herself. "We don't see each other every day, but knowing you weren't there . . ." She took a long drink. "Well, you've always been there, just like your mamas, and I didn't like the feeling of not being able to pop into the shop or your house whenever I wanted."

"Plus, all the drama was driving you up the walls, right?" Grace asked.

"Oh, yes it was," Beezy agreed. "Raelene, I want to thank you for fighting for Audrey and not letting that spoiled brat cut her face all up."

"You are welcome. But like I told Grace, it's what you do for family," Raelene said with a smile.

"Amen!" Grace and Audrey said at the same time.

The day was beautiful, so Travis drove with the windows down in his rental SUV so that he could smell the salty air and feel the sun on his face. He passed the Sugar Sands Motel on the way to the beach house, and he slowed down below the twenty-five-mile speed limit to take a good look at the place. Grace was staying right there in one of those units with her family, and he was in town—not with a single idea about charming her into selling anything to him but to spend time with her and relax.

You are acting like a teenager in love for the first time, the aggravating voice in his head said loudly.

"I'm not in love and might never be, but there is chemistry between us," he whispered as he sped up and drove the last half mile to the beach house.

He parked in the driveway, unlocked the front door, and dropped his suitcase in the foyer. Without stopping, he walked through the open-space living area and out onto the balcony. He inhaled deeply and took in the sight of nothing but a sandy beach and then water all the way out to the horizon. He hadn't realized how much he needed a few days to unwind until that moment. After a few minutes, he went back into the house, took a beer from the well-stocked refrigerator, twisted off the top, and sipped it as he walked through the place. His assistant in that area had done a good job of getting things ready.

His father had bought the three-bedroom house a year after Travis and Erica had gotten married. They had spent two short vacations in the place before they divorced. He had wondered if he would see Erica in every room and was glad that he didn't. Maybe memories of her—both bad and good—were finally fading into the past, where they belonged.

The company owned the property, from the bottom of the staircase leading down to the sand to the water. It hardly even seemed like his private beach since no one person or even any company should own something like that, so he didn't fuss if folks jogged across it or even set up a chair to sit in and watch the sunset.

He checked the time on his phone and muttered, "Three hours with nothing on my planner. I can't remember the last time I had this."

A dozen questions went through his mind about what he should do and how he should go about doing things that evening. Would Grace think that he was trying to impress her if he hired a limo to take all of them to the restaurant? Seven people would be a tight fit in his rented SUV. But if he got a limo, he could sit in the back with his guests and enjoy the ride rather than having to drive.

After he'd checked every room, he returned to the foyer, picked up his suitcase, and carried it to the master bedroom. He tossed it on the bed, unzipped it, and hung up his clothing, worrying about what to wear that evening. Would khakis and a knit shirt be too casual? He hadn't worried about what he should wear for years, until the night before. Thank goodness he had packed a lot of slacks, shirts, shorts, and even a pair of sandals for the beach. His suits and ties were back home in Texas, but he wished he had brought one along. Somehow, riding in a limo in casual clothes didn't seem quite right.

He finished unpacking and carried the rest of his beer out to the patio. He sat down in a chaise longue, pulled his phone out of his pocket, and called Delores.

"Don't tell me something else has gone wrong," she said.

"Nope. Flight was good, with very little turbulence, and I'm here at the beach house," he answered. "I have no idea which limo service we use when we're down here. I'm finding out real quick how much you do for me. I'm glad you have your intern soaking all of this information up!"

"It's nice to be needed," she told him. "I'll have your assistant text you the numbers of the service. I've already made arrangements for Julie to come in daily to clean or do errands for you while you are there, and to be ready to take the boat out. Now, go have a good time. Anything else?"

"That should do it," Travis answered, "unless you can tell me what I should wear to this place."

"It's basically a step up from a family restaurant." Delores chuckled. "Wear khakis. A knit shirt with a collar or a button-up will be fine, and casual shoes—not the Italian loafers. Just be comfortable and be yourself. You said that Grace was open and honest when she came to lunch with you, so you should do the same for her."

"Then no limo?" Travis asked.

"Depends on why you are ordering one," Delores told him. "If it's just to impress her, then no. If it's for more room and so you don't have to drive, then yes. For someone who makes billion-dollar deals on a daily basis, Travis Butler, you sure are a nervous wreck today."

"Yes, I am," he admitted, "and thank goodness I've got you to settle me down."

"I'm always here for you," she told him.

"Thanks, Delores," he said. "I'll try not to check in every day."

"You can if you've got personal questions, but do *not* call for business. As far as that goes, you are on vacation. It's my teatime, so good-bye. Have a good evening." She ended the call before he could even say goodbye back.

He waited a moment, and then a ping that told him he had a text sounded off. He called the first number on the list—the limo service—and made arrangements for a pickup at his house at six fifteen. Then he opened another cold beer, took a sip, and let the peacefulness of the ocean waves calm him. For the first time in . . . He tried to remember the last time that he'd had a couple of hours that weren't taken up with business and couldn't.

"Forever," he muttered to himself. For the first time in forever, he could look forward to seeing a woman with no agenda on his part. The idea of a business deal was off the table, and suddenly, he felt as free as those birds out there that were soaring through the air.

Chapter Seventeen

race was far too antsy that afternoon to sit around and wait on Travis. Under the pretext of going to the grocery store for milk and bread, she drove from the motel to the restaurant Travis had mentioned. If it was one of those super fancy places, then she would know not to wear jeans and a T-shirt with a dolphin on it. She even went inside and looked around to see what the lunch crowd was wearing and had a glass of sweet tea at the bar so she could peek at the menu. The place was cute, the food semi-expensively priced—at least in her book—and the atmosphere was cozy.

She found her room empty when she got back to the motel, so she put on her bathing suit and a big floppy hat. She had just filled the tote bag she'd bought at one of the thrift stores with snacks and drinks and was on her way to the beach when a beach ball came flying over the railing between her patio and the pool.

"Hey, throw it back to us!" Beezy yelled. "My aim might not be good, but I've still got lots of power. Come join us for some water aerobics."

Grace tossed the ball back toward the pool and noticed that Raelene and Audrey were out there with Beezy and two other ladies who were about Beezy's age. They all looked like they were having a great time batting the ball back and forth.

"No, thank you. When did y'all start doing aerobics?" she asked as she headed toward the gate at the end of the patio.

Audrey caught the ball and sent it over to Raelene, who tossed it to a gray-haired lady not far from her.

"We started this morning, and we've already got thirty minutes done," Beezy said. "We just met Bitsy and Annie when we came out for a swim. They go to the YMCA up in Alabama, and they're teaching us water aerobics. What's in the bag?"

"Snacks and drinks," Grace answered.

"We'll come join you when we get done here," Audrey said.

"See you then." Grace waved over her shoulder.

When she stepped off the hot concrete, the sand actually felt cool on her bare feet. "I could get used to living like this," she muttered, "but I bet that by the time we leave, we'll all be ready to go home to our normal world."

Her mother was back in her head with advice: *Enjoy the moment. Don't think about the past or the future.*

She was about to ask her mother how to do that when her phone rang. She saw that the call was from Travis, and her first thought was that he was canceling again. "Hello?" She could hear the disappointment and caution in her own voice.

"Good afternoon," Travis said. "I'm here at the company beach house and was surprised to see that I'm located less than half a mile down the road from that motel where y'all are staying. Seems like fate or the universe—whatever folks call it these days—is working for us. I had forgotten how peaceful this place is. Are y'all having a good time?"

"Yes, we are," she answered. "I'm glad you made it. We're all looking forward to having supper with you this evening."

"I wanted to ask about a couple of things before we go out," Travis said. "First is, do y'all have plans for tomorrow? Second is, if not, would you and whoever else want to take a trip over to Shell Island with me?"

"So far, our only plans are to enjoy the beach, but I can ask everyone if they'd like to do that. One of the brochures in the motel lobby mentioned a shuttle out to that island, and we had thought about it," she said as she sat down on a forgotten lounge chair next to the water's edge.

"Yes, but there's no bathroom on the shuttle. I can arrange to have the company boat and driver ready to go at whatever time is good for you, and we do have a bathroom on it, plus snacks and drinks. And later, if you want, we can make plans to go parasailing or something else fun," he suggested. "These are just ideas that you and the girls, or the whole bunch of you, might enjoy, but feel free to tell me no if you'd rather not. I don't want to come down here and start micromanaging your time."

"Oh, I will," Grace said with a chuckle. "But both ideas sure sound good, and I know Raelene and Audrey would love to do those things. Let me talk to them after supper tonight and call you later."

It was his turn to chuckle. "You're going to see if they approve of me."

"Yes, I am," she admitted, feeling a little bit vulnerable. "I can make up my own mind about people—and other than Neal, I've been a pretty good judge of character. But this is my family, and before I share you with them, I want to know what they think."

"I like your honesty," he said.

"I only know how to be me," she told him.

"That's refreshing in today's world," Travis said. "I'll see you later, then?"

"We'll be ready," she told him, and turned to see Sarah sitting beside her.

Grace shoved her phone back in her pocket, amazed that he had accepted her just the way she was and didn't criticize her for her comments about her family.

"So was that Travis?" Sarah asked.

"Yes, it was—and after y'all meet him, we're going to talk about taking a trip out to Shell Island tomorrow," Grace answered.

"I read that there's a shuttle that will take folks from here to there, let you collect shells, and then bring you back," Sarah said, "so count me out. There are no bathrooms on that shuttle or on the island."

"Travis said that he could take us on the company boat, and it has bathrooms," Grace said, "but don't say anything to the others until y'all meet him. I don't want Audrey and Raelene to get dollar signs in their eyes. I want their honest opinions without knowing that he has a beach house or a boat."

"I'm in," Sarah said.

"How do you feel about parasailing?" Grace asked.

"Not me," Sarah answered. "I like to have at least one foot on something solid, but the girls might like it."

Grace could hear Beezy huffing the last few feet that she walked toward the chairs. "I swear, that aerobic stuff will wear an old woman out in a hurry. Who would have thought that jumping around in water and batting a beach ball could be such a workout? What are we talking about?" she asked as she eased down into a chaise longue.

"Shrimp scampi," Sarah answered. "It's on the menu at the Perfect Pig, where we are eating tonight with Travis."

"With a name like that, I would think they would have barbecue," Macy said, holding up a bag of shells she had gathered as she and Raelene and Audrey all joined the others in the beach chairs.

"I checked out that place online," Audrey said, "and it's not a cheap date. Travis is going to have to cough up some serious cash to feed all of us."

"Maybe another evening, we can have a shrimp boil in the condo and invite him to join us to repay him for this," Grace suggested. "I saw a shrimp vendor on the side of the road when I went for groceries earlier. I bet fresh shrimp will taste a lot better than the frozen we get at home."

"I can make a dessert for that supper," Raelene offered. "I can whip up a mean chocolate cake."

"And I'll help," Audrey said.

Thank you again, Lord, for sending Raelene into our lives, Grace thought.

Grace could hardly be still that evening. She was dressed thirty minutes early but still had misgivings about whether she should call Travis and cancel, even at that late time. It would be downright rude, but after what had happened with Neal and Joel—well, it could be just the right thing to do.

Audrey wasn't helping one bit with the issue, but then she had never been invited to join her mother on one of the few dates she'd had through the years.

Grace had chosen a sleeveless pale green dress for the evening. It went well with the off-white sandals she had brought along in her backpack. She curled her blonde locks and applied a little lipstick and minimal mascara—no use in putting on a lot of makeup, she thought, because she'd just sweat it off, especially if Travis had made arrangements for them to eat at the tables she had seen on the patio.

Or quite possibly from sheer nerves, she thought again as she watched the two girls run back and forth between their rooms, modeling first one outfit and then another. Finally, Beezy took matters into her hands.

"If you girls don't get dressed in the next five minutes, I'm going to throw you out there in the pool myself and ruin all that makeup and those pretty curls. Wear the yellow polka-dotted sundress, Raelene. It looks good with your dark hair. Audrey, you put on that green gingham-checked one, and be ready to go when Travis gets here, or we're leaving you behind," Beezy said.

Both girls took off for their room in a blur.

"Thank you," Grace whispered.

"I'm starving, and I get cranky when I'm hungry." Beezy grinned. "You should be thinking about the date, not worrying with a couple of egotistical teenage girls. And besides all that, I'm not just another pretty face. I wear my bossy title with pride."

The girls had barely made it back when someone rapped on the door. Grace took a deep breath and headed in that direction. She let it out slowly and flung the door open to find Travis standing in front of her. She barely noticed what he was wearing because his smile and his expression when he looked at her made her feel more special than she had in years.

"You sure look beautiful," he said.

"Thank you," she whispered.

"Are we all ready?" he asked. "Your chariot awaits."

A vision of a horse-drawn carriage flashed through Grace's mind. If that was what he was talking about, then Beezy was going to be a whole lot crankier because it was at least twenty minutes to the restaurant in a car. A horse would take three to four times that long, and they would all be starving right along with Beezy.

She blinked away the vision. "Come in and meet my family."

"I'd love to do that," Travis said as he stepped into the room.

Grace made introductions.

Travis shook hands with each of them but didn't pass out compliments like Neal/Edward had done when he met the family. "Are we ready to go?" he asked. "Judging from the GPS, I think it's about twenty minutes to the restaurant, and I sure don't want to lose our reservation."

"Ready and getting hangrier—as the kids call it—by the minute," Beezy said and led the way outside. "Where are you parked?"

"Right across the street, in front of the laundry," Travis answered as he and Grace brought up the rear so she could lock the door. "I'm glad you're hungry. I've never eaten at this place, but several folks from my company have, and they recommend it highly."

"Honey, if they've got good shrimp scampi, I'll be a happy camper," Beezy said and looked back over her shoulder. "The black SUV?"

"No, the limo," Travis said. "I decided that I would rather sit and visit with all y'all than drive, and we would be really crowded in the SUV I have rented."

Grace heard Macy suck in air, and Sarah giggled under her breath. Audrey and Raelene whispered all the way across the narrow street. So much for two teenage girls coming up with an opinion of Travis based solely on his attitude and kindness.

"Too much?" Travis asked in a low voice.

"Not at all," Grace answered. "This is quite a treat. I know Audrey has never ridden in a limo, and I'm pretty sure Raelene hasn't, either."

"And you?" Travis asked.

"Nope," Grace answered.

"Well, well, well!" Beezy said when the driver opened the door for her. "I've got to take pictures to send to Mavis—that's my sister back in Devine. She'll never believe this."

"It's just a rental car," Travis said.

"To you, that's what it is," Grace said just above a whisper. "To all of us, it's something way out of our experience."

"I hope you don't feel like that about me," Travis said.

"I don't know you well enough to know how I feel about you," Grace told him.

That's a lie, the niggling voice in her head said loudly. *You like him, or you wouldn't be wasting time with him—especially on your first-ever real vacation.*

No sense in letting that cat out of the bag right here at the first, she argued.

"Well, I sure hope I can remedy that through this next week," Travis told her. "Looks like your girls are having a good time, and that makes me happy."

Audrey had her phone out, snapping pics of the driver and the stretch limo and making sure she got several selfies of herself and Raelene. No doubt the pictures would be all over social media long before they reached the restaurant.

When they were all seated and the door was closed, the driver got in behind the wheel and reminded them that there was champagne, both alcoholic and nonalcoholic, chilled and ready to pour, and a tray of fresh fruit for them to have on the way.

Grace leaned in close to Travis, who was pouring champagne into five stemmed flutes, and whispered, "Thank you for all this, and that getting to know each other works both ways. You might decide that you aren't a bit interested in a woman who's just part owner of a bakery shop."

"I kind of doubt that," Travis answered as he poured nonalcoholic champagne for the girls. Then he held up his own. "A toast to a good vacation that is long overdue for us all."

Beezy was the first one to touch her glass to his. "Hear, hear!"

"I know how Cinderella felt," Raelene said as she clinked her flute with the rest of them.

"Me too," Audrey said. "Does this thing turn into a pumpkin at midnight?"

"Have no idea, but after supper, we could ride around in it until then and find out," Travis answered.

"For real?" Audrey asked.

"Sure," Travis said. "We can go anywhere y'all want to go."

Grace glanced down at her dress and smiled. She was wearing a five-dollar thrift store dress, but she was riding in a modern-day golden chariot, and she had to admit that the excitement bouncing around in the back of the limo was contagious. The champagne warmed her insides, but not as much as Travis's shoulder pressed against hers heated her up on the outside. She wondered if the rest of her family could feel the electricity. That she was attracted to Travis couldn't be denied—but she still couldn't be sure he wasn't playing her by being nice to her family just so he could get what he wanted.

"So, Audrey, what do you want to be when you grow up?" Travis asked.

"I have no idea," she said, "but Raelene is going to help me get enrolled for some concurrent college classes next semester. I wish she wasn't going off to Oklahoma for college, because she is really good at explaining things. She should be an algebra teacher instead of a nurse, anyway. She's so smart in all things that have to do with math that it's not even funny."

"I may not go to Oklahoma," Raelene said with a shrug. "After the trouble we got into, those folks might withdraw their offer."

Grace knew how important it was to Raelene to be independent, but she would see to it that the girl went to college, no matter the outcome with the one in southern Oklahoma. Raelene was too smart to not have the opportunity to further her education.

"You're good in algebra?" Travis asked. "What else do you like?"

"I like learning new things and figuring out things," she answered.

"She's going to be the valedictorian of her graduating class this year," Audrey said in a bragging tone.

"And Audrey is a far cry from the teenager who didn't want Raelene to live with us," Sarah whispered in Grace's ear.

Grace nodded. "We're very proud of her and of all the hard work she's done for us and in helping Audrey bring up her grades."

"Valedictorian, huh?" Travis seemed to be thinking about things. "Are you going to have that honor when you graduate, Audrey?"

"Damn . . . ," Audrey stammered and blushed. "*Dang* straight. I can't let Raelene do better than me, but I'll have to work hard because I did some stupid stuff this past year, and it'll take some time to get my grades back up."

"Sounds like I'm riding with a couple of very smart girls," Travis said.

The limo maneuvered down a narrow street and parked behind the restaurant. The driver got out and held the door open for them again. "Y'all have a good time. I'll be right here when you are ready to leave."

"Thank you," Beezy said as she put her hand in his and allowed him to help her out of the limo. "You make an old woman feel like a princess."

"You're not old, ma'am, and it's my pleasure." The driver flashed a smile.

Grace and Travis followed along behind everyone else. Audrey took pictures of everything again, including more selfies of her and Raelene. The two of them were certainly showing their tourist colors, but Grace didn't care. Maybe when they had been here a dozen times, it would be old hat—as her mother used to say—but today, this was their first ride in a limo, and this place was gorgeous. Huge pots of green plants lined the short alleyway between two buildings. A gentle breeze from off the nearby ocean blew the girls' hair back and away from their faces, making for the perfect picture.

"Oh. My. Goodness!" Beezy giggled when she turned the corner. "Girls, come quick and let me take a picture of the two of you kissing the pig."

"I love you, Beezy, but I'm not . . . ," Audrey said and then turned the corner right ahead of Grace and Travis.

"It's not a real one." Raelene pointed to a concrete pig sitting on a stand by the door.

"They're having so much fun," Travis said. "I'd forgotten what it was like to be that happy with something as simple as a limo and a nice restaurant."

Grace nudged him with her shoulder. "You've done something special. We spend more than enough time in a restaurant setting at the bakery. They're used to that, but I'm still glad that they're not embarrassing you."

"But you really wouldn't care if they were, because you like to see them having fun, right?" Travis ushered her past the pig and the outside tables, then into the restaurant.

"We're not eating outside?" Audrey asked. "This is what I imagined it would be like to eat outside in one of those cafés in Paris, France."

"I'm sure they already have a table ready for us inside, but I could arrange for us to have dessert out here," Travis answered and then held the door open. "There's a small gift shop inside that you girls might want to check out for a T-shirt between our meal and dessert."

Audrey and Raelene were the first ones in the restaurant; Beezy, Sarah, and Macy went in right behind them. All five were looking at T-shirts and souvenirs when Grace and Travis made their way inside and to a small counter to the right.

"Butler, party of seven, right?" the girl behind the desk asked.

"Yes, ma'am," Travis said, "and we would like to have dessert outside when we finish dinner."

"We'll get that set up." The girl smiled up at him. "This way, please."

Grace wondered if Travis walked into the restaurant and asked to buy the place—like he had her doughnut shop—whether the owner would agree to sell on the spot.

"Okay, girls. We are being seated. We'll get shirts before we leave, I promise," Macy said. "This is really an interesting place. I love the decor and all the antiques. Whatever made you decide to bring us here, Travis?"

"The company has a beach house not far from the motel where you are staying. One of the benefits of working at Butler Enterprises is that if our employees want to come to Florida for vacation, they can claim it for a week. My close friend, Calvin, told me if I came back to this area, I should make a point to eat here," he answered as he seated Grace first and then the rest of the ladies.

"Man, I'd like to work for you, then," Raelene said with a sigh.

"Me too," Audrey agreed. "Just think, Raelene—if we both worked for Travis, you could take a week in the spring and I could take one later, and we could come down here two times in a year."

"Looks like I've got the prospect of new employees." Travis chuckled.

Sarah, Grace, and Travis were seated on one side of the table while the other four sat across from them. Sarah leaned over and whispered to Grace, "Can you believe this is the same kid that we were about to send to a convent a few weeks ago?"

"It's a miracle," Grace said out the side of her mouth.

The clock on the stove said that it was midnight when Macy and Sarah slumped down on the sofa in their motel unit. Beezy eased into an upholstered side chair, kicked off her shoes, and propped her feet on the coffee table. Audrey and Raelene started to make their way across the room toward their bedrooms.

Macy held up both palms. "Oh, no you don't. Pull up a couple of those barstools or sit on the floor. Grace and Travis have walked down to the beach, and that means we've got a few minutes to talk about him without her hearing what we say."

The girls opted to sit on the floor beside the coffee table. This whole thing with Travis was tough on Macy. On one hand, she was happy for Grace because she loved her so much. On the other, she could still feel the horrible pain of Neal's betrayal, and even though she knew that jealousy was a sin, she had more than a healthy dose of it!

"She probably did that on purpose," Beezy said. "I like Travis. He's a gentleman, and he was attentive to all of us at dinner tonight. Then he had the limo driver park, and we all got to walk out on that long pier. I needed that after all that food."

"When he asked me about my plans, he listened to me. Most adults ask, but then you can see by their expression that they've tuned you out," Raelene said and covered a yawn with her hand.

"I like the way he looks at Mama, and I feel like she hasn't dated because of me all these years. She kind of put her life on hold to be a mother, and she deserves a life—especially a fantastic evening like this," Audrey said, yawning out the word *fantastic*. "But I'm not so sure I'm ready to bring someone else into our family, or even just our vacation."

"Sarah?" Macy asked.

"You first," Sarah answered.

"I'm on the fence," Macy admitted with half a shrug. "I just went through the con of all cons. I think Travis is an honest man, but I'll need more time to see which way I'm going to fall off this fence before I pass judgment."

"How long is 'more time'?" Beezy asked.

"A year, at the very least," Macy said. "I'm living proof that falling in love too quick can get a woman in trouble."

Grace knocked on the glass doors, and Audrey jumped up to open them for her mother. She pulled out a barstool for her, and Grace hiked up a hip on it.

"Okay, give it to me," Grace said. "What did you think of Travis?"

"First, you tell us . . . ," Macy said with a grin. "Did you get a good-night kiss?"

"I did not," Grace answered.

Sarah chuckled. "Then it wasn't a real date. It was just a family outing with a new friend."

"Something like that." Grace slid off the barstool and got a bottle of water from the refrigerator.

"We *have* been talking about Travis," Macy said, "and the consensus is that he appears to be a nice guy—but then, so did Neal. If you are interested in him, and he is in you, we think you should give it lots of time and not fall too fast and hard like I did."

Grace twisted the top off the bottle and took a long drink of water. "Audrey?"

"I'm not sure I'm ready to share you with anyone, but Travis does seem to be a nice man," she answered. "And, Mama, you deserve to have a life. I'll be graduating in a couple of years, and you'll be lonely without me and Raelene in the house."

"Is he nice enough to go out to Shell Island with him on the company boat—with a bathroom on it—tomorrow?" Grace asked.

Raelene gasped "He's got a boat *and* a beach house."

"They belong to the company, not really to him," Grace answered.

"I suppose I could share you *one* more time before I go off to college," Audrey answered. "What time do we need to be ready?"

"Ten o'clock, and take a tote bag with your bathing suits if you want to do some snorkeling," Grace answered.

Raelene stood up and held out a hand to Audrey. "This isn't a vacation. It's a slice of heaven."

Audrey put her hand in Raelene's. "I agree. Is the limo taking us to the boat?"

"No, we're meeting Travis at the dock. I have the address already plugged into my phone," Grace replied. "But if you want to spend the day right here with me, I can always tell him not to have the boat ready."

"I'm going!" Beezy declared. "Travis is good company, and if I was thirty years younger, I'd give you some competition for that man, Grace."

"I would love to go," Sarah chimed in.

"We'll be here," Raelene said. "I wouldn't miss that trip for anything. And Audrey's Instagram has been blowing up with the pictures from the restaurant." Macy could hear the wistful tone in her voice.

"Why don't we get you a phone of your own tomorrow?" Sarah said, clearly picking up on that. "We'll go by the phone store on the way to the boat, buy you one, and get you set up on my plan. You'll need one when you go to college, so we might as well get it right now."

"For real?" Raelene asked.

"For real," Sarah said. "Now, you two get on out of here. Us old ladies need our beauty rest."

"Who are you calling 'old'?" Beezy teased.

The girls' giggles followed them out of the room, and then Macy got to her feet. "I get first shower—and, Grace, maybe the third time is the charm."

"What does that mean?" Grace asked.

"Sarah and I both didn't have things turn out right, but maybe this will work out for you. All I ask is that you give it time, and a lot of it." Macy crossed the room and gave her cousin a hug, feeling a little wetness on her shoulder as Grace's body tightened and relaxed.

Grace released Macy, running the back of her wrist across her eyes. "Don't any of you worry. I'm not in any hurry—and just so you all know, Travis told me that he's no longer interested in our land or our shop. He's here with no agenda, which means we aren't talking business at all. Don't tell the girls, but if tomorrow goes well, he wants to take whoever wants to go parasailing the next day."

Beezy got to her feet and began to unbutton her blouse. "The way to a man's heart might be through his stomach, but the way to a woman's heart is through her family. I'm going to bed. I'll have a morning shower. Good night to all of you."

"Good night," Macy said. In spite of the jealous streak that shot through her heart, she wanted to be happy for Grace, and she hoped that she and Travis would develop a good relationship . . . but with the luck all three of them had been having recently, she wouldn't put money on it—not just yet.

Chapter Eighteen

S *o this is what it feels like to have a family,* Travis thought as the boat moved slowly through the emerald-green waters toward Shell Island. In his imagination, the two girls belonged to him and Grace. Beezy was the grandmother figure. Sarah and Macy were his sisters-in-law.

Two outings do not make a long-term relationship, his grandfather's voice whispered in his ear.

I know, Granddad, but it's nice to pretend, Travis thought.

"Thank you . . . again," Grace said. "We're making memories that we'll talk about for years to come. And I want you to know that I appreciate knowing the information about you withdrawing your interest in our business."

Travis slipped his arm around her shoulders. "What business? I don't know what you are talking about. We're just a couple of adults down here in the sand and surf, having a good time with the family. With that said, thank you for sharing them with me."

Grace moved a little closer to him. "You are so welcome."

His arm lay around her shoulders so comfortably that it was like they were meant to stand together. She didn't have a bit of makeup on, and the breeze had caused a few errant strands of her blonde hair to escape her ponytail. Travis liked that she was comfortable in her own skin around him. Most women that he had dealt with—or even dated a couple of times—weren't.

"I've got to admit that I'm having a wonderful time with such beautiful women around me, especially you."

"But, honey, you might ought to have your eyes checked and get stronger glasses," she teased.

"Never underestimate the power a woman has on a man when she is just herself." He gave her shoulder a gentle squeeze.

"It's too much trouble to be anything else." She smiled up at him and then changed the subject. "I thought that you would be the one driving the boat."

"I would," he said, "but then I would have a job, and I'm on vacation. Julie does a fine job of managing the boat and the house for us. Our HR department runs a calendar for folks who need to come down here for a week. That way, Julie knows when to get the boat ready for short trips like this or longer ones for some deep-sea fishing, or when to have the house cleaned and stocked with food and liquor."

"That's pretty amazing," Grace said.

"If you don't use money, it's nothing but dirty paper stacked up in a bank somewhere. I like to make people happy—and who doesn't like the beach and a boat ride?" Travis asked.

"Certainly not any of us," Grace answered.

"Like I said before, you are treating me, not me treating you," Travis told her.

"Mama, come and look," Audrey yelled from the other side of the boat. "There's a dolphin."

"And you get to swim with him as soon as we dock," Julie said over her shoulder as she steered the boat toward the island that was coming into view. "The dolphins are very gentle, and it's quite the experience to be close to them."

"I can't wait," Raelene said and pointed to a dock not far from them. "Is that where we stop?"

Julie steered the boat that way. "Yes, it is. Who wants to swim before we gather shells? I've got blankets for anyone who just wants to sit on the beach and rest." She glanced over at Beezy.

"Honey, I'm swimming with the dolphins." Beezy held up her tote bag. "I've got my bathing suit right here, and I don't give a rip if my hair gets wet. At my age, we got to do what we can when we can, because tomorrow we might be too old and decrepit to even feed ourselves."

Beezy reminded Travis so much of his grandmother—full of sass and always with a positive attitude.

"Can I grow up and be just like you?" Julie asked with a giggle.

"I've already called dibs on that," Sarah called out from her lounge chair. "I've been studying this woman my whole life so I can be as strong as she is when I grow up."

"Me too," Macy chimed in.

"You've got a great role model to study," Julie said and then expertly steered the boat right up next to the dock. "If you want to swim first, you can go down the steps into the cabin to change." She removed her shirt and shorts to reveal a black one-piece bathing suit and then pulled up the top of a bench. "I'll have enough gear out for anyone who wants to get in the water first, and there are bags for each of you to use for your shells."

Julie tossed everything from masks and snorkels to plastic bags with the Butler Enterprises logo on them into a net bag and carried it all out to the beach.

"You're not going to swim?" Travis asked when Grace didn't head down the stairs.

"I'd rather sit on the beach with you and watch the others. Seeing them have such a good time is more fun for me than getting in the water," she answered.

"And here I was looking forward to seeing you in a bikini," Travis said with a grin. "But then, you couldn't be any more beautiful than you are right now."

"You really should get your glasses strengthened," Grace teased.

227

"Beauty isn't just what you see with your eyes," Travis said, "but it's what you see with your heart, too. You've got both covered really well."

"Thank you," Grace said. "I believe that just might be the most romantic thing anyone has ever said to me."

"Then you've been spending time with the wrong men," Travis told her as he picked up a couple of blankets.

Grace helped spread out a blanket and blinked a few times to be sure that she was awake and not dreaming. Last week at this time, she had just been finishing up her day at the shop, cleaning all the bowls and trays and getting ready for the next morning, when it would all start again. She had been happy doing that and letting her money grow in the bank. Travis was right: if she didn't use it for something, it was nothing but dirty paper that Audrey—or maybe the generation after her—might go through in a short time.

Maybe this was the universe telling her that she and her family could slow down. If they took a couple of days off each week, she could spend more time with Audrey these last two years that she would be in high school. She wasn't ready to close the shop, but she was more than ready to cut back on the days when it was open.

All those thoughts vanished when Travis set a small cooler on the edge of the blanket, opened it up, and removed two bottles of beer. He twisted the top off one and handed it to her; then he pulled his shirt up over his head, tossed it to the end of the blanket, and sat down beside her. "I wasn't sure what brand you like. I hope this is all right."

"It's fine," Grace told him, but her tone sounded breathless in her own ears. Travis had an abdomen that would make most male models jealous. "I'm not particular about my beer. It just has to be icy cold."

"I agree with you," Travis said with a nod. "I haven't had a chance to get out in the sun for a while, so I'm going to depend on you to tell me if I'm getting too pink."

Grace glanced over at the soft black hair on his chest and clasped her hands together to keep from reaching out to touch him. "Of course. Want me to put sunscreen on for you?"

"I sprayed down good before we left, but now I wish I had that kind that rubs on," he said and shot a broad wink her way.

"Are you flirting?" Grace asked.

He grinned and locked gazes with her. "I'm trying to, but it's been a long time since I gave it a shot. How am I doing?"

"Not too bad. I'd give you a high B." She chuckled.

"That's probably higher than my ex-wife would have given me." He blinked and looked away.

"So you were married?" she asked.

"Yes," he answered. "I'm surprised that you didn't know that, at least through the grapevine. Claud and the guys brought me up on all the gossip about you. I figured they'd do the same about me."

"Nope, not a word." Grace wondered what "all the gossip" entailed.

"Erica and I got married right out of college and divorced ten years ago. We were both workaholics, which isn't good for a marriage, but then she got a huge opportunity to make a career move. The only drawback was that she had to live in London. We soon became living proof that long-distance relationships don't work so well. End of story," he said. "I haven't dated much since then, and Delores says I'm married to the job."

Grace opened her mouth to say something, then closed it without saying a word. She was proof that it didn't have to be a long-distance relationship to not work, and even though there hadn't been a divorce, she hadn't dated much since then, either.

"According to what the guys told me, I guess we have a lot in common," Travis said.

"I agree," Grace said with a nod. "Different circumstances but pretty much the same outcome."

"On another note, I've got something I'd like to run past you," Travis said.

"What?" Grace's Spidey-senses—as Audrey would say for a week after she saw any *Spider-Man* movie—went on alert. Had he just figured out a new angle to try to talk her out of her property?

Travis opened his beer and turned the bottle up for a drink. "Is Raelene think-tank smart?"

"I'm not sure how smart that has to be," Grace answered.

"Every summer we hire an intern for the think tank. Some high school graduate who shows signs of being able to compete with our first-floor kids. We pay minimum wage, with a bonus at the end of the summer, and expose them to the world of looking out for corporate opportunities. Lucy, our supervisor in the group, was like Raelene," Travis said.

"Hey, Mama." Audrey came over to the blanket. "Aren't you going in the water?"

"Not this time. I'm going to watch y'all."

"Will you take pictures for me?" Audrey held up her phone.

"Of course," Grace answered.

Audrey tossed her phone onto the blanket, and then she and Raelene headed for the edge of the water, with Julie right behind them, giving them instructions about the masks and snorkels.

Grace picked up the phone and turned to Travis. "Were you asking me if I thought Raelene would be interested in interning for you?"

"Yes, I was, but that's not all. I also hire an intern to work with Delores and her assistant, and she's been on my case to find one for her this summer. She says she's going to retire in six years, when she gets to be eighty, and she needs to be training someone to take her place," Travis replied. "Maybe Audrey could work out as she grows up. As she learns more and more, Audrey might be a big help to her and eventually step into more responsible positions."

"Sweet Lord!" Grace gasped. "Are you serious?"

"I have a vision, and I believe those two girls are going to grow up to be just like me and Calvin—best friends who want to work together," he answered. "Just think about it. I won't even make either of them an offer if you don't think I should. But when someone works out in my think tank, or if Delores finds her own protégée, it also means a full scholarship to the university of their choice. The only string is that they have to come work for the company in the summertime. Except for Lucy, all the employees on that floor were interns."

"Are you that good at judging people?" Grace asked.

"I make a mistake every now and then. Remember, I *am* divorced," he reminded her.

Grace's mind went into overdrive. If Audrey had a job working for the same company as Raelene this summer, she could learn responsibility, how to take orders, and the value of a dollar. Seeing her family run a shop hadn't done that so far. If the girls liked those corporate jobs, they wouldn't move a thousand miles away from Devine, and Grace could see them both often.

Her mother's voice popped back into her head: *That's selfish.*

Yes, it is, but I'm not taking it back, Grace thought.

"You're already weighing pros and cons," Travis said, "and you are wondering if I'm offering this just to ingratiate myself to you. I assure you that I am not. I'm not that kind of man, and you aren't the type of woman that would do anything other than what is right for your family. I trust your judgment, Grace."

Grace picked up the phone and snapped a couple of pictures of Beezy and the girls watching Julie demonstrate how to use the masks. "That's quite an opportunity—but don't most interns work for free?"

"Some do, but I always pay mine minimum wage," Travis answered and pointed. "There's the first dolphin, coming in close enough that they can touch him."

Grace quickly took a picture of the girls with the dolphin. Her thoughts weren't on summertime or the money the girls would make; they went way beyond that. She found herself wishing that Justin would have stuck around and been a husband to her and a father to Audrey, and that as a family, they could have gone on vacations like this.

Chapter Nineteen

Sarah picked up a pretty shell and slipped it into her tote bag, then wandered off away from Macy and several other groups who were scattered along the beach. More people arrived by the minute as boats came in to drop folks off in the shallow water close to the shoreline and others gathered up their passengers and left. The traffic reminded her of the streets during the five o'clock rush in San Antonio. Of course, here on the island, folks were rushing off and onto boats rather than driving cars. Everyone wore bathing suits and floppy hats, and most of them had something in the way of a bag to use for gathering up shells.

She had left the sandy area and wandered back to where the sea oats grew wild when she heard something that sounded like a child weeping. She passed it off as bird sounds, thinking that maybe one was fussing at her for getting too close to a nest. She picked up another nice-size shell that she could use as a ring holder on her dresser and then heard the noise again.

"That's not a bird," she whispered.

"Daaadddy, I'm scared."

This time Sarah was positive that she had heard words, not just sobbing.

"Hello?" she called out. "Where are you? Are you hurt?"

A little girl stepped out from behind a clump of sea oats. The ocean breeze blew the strands of hair that had escaped from her thick black braids across her face, and her big brown eyes were filled with both fear and relief.

"I want my da . . . ddy," she moaned, drawing out the last word into a whine that had several syllables. Then she crossed the distance and threw her arms around Sarah's legs. "Help me find my daddy."

"Angela!" a deep voice yelled from somewhere behind Sarah. "Angela, where are you?"

"Daddy! You found my daddy!" the little girl squealed and peeked around Sarah's legs. "I'm right here."

The man raced across the sand and through the clumps of grass as if the devil himself were licking his heels. He dropped down beside Sarah and wrapped Angela up in his arms. "I was so worried, baby girl. I told you not to leave my side."

"I saw a lizard, and I chased it," Angela said and pointed up at Sarah. "She found me, and then you came."

"Thank you." The man stood with his daughter still in his arms. "I'm Brock Stephens."

The guy looked to be part Hispanic with his dark hair and brown eyes—just like his daughter's. His bright smile warmed Sarah's heart.

"Pleased to meet you. I'm Sarah Dalton," Sarah said. "And this must be Angela."

"Yes, I am, and today is my birthday. I am five years old," the child said. "Daddy, can we take her home? She saved me and it's my birthday, and I want to keep her."

"Sorry, sweetheart. I have to stay here for a few more days, but I'll walk back with y'all to the beach area. She sure has a big vocabulary for her age," Sarah said, muffling a laugh. Angela reminded her of Audrey when she was five years old.

"She has always talked big for her age—but then, it's just been me and her since she was a year old," Brock said. "Right now, we'd better get back to the shuttle. It leaves in ten minutes, and we've got a plane to catch back to Texas this evening."

"Where in Texas?" Sarah picked up her tote bag and walked beside him. Maybe if he lived close to Devine, their paths would cross, and she could see that precious child again. That idea put a warm feeling in her heart and a smile on her face.

"Little town west of San Antonio named Castroville," he answered, and bent to pick up a bag filled to the brim with shells. "You probably haven't heard of it."

"I thought I heard a familiar accent," Sarah said with a smile. "My family and I run a little doughnut shop in Devine, not far from Castroville."

"Small world," Brock said and winked. "Thanks again for saving Angela."

"Can we go see her doughnut shop when we get home?" Angela begged.

"If you bring her to the shop, the doughnuts are on me," Sarah promised, crossing her fingers like she did when she was a little girl.

"Maybe we will, and you can pick out one pretty shell to take to Miz Sarah for saving you," Brock said and then he waded out to the shuttle.

"Wave at me until I'm gone," Angela yelled as she and Brock boarded the boat.

Sarah didn't even consider not doing what the little girl asked. She stood right there on the beach in the sun and waved until the boat looked like nothing but a dot out there in the water. She coveted that child more than she had ever wanted anything in her life, and she wondered if her father—Brock didn't have the letter *L* in his name, which was a good sign—would bring her to visit.

"Get a hold of yourself," she muttered as the boat disappeared altogether.

Macy tilted her head to get more sun on her face as Julie maneuvered the boat away from the island. She couldn't help but think about Darla Jo and Neal—he would never be Edward to Macy—somewhere out there on an island. Did they gather shells with their sons, or were they already bored with the whole idea of settling down and being a family? Was the thrill of the con what made them happy?

Beezy nudged her on the shoulder. "Does leaving the island make you sad? Are you jealous of Grace and Travis?"

Macy lowered her chin. "Yes, a little, and no, not at all. I was thinking about Darla Jo and Neal. Do you think they'll be happy without the excitement of their con games?"

"Probably not. People like them survive on the danger in their lives," Beczy answered. "On a different note, y'all have lost your place at the top of the gossip list in Devine. My sister called while we were gathering shells. The preacher at our church has been offered a position in Amarillo. Everyone in Devine is talking about who might come to pastor for us. Some folks are hoping it's a young man with intentions of putting down roots. Others hope it's a married man with children so that he'll be more stable."

"I'm glad to give up my place at the top of the rumor list," Macy said.

"I never really made it on the list, since no one knew about Joel," Sarah added, "but I fell in love on the beach today." She crossed from one side of the deck and sat down on the other side of Beezy.

"With seashells?" Beezy asked with a chuckle.

"No, with a little girl named Angela," Sarah answered and told her about her brief encounter with the child and her father. "My biological clock screamed in my head the whole time I waved goodbye to her. I wondered if it was an omen. Maybe I was saying so long to any hope of ever having children of my own."

Beezy draped an arm around each of their shoulders and gave them a sideways hug. "Be patient, darlin' girls. Fate is working things out for Grace." She nodded across the deck toward Travis and Grace, who had their heads together, whispering about something or other. "Your turn is coming."

"I hope it is," Macy agreed, pushing herself out of her doldrums.

Grace had given the idea of the girls working for Butler Enterprises that summer some thought and decided that she should tell them about the offer. She might regret it on down the road, but she would really be surprised if her decision to give them a chance like that would change the path of their lives for the *worse*.

Audrey was a professional at eavesdropping and could hear a cat walking across carpet, so Grace kept her voice barely above a whisper as she told Travis about her decision.

"That's great," Travis said. "I'll let Delores, Calvin, and Lucy all know when I get back. This has been a wonderful day. I can't remember when I've had more fun or wished that I had a family like you have. But . . ." He paused.

"Why does there have to be a *but*?" Grace's Spidey-senses went on alert for the second time.

Travis slipped his arm around her waist and drew her closer to his side. "I still want to spend time with your family. They are so much fun, but . . ." He hesitated again and looked down into her eyes. "I want to spend some time with just you, also. I like you, Grace Dalton, and I'd like to see where this attraction that is between us might go."

When she gazed into his eyes, she felt like she was looking straight into his soul—and everything felt right. "I can live with that *but*," she whispered.

Chapter Twenty

Beezy needed to go into town for souvenirs, and the girls wanted to check out Pier Park—maybe ride the Ferris wheel at the small carnival there and get some cotton candy. The speed limit on the two-lane highway from the motel to the shopping center was twenty-five miles an hour, so Grace kept an eye on the speedometer and on the golf carts, bicyclers, and joggers at the same time. Five miles from one spot to another in Texas usually meant less than five minutes. At the rate she was driving, it would take three to four times that long to get to Pier Park.

"Stop!" Macy yelled from the passenger seat.

Without hesitation, Grace stomped the brakes and sent up a prayer that she had not hit one of the several dogs she'd seen running along beside their jogging owners.

"What?" Grace's heart thumped so hard that she had trouble breathing.

Macy pointed over her shoulder. "Travis is waving at us. That house right behind us must be where he is staying."

Before Grace could gather her racing thoughts, Travis had jogged over to their rental SUV. Macy pressed the button to roll down the window, and he leaned his elbows on the edge. A soft breeze blew his woodsy cologne across the front seat to Grace. Added to his bright smile and the twinkle in his eyes, the whole effect sent vibes bouncing all around the inside of the SUV.

"Good mornin', ladies," he said.

"Mornin'," Grace chimed in with the others.

"We're off to Pier Park and to buy souvenirs," Beezy said from the back seat. "You want to go with us?"

"Not this morning," Travis answered. "But after a day in that place, y'all are going to be too tired to go out for supper or to fix anything at the motel, so why don't you let me cook tonight? There's a fancy grill out on the patio. I could make us some steaks."

"That sounds wonderful," Beezy said. "What time should we be here?"

"Anytime you want," Travis answered, but his eyes were on Grace. "Bring or wear your bathing suits, and you can play on this end of the beach. We'll go completely informal tonight and even eat out on the patio."

"We'll bring dessert," Grace said.

"Ice cream would be great," Travis said and slid a slow, sexy wink at her.

The way I feel right now, I might need to cover my body in it. Grace fought the urge to fan herself with her hand.

"Any particular flavor?" she asked.

"Whatever sounds good to y'all. There's not a flavor I don't like— except maybe bubble gum," he answered and straightened up. "See y'all later, then. Have fun on your shopping trip."

Grace watched him jog the short distance back to his house and almost blushed when he turned around and blew her a kiss.

"Mama, we can go now," Audrey said from the third seat.

"Give her time to let her heart stop racing," Beezy said with a giggle. "First, she probably thought she'd hit someone when Macy yelled at her to stop, and then"—she fanned herself with a map of

Pier Park—"Travis's face was framed up in the window. Sweet Jesus, that would put any woman's pulse in overdrive. She needs to catch her breath."

Raelene turned around and pointed out the back window. "I can see our motel back there. I didn't realize Travis's house was this close to where we are staying."

"Looks to be less than half a mile," Sarah said, "and tonight, we get to see the inside of his beach house."

"And eat steak," Raelene said. "I will probably never stop talking about this vacation."

"Me either," Audrey added.

Or me for sure, Grace thought as she started driving on toward Pier Park.

Travis heard the ringtone that said Delores was calling. He pulled his phone out of his pocket and hit the accept button at the same time the doorbell rang. "Hold on just a minute, Delores," he said. "My dinner guests have arrived."

"A minute is about all I can hold on," she said in a tone that scared Travis to his very core. He hurried to the front door, flung it open, and motioned for everyone to come inside. It sure wasn't the welcome he had planned, but that's all he could do at the time.

"What's wrong?" he asked Delores.

"I'm sorry, but you are going to have to cut your vacation short," Delores told him.

His mind went to the worst-case scenario: Calvin had had a heart attack, or Lucy had dropped with an aneurysm.

"Calvin and I both are down with the flu. The think-tank kids all went home yesterday afternoon. They must've gotten it at the conference. Calvin called a little while ago and said that he and his whole family are sick, and now I've gotten it. We need you home by Monday morning to run the business. It's just one day earlier than you planned. Daniel will be at the airport at noon tomorrow to fly you home. I've made arrangements for the car-rental place to pick up your vehicle at the airport," Delores said.

Travis glanced up at the calendar hanging on the kitchen wall and realized that it was the first day of the month. "Is this an April Fool's joke?"

"No, it is not, but I sure wish it was," Delores said. "My body aches all over, and I'm going to bed with a heating pad. The doctor says rest and fluids, so I've started drinking lots of hot tea with lemon and honey. I'll see you about Wednesday, if I'm lucky."

Relief washed over Travis. The news could have been so much worse. "Take care of yourself, and don't worry about work. It will be there when you feel like coming back."

"Will do," Delores said and ended the call.

He turned to see six people staring at him. "I'm so sorry about that—but even more sorry that I have to leave tomorrow," he said. "Calvin and Delores, my top staff at the company, both have the flu. A big group from our company went to a two-day conference and evidently brought it home from there. But we have tonight, so let's make the best of it."

"When are you leaving?" Grace asked.

"I have to be at the airport at noon tomorrow," Travis answered. "But like I said, we've got tonight. So . . . welcome to the beach house! Make yourselves at home. Appetizers are on the kitchen table. The bar is stocked, so help yourself to anything there, and soft drinks are in the refrigerator for you two underage girls," he managed, even though he felt like his mind was on a hamster wheel and his emotions were on a roller coaster.

When he got back to San Antonio, there would be a hundred little details to work out for the big meeting on Wednesday morning, but the worst thing was that he would be leaving Grace. He wanted more time for just the two of them, but that would have to wait until they were all back in Texas. He bit back a sigh when he thought of the romantic walks on the beach at sunset—or even sunrise—that he had hoped for in the next few days.

"April Fools!" Audrey said with a giggle. "You almost had me there, and then I remembered that Raelene pulled a good one on me this morning. She told me I'd flunked my history test. I thought I'd aced it."

"Got her good," Raelene said. "She rushed over to her computer to find out that she'd made a hundred on the test."

"It would be wonderful if it was an April Fool's joke, but it's not," Travis said with a sigh.

"I'm so sorry for all your people who are sick," Beezy said. "I had that miserable stuff a couple of months ago. It's not fun. I sure hope they get along all right. Lots of rest and plenty of fluids."

"That's what the doctor told Delores," Travis said. "But for right now, let's enjoy our last night together. Dinner will be served in about twenty minutes. Steaks are on the grill. Does anyone have a particular way they like them cooked?"

"Medium rare," Grace answered.

"Me too," everyone else chimed in at once.

"That makes it easy. Y'all feel free to look around. There are bathrooms off each bedroom. Make yourselves at home. We'll be eating out on the patio," Travis said.

Audrey pointed toward the kitchen and led the way to the appetizers. "I see stuffed mushrooms. Did you make them, Travis?"

"No, ma'am. Julie knows a little local place that did up the appetizers for tonight," he answered.

Travis draped an arm around Grace's shoulders and pulled her close to his side. "I really wanted to spend more time with you."

"We can still do that in Texas," she told him.

"I hope so, but we're free of work and time is ours here in Florida," he said. "Could we at least have a long walk on the beach after supper?"

"I would love that," she answered, and turned to face him. She rose up on her tiptoes and brushed a soft kiss across his lips.

His arms went around her waist, and his lips found hers in a long, passionate kiss that heated up his whole body. He had not been celibate since his divorce, but not a single kiss from another woman had set him on fire like Grace's, and that included his ex-wife, Erica.

"Mama, you've got to try these fried green tomatoes," Audrey called.

"I guess that's our cue to stop making out," Grace panted.

"And I guess"—Travis sucked in air—"that from your breathlessness . . ."

"Yes," she butted in and took a step back. "If I was wearing socks, they would be flying through the air toward the surf about now."

"Good thing neither of us are wearing any, then, isn't it?" Travis said with a grin.

"Mama, where are you?" Audrey called out again.

"I'm on my way," Grace answered.

"And I've got to check on the steaks," Travis whispered as he bent and kissed Grace on the forehead.

Grace would have gladly given up the best steak dinner she'd ever had to spend more time alone with Travis. She would have bypassed the walk if she could have taken Travis back to her condo, locked the doors, and spent time with him in the bedroom. But with all of them having keys to both rooms, that wasn't possible.

Later, after supper, when they were alone at last and walking toward the setting sun, she found it hard to think of anything to talk about. Was that an omen? If they ever did enter into a serious relationship, would their worlds be so far apart that they would be like strangers?

"I love this," Travis finally said.

"The beach?" Grace asked.

"No, that the two of us can find joy in something this simple," he answered.

"Without words?" she asked.

"Just being together, but"—he dropped down on the sand and pulled her down beside him—"the selfish side of me doesn't want to go back to work, and that's quite a thing for a workaholic to admit."

"I understand," she said.

He tipped her chin up with his fist and kissed her.

She leaned in for more, but as luck would have it, a group of teenagers jogged past, and one of them yelled, "Get a room!"

"I guess we *are* acting like love-starved high school sophomores," Travis said with a chuckle.

"But isn't it fun?" Grace moved a few inches away from him.

"Got to admit it is," Travis agreed. "I'll miss you, Grace Dalton."

"I'll be back in Texas next week," she said. "I got a phone call from the principal of the girls' school this evening just before we left to come here. I haven't had time to tell them yet, but they'll be heading back to school in person soon. Several other students came in with documented proof that they had been bullied by Crystal and Kelsey. I guess some of them had told Raelene about the problem, and she had advised them to write what had happened and to add dates and times. When the investigating committee went back and checked the material from the cameras scattered around the school, they found the kids were telling the truth and not just jumping on a bandwagon."

"And?" Travis asked.

"And Crystal and Kelsey will be on distance learning the rest of this year for their acts of bullying other students. If they want to come back to regular classes next year, they'll be on probation," Grace said. "But here we are, on our last night together, talking about the kids."

"Yep, and I love it." Travis leaned across the distance and kissed her on the cheek. "Not as much as I like being alone with you or those scalding-hot kisses, but I like the family side that you bring to the table, too."

"That's good," Grace said, "because that's part of who I am."

"I know that, and everything about you is charming to me," Travis told her.

"Well, darlin', I'm glad, but I don't think anyone ever called me *charming* before. I've been called *bossy*, *demanding*, and *overprotective* but not *charming*," Grace said. "And I like being alone with you, too. You have a kind heart, and I feel like I can be myself with you."

"What makes you say that about me?" Travis asked.

"I see the way you treat your coworkers and my girls—and whole family, for that matter—and you have accepted me for who I am," she answered.

"Thank you. That all comes from my raising. My grandparents and parents alike taught me from a young age to work and to be accountable."

"So did my mother and dad," Grace said.

"One thing I have to admit, though, is that I'm glad that I'm the only one who thinks you are charming, because that means I might have a chance at winning your heart," Travis said.

"Just why would you want to win that?" she asked.

"Because you make me happy," Travis answered. "We can be content sitting right here on the sand, or making out in the living room, or even eating pizza in my office."

"That's because we are together," Grace said.

"Yes, ma'am, it is," Travis agreed.

Chapter Twenty-One

*M*acy was jealous, and she knew that was as much a sin as robbing a bank in God's eyes. Sin was sin, no matter the caliber. That's what she'd been taught since she was a child, anyway, and she knew that down deep in her heart and soul—but somehow, she just couldn't let go of the envy she felt toward Grace and Travis.

"What's going on with you?" Sarah adjusted her hat to shade more of her face and lay back in the chaise longue. "Are you sad that we've only got a little while longer in this little bit of paradise?"

"Why are you asking?" Macy answered with a question of her own.

"Because you've been upbeat and happy ever since we got here, and this morning you look like you've lost your best friend," Sarah told her.

"I'm jealous," Macy admitted, "and I'm ashamed of myself for feeling this way. I should be happy for Grace. Besides, jealousy is a sin that will eat away at your soul if you don't get control of it."

"Well, then, I guess we should both be ashamed," Sarah said, "because if envy really turned a person green, I'd look like a leprechaun, for sure. Grace is the one of us who didn't even care about a relationship, and it's easy to see that she is falling in love with Travis. I want to start a family so bad that my heart aches, and all I ever seem to meet is men like Joel."

"Yep, and I walked right into a con," Macy said with a nod. "Do you think we just need to be content with the idea that we'll never find someone to look at us the way Travis looks at Grace?"

Sarah shook her head. "Not me. I'm not giving up."

"If you found someone, would you move out of the house and leave the business?" Macy asked.

"Maybe," Sarah answered. "If it meant a choice between the business or love, I'd take love. I thought after a couple or three days, I would be ready to leave this place but I'm not, so what does that say about my commitment to stay at the shop forever? What about you?"

"In a heartbeat," Macy replied. "All three of us don't need the money, and the shop has had a good run for several generations."

"Yep," Sarah agreed. "But I'd sure miss seeing you and Grace every day."

Macy sat up straight and removed her hat. "That's the one thing I would miss, too, but I could sure get used to sleeping past three o'clock every morning. I wonder, though, if that drastic of a change for the rest of our lives would bring about regrets."

"Or if *not* changing when we had a chance at a family would bring about even worse disappointments?" Sarah asked.

Grace set a tote bag beside the third chair in the row and eased down into it. "I've loved every minute that we've been here, but . . ."

"But you are ready to go home so you can see Travis," Macy finished her sentence.

"There's that, but that's not my *but* for today," Grace said with a smile. "I was thinking that maybe our next vacation could be over the girls' fall break, and we could go to Colorado or Utah to learn to ski. Wouldn't it be great to see snow and lots of it? When we do get it in our part of the world, it's usually just barely enough to cover the ground, and then it's gone the next day."

"I love that idea," Macy said. "And then over their Christmas break, we could come back down here for a few days."

"Maybe by then Grace and Travis will be a couple, and he'll invite us to stay in the beach house," Sarah teased.

"I'd rather stay here." Macy dug around in her tote bag and brought out a bottle of sweet tea. "It's closer to the beach, and we don't have to climb down as many steps, and . . ." She stopped for a breath.

"And that ain't likely," Grace finished for her. "I promised you both I wouldn't get in a hurry about anything and that I'd go slow."

"Has he kissed you yet?" Macy asked.

"Don't answer that," Audrey said as she set her hat and bag down in her chair and started out into the water with Raelene right behind her. "I don't want to hear about any kissing going on between old people."

"I don't kiss and tell," Grace called out, and then winked at Sarah and Macy.

Another surge of jealousy shot through Macy's heart like a spear. Yes, ma'am, she was surely going to have to seriously work on that.

On Wednesday, Beezy announced that she was treating them all to lunch that day in celebration of their last day at the beach. She had chosen an Italian place in Pier Park, and she suggested that while they were there, they could all pick up suitcases. Grace was glad to have something to do that day. For the past two days, she and Travis had texted several times, but today he was in back-to-back meetings, and she wouldn't hear from him until he called later tonight. She had figured the day would drag by like a snail slogging through molasses, and she really needed something to keep her busy. She hadn't realized how strong the attraction between them had become until he wasn't there anymore.

"You need something to take home all your new things in, plus the half ton of shells you've each collected," Beezy reminded them.

"We could hit the thrift stores again," Raelene said.

"Nope, you will not!" Beezy declared. "I don't mind thrifting for clothes. You can wash them if they aren't brand-new, but in today's world, you never know what might have been in a suitcase. What if they've got drug-sniffin' dogs at the airport, and the previous owner had that kind of thing in their suitcase? You've saved enough money on your wardrobe that you can buy new suitcases. Besides, now that you've all got a taste for vacations, you'll be using them again."

"Never thought of that," Raelene said. "It would be so embarrassing."

"And just think of the gossip if it got back to everyone in Devine. The girls who got Crystal and Kelsey in such horrible trouble were caught trying to smuggle drugs," Audrey said.

Grace finished heating up sausage biscuits for breakfast and set them on the bar. "Speaking of those girls who are declaring that this is all your fault"—she glanced over at Raelene and Audrey—"the principal called me. The investigation is over. Neither set of parents wanted to appeal the decision that was made. You two will be going back to school on Monday morning."

"Why didn't their parents fight for them?" Raelene asked. "I figured that their fathers would use their positions to go to battle for the girls. Their mothers told everyone that we were the ones that got Crystal and Kelsey in trouble and none of it was their fault. I figured those two women wouldn't be happy until the day they saw me and Audrey in jail for assault."

"We'd never let that happen," Beezy assured her with a pat on the shoulder.

"It was all verified when the investigation team looked at tapes from the school cameras," Grace added.

"What about my scholarship?" Raelene asked.

"That's still up in the air. We can look into things better when we get back," Grace answered to soothe her. "Y'all come on over here and grab a biscuit and some juice. Are you ready to get back in school?"

"I am," Audrey said. "My old friends have been texting me and Raelene. And guess what, Mama? I've pulled all my grades up while we've been on vacation."

Sarah poured herself a glass of juice and picked up a biscuit. "Looks like everything is working out."

"Except for my scholarship," Raelene said with a sigh as she slid off a barstool and headed toward the kitchen.

"Girl, don't you worry one bit about that," Sarah told her. "I'll make sure you get an education if that scholarship falls through."

Raelene got the milk from the refrigerator and poured two glasses full. "I couldn't let you do that—not after everything you've already done."

Grace wasn't sure if it was the right time to bring up the internship for Butler Enterprises or not. She remembered her mother saying something about seizing the opportunity while it was there instead of waiting to chase it down the road when it was a mile away. "Just how much do you have your heart set on that nursing program, Raelene?"

"That junior college was the best offer I've gotten, and the two-year program for nursing would give me what I need to support myself quicker than any other job," Raelene answered and handed off one of the glasses of milk to Audrey. "I wouldn't have the money to go on to a university without borrowing a lot—and I mean a lot—to go on for two more years. It seemed to be the best chance I had."

"But do you really want to be a nurse?" Grace pressed on. "What was your dream when you were a little girl?"

"*I* wanted to be a princess, and then last year I wanted to be famous," Audrey piped up, and then downed half the milk. "Both of those seem kind of silly right now."

"Nursing wasn't my first choice," Raelene admitted. "I just wanted to be smart, and my Granny told me that it didn't matter what other people thought of me, or what they said, or how I dressed. She said it didn't take money or beauty to use my brain."

Grace might not have believed in fate before, but she sure did at that moment. What else could explain everything that had happened in the past few weeks?

"How about you, Audrey? When you got past being a princess and being famous, what's been your dream?" Grace asked.

"Why are you so interested in all this? Do you know something the rest of us don't?" Macy asked.

"I do," Grace replied with a nod, "but first, I want to hear what Audrey has to say." She turned to face her daughter. "You've got two more years before you go to college and try to figure out what you want to do—but if you had to decide today, what would that be?"

Audrey fidgeted on the barstool. "I don't want to hurt y'all's feelings, but I would not want to run a doughnut shop. I want a job where I . . ." She hesitated.

"Where you what?" Grace pressured.

"Speak up, child," Beezy said. "You're not going to hurt our feelings. The shop has had a good, long run, and everything has an expiration date at some time. Maybe not this year or even this generation, but nothing on this earth lasts forever."

"Dinosaur bones seem to," Audrey argued. "But I want a job where I go to work at nine, get off at five, wear pretty shoes, and have an office of my own." She paused again before adding, "With a view. Now, why are you asking all these questions, Mama?"

Fate or opportunity or the universe has surely come knocking on our door, Grace thought. She inhaled deeply, finished the last bite of her sausage biscuit, and took a drink of orange juice.

"Delores hires one intern each summer to help her in the office at Travis's company, and he hires one intern each year to work with a team that he calls his 'think tank kids.' He asked about you girls, and I told him it was up to you. You would get paid minimum wage for the summer, a bonus at the end of the year. If you work out, Raelene, in that particular job for Travis, then you would have a scholarship to whatever college you want to go to, and you can study whatever you really want to study. The catch is that he would want you to come back to Butler Enterprises and work for him in the think tank, depending on what your master's or doctorate direction turns out to be," Grace explained.

Tears streamed down Raelene's face, dripped off her jaw, and left wet spots on her Perfect Pig T-shirt. "Yes," she whispered, "but are you serious? I could go to school at the University of Texas right there in San Antonio and live at home?"

"Halle-damn-lujah!" Beezy pumped her fist. "Hilda would be so proud of you."

"This is a dream." Raelene reached for a tissue on the bar and wiped her eyes.

Audrey let out a squeal and pumped her own fist. "You won't have to leave and go all the way up into Oklahoma if you get that internship. This is the best news ever. Take that, Crystal and Kelsey!"

Grace pointed to Audrey. "And you might have a chance to be that intern with Delores, the person that Travis swears knows more about his company than he does. You'll both have driver's licenses by then, so you can take my car and go to work each day. But, girl, you will have to take orders and learn what Delores has to teach you from the ground up."

Audrey sucked in air and let it out slowly. "I would count paper clips or file papers all day to get a job like that. Would I get a scholarship, too?"

"Yes, you would," Grace answered.

"I'll start concurrent classes in business as soon as I can," Audrey whispered.

"Can you believe that we would be working in the same building?" Raelene asked.

"This is the perfect ending to our vacation." Audrey slid off her barstool and hugged Raelene.

"No, it's not," Beezy said. "The ending won't be until we watch the sunrise one more time. We'll tell the beach goodbye and promise to come back at Christmas for a few days. But right now, we need to go buy suitcases for all five of you. And then we're going to lunch. After that, we'll get all packed up and ready to leave by seven in the morning because we board our plane at ten. One more thing, we've all got to be at the church at seven thirty tomorrow night to vote on whether to hire the new preacher or not."

"How are you going to vote?" Macy asked.

"I listened to his Sunday sermon on the phone earlier this week," Beezy said, "and my sister snuck a picture of him so I could see what he looks like. He's thirty-five and never been married. He's not a big man, but . . ." She pulled her phone from her shirt pocket and hit a few icons. "Take a look—but remember, we're not hiring him based on his looks. If we were, I wouldn't vote for him. He's kind of generic looking. But let me tell you, when he presented that sermon, I was on the edge of my seat. So I'll be voting for him."

Macy took the phone from her. "What's his name?"

"James O'Malley. That red hair and green eyes say he's Irish as much as his name does," Beezy said.

"If he can stir your spirit that much," Grace said, "then he's got my vote."

"Yep," Sarah agreed with a nod.

Grace wondered if Travis would be the kind of guy to go to church with her or if he would want to continue to go wherever he went in San Antonio.

That's silly, she scolded herself. *Two or three kisses does not mean wedding bells or three-tiered cakes.*

Chapter Twenty-Two

"It's hard to believe that we are on a plane in Florida and will be home in time to vote on our new preacher tonight," Macy said as she fastened her seat belt.

"Or that Raelene and I will be in school on Monday morning," Audrey said from across the aisle.

"Excited about that idea?" Sarah asked from the seat behind Audrey and Raelene.

"It'll be a whole new experience," Raelene answered. "I just hope that what happened to Crystal and Kelsey put some fear into the other bullies."

"If it didn't and we have to fight them off us, do we get to go back to Florida?" Audrey teased.

"Not until Christmas break," Grace answered.

"Is Beezy going with us?" Audrey asked.

"Anytime you pack your suitcases, I'll get mine ready to go," Beezy answered. "This has been the most fun I've had in years. Not even that cruise could compare to these past few days."

Once the plane was in the air, Macy stared out the window at the land beneath them getting smaller and smaller. Each plot down there was no bigger than a postage stamp. In the grand scheme of things, that's the way her anger over Neal and her jealousy about Grace looked.

She should let them go now before they grew into acres and acres and consumed her.

Macy sighed and turned around to find Sarah sound asleep. Audrey and Raelene were deep in a whispered conversation, most likely about the possibility of their summer jobs with Butler Enterprises. Grace and Travis had been in communication every day since he left, so she would be glad to get home to see him. Beezy, bless her heart, would get right back to whatever gossip was going around town.

Macy glanced back over at Sarah. *Just me and you, darlin' cousin, who have nothing to go home to but the same old routine.*

Sarah awoke when the plane began to circle Dallas. "Are we home?"

"Nope," Audrey answered. "But we're close. We've got an hour lay-over here in Dallas, and then a quick flight home. We should be there by noon—and this might sound crazy, but I'm starving for doughnuts."

"I'm not cooking doughnuts until Monday morning," Sarah declared.

"How about we just make one batch at home?" Macy winked at Audrey. "Just to be sure we haven't lost our touch."

"Maybe," Sarah said and covered a yawn with her hand. "But not today. We've got to unpack, and then we have to go vote on the preacher."

"We should either get a bite of lunch in San Antonio or else make a stop by the grocery store in Devine and eat at home," Grace said.

"My sister is picking me up, and I promised to feed her for coming to get me. You are all welcome to join us," Beezy told them as they began the descent to the runway.

"I just want to go home, but you have to promise to tell us all the gossip after church tonight," Sarah said.

"I'm old and forgetful," Beezy said with a chuckle, "but I'll take notes if it's something really important. You can bet that my sis won't miss a single thing, and she'll tell all while we're eating our lunch."

"Can we stop at the burger shop and get takeout?" Audrey asked.

"Sounds good to me," Sarah said. "I'll volunteer to do our grocery shopping this afternoon."

Home!

The vacation had been wonderful, and Sarah wouldn't have minded booking a flight to go back as soon as they were on the ground in Dallas, but her own bed in her own room surrounded by her things sounded really good, too. Too bad she couldn't have both in one place, she thought.

Macy nudged her shoulder. "You had a smile on your face when you were sleeping. What were you dreaming about?"

"I was on Shell Island again. That little dark-haired girl and I were picking up shells together, and she called me Mama," Sarah answered.

"What was her name?" Macy asked.

Sarah sighed and shook her head with a twinge of sadness. "Her name is Angela, but I called her Angel in my dream, which may be the closest I will ever get to having a daughter of my own."

"Hey, don't give up," Macy told her. "It's not like you're over the hill just yet. Your dream may be an omen."

"I won't give up if you won't," Sarah told her as the captain began his "thank you for traveling with us" speech.

"It's a deal," Macy agreed, "but I'm having ornery boys, not little angels."

Grace was so tired by evening that she just wanted to curl up in front of the television and binge-watch old episodes of *Justified*. Instead, she had to do her spiritual duty and vote on the new preacher. She would have gladly sent her vote with Macy, but that wouldn't have been right. Beezy had made her listen to part of James O'Malley's sermon from the previous Sunday on the plane. Grace had checked his credentials—six years at a small church in Alvord, Texas; three in Breckinridge; and three in Waco. He had said he felt like he had a *divine* calling to leave the big churches and come back to a smaller one. Grace didn't think the older folks would pick up on the subtle divine/Devine joke, but she appreciated it in a sermon.

All three of them were quiet on the ride from their house to the church that evening. They filed into the sanctuary, and Grace stood to the side and let Macy and Sarah sit down first, then took her place at the end of the long oak pew where the rest of the committee already waited. The president of the hiring committee stood up, cleared his throat, and began to talk to them about the new preacher.

Grace wondered why she had let Beezy talk her into sitting on this committee ten years ago and vowed that as soon as she helped hire the new man, she would resign. Holding someone's future in her hands wasn't something that she enjoyed. The president went over all James O'Malley's credentials and then told them a little about James's personal life. He had been born and raised in Post, Texas—a small town in the Texas Panhandle—had gone to seminary on a basketball scholarship at Oklahoma Baptist University, and had begun his ministry at the age of twenty-two. His grandparents and his family still lived in Post, where they owned a cotton farm. Then President Henry passed out copies of letters of recommendation from the three churches where James had ministered.

"I'll give you a few minutes to scan these, and then, for those of you who weren't here Sunday to hear James preach, we are having a little meet and greet in the fellowship hall so everyone can visit with him. After that, you can cast your vote on the way out, and I will send out a group text to let you all know the result," he said.

Grace leaned over. "Thirty-four or thirty-five years old and unmarried?" she whispered to Macy.

"Sarah is that age, and she's not married," Macy reminded her.

"Touché," Grace said with a nod. "Do you think he goes by James or Jimmy?"

Macy glanced over the raving recommendations, stood up, and headed out of the sanctuary. "That'll be the first thing I ask him as soon as we get to the fellowship hall. And after that, I'm inviting him to Sunday dinner. There's no telling what rumors he's heard about all of us, so maybe if he gets to know us before he hears the gossip, he'll see that we are good people."

"Brave little soul, aren't you?" Grace followed her, thankful Macy's back was turned to her sudden smile.

Sarah fell in behind Grace. "Hide that grin. I wouldn't mess with her—not after seeing her go all Kickboxing Queen on Neal."

They were the first ones in the fellowship hall, and Grace was surprised to see that the picture she had seen of James O'Malley did not do him justice. To begin with, he was only a couple of inches taller than Macy, who was the tallest of the three of them at five feet, five inches, and to end with, he looked like he lifted weights every day. His biceps stretched the sleeves of his dark green knit shirt, and his thighs filled out his jeans really well.

She thought of how surprised she'd been when Travis shed his shirt at the beach and she had seen how muscular he was. In some cases, a picture was not worth a thousand words.

He crossed the room and held out a hand to Macy. "Hello, ladies. I'm James O'Malley, but my friends and any members of my past congregations all called me Brother Jimmy."

"Macy Williams, and these are my cousins, Grace and Sarah," she said. "And before everyone else gets here, we would like to invite you to dinner after services on Sunday."

"If I'm your new pastor, I'll be glad to accept," Brother Jimmy said with a smile.

"Even if you aren't and you are still in town, you are welcome," Sarah told him.

"That's even better, and thank you so much." Brother Jimmy patted Macy's hand and then dropped it. "Excuse me while I go meet these other folks. There's refreshments on the table. Please, help yourselves. Electing a new preacher is hard work, and you might be thirsty or in need of a freshly baked chocolate chip cookie. I made them myself."

Sarah nudged Macy's shoulder. "I'm reminded of that old country song about somebody knockin'."

"The one that says the devil has blue eyes and wears blue jeans," Grace whispered. "And then there's something about having a heavenly night. His red hair is almost the same shade as yours. His eyes aren't the same color as yours, but hey, he might still be knockin'. Can't you just imagine little redhaired boys running around the church sanctuary?"

"Oh, hush!" Macy hissed at them. "I'm not preacher's-wife material, even with all that Sunday school teaching. Remember, I was at the top of the gossip-vine list not all that long ago. Brother Jimmy would never be interested in me."

"You are so right," Sarah told her. "He would want a sweet, submissive little wife who wouldn't try to kick a man's ribs into pieces small enough to pass through the eye of a needle."

"Amen!" Macy said and headed over to the refreshment table.

Grace had just finished marking her ballot in favor of hiring Brother Jimmy and had slipped it into the ballot box when her phone rang. She fished it out of her purse, saw that the call was from Travis, and answered it. "Hello, how was your day?"

"Hectic, but productive," Travis answered. "Delores came back to work today, and my first-floor kids are all back at their jobs, but Calvin is going to need another day and the weekend to fully recover. But I didn't call to talk about my day, other than to say that I missed you horribly all week, and I'm so glad you are home."

The tone of his voice meant as much as his words.

"Thank you, and I've missed you, too. Today was also pretty hectic for me. We barely got home when we had to come back to the church to vote on a new preacher, and now I think I may have some jet lag," Grace said. "Are we still on for dinner tomorrow night—just the two of us?"

"Yes, ma'am, but I can't wait that long to see you. I'm on my way to Devine—just passing the city limits sign. Think we could go get some ice cream when you get finished with your meeting, or are you too tired for that?" Travis asked. "If you get sleepy, I'll be glad to let you sleep on my shoulder."

"We're just finishing up here at the church. First one on your left as you come into town. I'll be waiting on the porch for you," she told him and tossed the keys to her SUV to Sarah. "Travis and I are going for ice cream. Don't wait up for me."

Sarah caught them on the fly. "There's a motel in Hondo, if you want to be discreet."

"I *said* ice cream," Grace told her as she was walking out the door.

"You might need some ice cream to cool down," Macy teased. "And remember, you are not like Cinderella. You won't turn into just a doughnut maker at midnight, and we will watch over Raelene and Audrey until you get home."

"Thanks," Grace said as she closed the door behind her.

The parking lot didn't have many vehicles in it, but even if it had, Travis would have been hard to miss. He had turned on his headlights, and when she stepped off the porch, he got out of his SUV and started toward her. She didn't care if she seemed too eager as she met him halfway and walked right into his open arms.

"I have missed you so much," Travis whispered into her hair. "Miz Grace Dalton, I think I could fall in love with you." He tipped up her chin, looked deeply into her eyes, and kissed her.

She wrapped her arms around his neck and leaned into his body. The kiss said as much as—or more than—his words. "Me too, but . . ."

"No *but*s today, darlin'," Travis said. "We can take it slow and be sure."

"Then there are no *but*s. However," she said with a smile, "just how slow do you want to go?"

He returned her smile. "Your foot is on the gas pedal. You tell me. I've got a feeling you won't be one bit bashful."

"You got that right." Grace wished that she could take him by the hand and tell him to drive to the motel in Hondo. But their first night together shouldn't be at the end of a long day when she was worn out. It should be something special. "Right now, let's go get ice cream. After those kisses, I do need something to cool me down."

"Yes, ma'am," he said and drew her even closer for another kiss.

Chapter Twenty-Three

This is going to be a long day," Sarah said as the three of them made their way from the house to the shop that Monday morning.

"Yep," Macy agreed.

"Are you pouting because our new hunky preacher didn't come to dinner yesterday?" Grace asked.

"I believe she is," Sarah teased.

"I. Am. Not. Pouting." Macy punctuated each word with a stab of her forefinger toward Sarah. "I understand that it is tradition here in Devine for the outgoing preacher to take him to dinner to celebrate his last day and Jimmy's first day in the parsonage. Let's go make dough and get our minds off dreams of dark-haired angels and con men."

"*You* are dreaming about that little girl?" Grace asked.

"No!" Macy snapped. "Sarah is, though."

"My biological clock is ticking, and Angela has been surfacing in my dreams. I want a family and a baby," Sarah admitted.

"What about you, Macy?" Grace teased. "Are you dreaming about little redhaired boys?"

"I'm not talking about my dreams," Macy said as she unlocked the door and flipped on the lights. "I need to be busy, so let's get our hands in some dough. And"—she paused as she set up three bowls—"I got to admit, I'm hungry for one of our doughnuts, too."

Sarah put two cups of warm water into each bowl. "Do y'all feel change in the air?"

Grace added half a cup of sugar and two tablespoons of yeast to each bowl and used a whisk to mix them well. "I do, but then we've always been open six days a week, and we're talking about cutting it down to four. That's a radical change. I bet Claud and his cronies won't like the idea at all."

"Probably not," Sarah said, "but I'm looking forward to it, and I wouldn't even mind if we were only open Thursday, Friday, and Saturday."

"What would we do with all that free time?" Macy asked.

"Well"—Grace added flour to the mixture in one of the bowls—"on our days off, for the first six months, I would sit in Mama's rocking chair out on our porch."

"And after that?" Sarah asked.

"I might start it to rocking," Grace said with a soft giggle.

"That sounds like retirement, not starting a new life with Travis Butler," Macy told her.

"Grace didn't say why the chair started rocking, Macy." The joke only kind of dulled the ache in Sarah's heart for a family and home of her own.

"Right now, we're just enjoying each other's company and getting to know each other. We're barely in a relationship, and we sure haven't talked about things that far in the future. Besides, I've got a whole year before I even intend to open one of those bride magazines that you still have in your bedroom, Macy," Grace answered. "Now, getting back to the shop. Let's keep to four days a week until the girls are out of school. We can start next week so our regulars get plenty of notice that we won't be here Sunday, Monday, or Tuesday. Later, we can decide whether to cut back another day. If the girls don't get jobs at Travis's company, they might want to be put on the shop's payroll this summer."

Macy added the rest of the ingredients to the dough she was mixing up and kneaded it right in the bowl a few times before setting it back and starting a second round. "Sounds like a plan to me. This flour reminds me of the white sand down at the beach."

Sarah finished kneading her first bowl of dough and set about working on the next one. "The sugar reminded me of the beach, too, but part of me hopes they don't take those internships in San Antonio. Having big-people jobs with that big of a company brings it all home that they are growing up too fast."

"Let's don't think about that," Grace said with a long sigh.

"Amen," Macy agreed. "I'm going to the dining room to put on a pot of coffee. After two weeks of sleeping until I was ready to get up, this three o'clock a.m. business is kicking my butt."

"I hear you, sister," Sarah told her.

The display cases were full, and Macy was still working on putting the icing on the last six dozen doughnuts when Sarah flipped the "Closed" sign around to "Open" and unlocked the front doors. Sure enough, Claud, Ira, and Frankie were the first customers, and they quickly claimed their regular table.

"Good mornin'," Sarah greeted them with a smile. "What can I get y'all?"

"Girl, we missed y'all so much that us three grown men cried every morning that you were gone," Ira teased, and wiped fake tears from his eyes.

Frankie patted his stomach. "I bet I lost ten pounds. I might even have to buy new overalls."

"Don't pay no attention to them," Claud said. "What they're full of ain't yesterday's Easter ham. Bring us three cups of black coffee and a dozen doughnuts. Just mix 'em up this morning, and we'll fight over who gets the maple ones. Lord, I'm glad y'all are back. I ain't had a decent doughnut since you been gone."

"We had a wonderful vacation, but we're glad to be home," Sarah said. "Thanks for missing us, and I'll have that order right out."

Claud's comment about Easter brought a vision of Audrey and Raelene to Sarah's mind. Audrey had worn a baby-blue dress with white polka dots, and Raelene had chosen one with yellow sunflowers for that special Sunday. Although neither of them would have admitted it, Grace could tell they had been nervous about going into the Sunday school room with Crystal and Kelsey. The girls hadn't said anything to her about the fact that Crystal and Kelsey weren't in attendance that morning, but Beezy had whispered that they wouldn't be back to their church.

Sarah left the lid on the box open and set it on a tray, then poured three cups of coffee and carried it all to the table, where the guys were already deep in conversation about the new preacher in town.

"Did you hear that four families left our church and went to another one?" Claud asked as he took a doughnut from the box.

"No, is that why Crystal and Kelsey weren't in Sunday school with our girls yesterday?" Sarah asked.

Ira reached for a doughnut with sprinkles. "Probably so. Those two have always been little hellions. My sweet wife, Martha Jane, used to put up with them in the church nursery. She could put a halo on the devil himself, but those girls were a different matter. Their mothers wouldn't believe a thing when Martha Jane told her what they'd done."

"Macy will probably have a better class without them. But I got to admit, I kinda feel sorry for whatever church they moved to," Claud said and took a sip of his coffee.

Sarah sidestepped having to make a comment and pointed out the window. "Looks like we're in for a busy day. You guys just holler when you get ready for a warm-up on your coffee."

She hurried back behind the counter and quickly put on the second pot of coffee. When she turned around, people had not only filled all the tables but were lined up for take-out orders. She was just about to yell at Macy and Grace when they both came in from the kitchen with full trays in their hands.

"Looks like we're going to sell out early today," Macy said as she picked up an order pad and a pen and headed over to one of the tables.

"I've got one dozen saved back in the kitchen for the girls' breakfast and for us to snack on when things slow down," Grace said as she took her place behind the register.

Sarah filled a box with half a dozen glazed. "*If* they do slow down. It looks like we might run out by midmorning."

At ten o'clock the items in the display case were sparse, but there were still a few of each variety left. The dining area and the parking lot had emptied out. Macy had just finished sweeping up crumbs and taken the broom and dustpan to the kitchen. Grace poured herself a cup of coffee and sat down at a table.

"Mercy! What a morning!" Macy said. "I think everyone missed us."

"Yep, I believe they did," Grace agreed with a nod.

Sarah was about to join them when she heard a car door slam. She set a bottle of sweet tea to the side. "I'm still up. I'll take care of this one."

"Sarah Dalton," a child squealed when the door opened.

Sarah looked out over the counter to see Angela with her father, Brock, right behind her. For a split second, she thought she was dreaming again, but then the child ran around the end of the counter and threw her arms around Sarah's legs.

"I chased the lizard and you found me," Angela said, looking up at her. "And now *I* found *you.*"

Sarah reached down and gathered the child up in her arms. "Yes, you did. Would you like a doughnut and some milk?"

"Will you have one with me?" Angela asked.

"I guess I could do that," Sarah answered and looked over the counter at Brock, who was standing there with a smile on his face.

"You are a hard woman to track down," he said, "and I hope we aren't intruding. Angela has been asking when I'm going to find you every morning at breakfast, and when she says her prayers, she asks God to let her find you."

"I'm glad you kept looking. What can I—" Sarah began, but Grace appeared by her side, seemingly out of nowhere.

"I'll take care of this. You go on and sit down with your guests." She turned to face Brock. "What can I get y'all this morning?"

"Chocolate and sprinkles," Angela said.

"Half a dozen glazed. Coffee for me and milk for Miss Bossy Britches," Brock answered with a smile.

"Some dreams come true," Grace whispered for Sarah's ears only.

"I'll have a cream cheese–filled one," Sarah said. She lowered her voice: "And from your lips to God's ears."

Grace filled the order, put it all on a tray, and took it to the table that Claud and his cronies had vacated. "I'm Sarah's sister, Grace Dalton, and that redhead over there at the other end of the dining room is Macy, our cousin."

"I'm Brock Stephens and this is my daughter, Angela."

"Daddy, if she's a sister, does that mean if I take Sarah home that she can be my sister?" Angela asked.

"Remember what I told you." Brock's face turned slightly pink. "We can come see Sarah, but we can't take her home."

Angela cocked her head at her father. "I prayed and God said I could take her home."

"Did God say today?" Brock asked.

Angela's lower lip protruded in what Grace figured was a well-practiced pout.

"No," the child finally answered, "but maybe she can go to the park with us?"

"We can ask her if she can do that," Brock replied.

"I would love to," Sarah said. "We've got one here in Devine with swings, but I have to work until noon."

"We've got this place covered," Grace said. "If Angela is going to the park after she has her doughnuts, then there's no reason why you can't go with her. It's a pleasure to have met y'all, but I hear a car door slamming, so I'd better get back to work."

"Thank you," Sarah mouthed.

Grace had barely made it back to the counter when Brother Jimmy came through the door. "Good mornin'," he called out. "Is Macy . . . oh, I see her . . ." He made an abrupt turn to the left and headed toward her table.

"Can I get you anything?" Grace asked.

"A cup of coffee and maybe two glazed doughnuts," Brother Jimmy answered. "I've been hearing all about how good your pastries are."

Macy sat up a little straighter and tucked a strand of red hair back behind her ear. "Good mornin' to you. Are you settling into the parsonage?"

"Yes and no," Jimmy said. "My furniture hasn't arrived, so I'm sleeping on a pallet until the end of the week. Miz Beezy sent me to talk to you about helping me with the youth program at the church. She says you'll be the best person in town."

Grace took the order to their table and then went back to the counter. She would bet that Beezy had had more than the teenagers at the church on her mind when she had talked to the new pastor. Grace could already hear the rumors that would soon be flying around town. They would say that he had come to Devine because he and Macy had met somewhere in the past and already had a romance going.

Grace's mama popped into her head. *And what about Sarah? The gossip will be that she met Brock in a bar and has broken up his marriage. He did tell Sarah that he and Angela have been on their own since the little girl was a year old. I'm guessing the mother passed away or left them.*

Grace loved the times when she could hear her mother's voice, but before she could say another word, the bell above the door jingled, and Travis's bright smile greeted her. She looked at Brock and then over at Jimmy. Could it be possible that, on down the road, Macy and Sarah would find someone to make them as happy as she was with Travis? She surely hoped so.

"Good mornin', lovely lady," Travis said as he crossed the room. "I am here to buy six dozen doughnuts for the break room at the company, but it looks like I'll be lucky to take home five."

"Thank you, and good mornin' to you. It looks like five is about what I have," Grace said as she started boxing up his order. "Got time for a cup of coffee or a sweet tea?"

"Always," Travis answered. "Sweet tea sounds good."

Grace finished the order, set the boxes on the counter, and ran Travis's credit card through the reader. "Give me a minute to lock up, and we'll take our tea to the kitchen."

Travis looked around at the two tables and raised an eyebrow.

"Macy and Sarah will let them out when they are ready," she said with a bright smile.

Suddenly, it didn't matter if the Devine Doughnut Shop came to an end in the next year or lasted on to another generation or two. What really mattered was that there were three very real possibilities for happiness and a future right there in the shop at that moment.

Grace Dalton was as sure about that as she was about her feelings for Travis Butler.

Epilogue

ONE YEAR LATER

Audrey and Raelene had decorated the dining room of the Devine Doughnut Shop with pink and blue balloons and were even more excited than Angela was that morning. She was bouncing around the whole shop, asking so many questions that Sarah couldn't keep them answered fast enough.

Today was the gender-reveal party for Macy and Brother Jimmy's first baby, who would arrive in late summer. The due date was the same as their first anniversary.

Grace brought in the cake she had made in the kitchen and set it on one of the tables. It had pink icing on one end and blue on the other. Audrey and Raelene were the only ones who knew the gender and would cut either a pink slice if it was a girl or a blue one if it was a boy, and serve it to Brother Jimmy and Macy.

"Beautiful cake. You did a good job," Sarah said and gave her sister a hug. "Has Audrey told you if she'll be cutting pink or blue?"

"Nope, she and Raelene are doing a good job of keeping it a big secret," Grace answered and waved at Travis, who came in through the kitchen. "We've sure come a long way since this time last year, and I kept my promise about waiting a year—not that I can say the same for you and Macy."

"Hey, we didn't make a promise," Sarah told her. "And I never believed in love at first sight before, but I think I fell in love with Brock that day on Shell Island. Are you sad that we closed the shop right after Macy and Jimmy's wedding?"

"Not one bit, and I'm not sad that I can sit in Mama's rocker each evening and wait for Travis and the girls to come home. Every now and then, I whip up a few dozen doughnuts in the kitchen for Travis to take to the break room. I've been helping Macy fix up her nursery and volunteering with the new youth program at the church. Audrey and Raelene are really enjoying all the fellowship with the teenagers that are flocking to our church now. I've been so busy that I don't know when I would have time to make doughnuts. And then"—she smiled—"I'll be busy helping you out with your nursery before long. Plus, I'm so excited that I can be more involved in Audrey's senior year."

Sarah laid a hand on her small belly bump. "I'll sure enough need help, but mostly to keep Angela from trying to put a kiddie swimming pool and swing set in the nursery so the baby will have something to play with."

"She reminds me so much of Audrey at that age that they could share DNA," Grace said.

"Think you and Travis will ever have kids?"

"We wouldn't mind having one or two, but Travis says the two girls we've got are enough if it never happens. Speaking of *our* girls, they are eager to get back to full-time work this summer. Delores says that Audrey is a natural, and there's real hope that she can grow into bigger positions after Delores gets ready to retire. And Lucy says that she's never had an intern as smart as Raelene. That girl aced every single one of her college classes this year," Grace said and pointed out the window. "Look! There's Jimmy and Macy coming now."

"What's your guess: Boy or girl?" Sarah asked.

Brock slipped up behind Sarah and put his arms around her waist. "I'm guessing it's a boy because she's already settled on a name."

"I'm not guessing," Grace said.

Travis kissed Grace on the forehead. "Let's get this over with so I can sit on the porch with you and watch the sunset. I'm loving this country life and having a family to come home to at night."

"And I'm loving that we have kept this building, and that Sarah, Macy, and I can have our sister day every couple of weeks here to have a catch-up afternoon," Grace said.

Sarah glanced over at Travis. "You don't miss your penthouse apartment or mind the commute?"

"Not one bit," Travis answered. "Brock says he doesn't know how he ran his business without you. Do you regret not coming to the shop to work every day?"

"Love before business." Sarah winked at Grace.

"Right," Grace agreed and stood on her tiptoes to plant a kiss on Travis's cheek. "Every single time."

"Hello, everyone," Brother Jimmy said as he held the door for Macy. "Beezy says not to start without her. She's parking her car right now."

"Wouldn't dream of it," Grace said. "I see you both wore blue. Is that an omen?"

"I don't care if we get pink cake or blue," Brother Jimmy said. "I'll be happy with either."

"I didn't even realize that I'd chosen a blue one"—Macy smoothed the front down over her belly—"but we have decided that if I get pink cake, we will name her Molly Elizabeth after our mothers. His mother's and grandmother's middle names are the Elizabeth, so we'll be hitting all of them," Macy said.

Beezy hurried into the dining room, out of breath but yelling, "I'm here! I'm here! Let the party begin."

"Is everyone ready?" Audrey asked.

Macy nodded.

Brother Jimmy slipped his arm around her and kissed her on the forehead.

Raelene picked up a knife and held it above the blue end of the cake.

Audrey did the same with the pink end. Then Raelene stepped back, and Audrey cut a slice of pink cake, put it on a plate, and handed it to Macy. "Welcome to the family, Molly Elizabeth! We can't wait to see you."

"I get a baby sister!" Angela squealed.

No one had the heart to tell her that she would really be her cousin.

"And the legacy lives on, even if it doesn't live through the doughnut shop," Sarah whispered. "I love that name, and I am a little jealous that I can't use it."

"You can always go back a little further in our family tree and use Edith Agnes," Grace teased.

"No thank you," Sarah said and tucked her hand into Brock's. "Let's go get some of that blue cake, darlin', and hope it means we'll get a boy."

"That would be nice." Brock took the time to kiss her on the cheek. "I'm not sure either of us can live through another Angela."

"Who knows? Maybe you'll have ornery twin girls just to show you that blue cake doesn't work," Travis said. "Grace and I sure enjoy our girls, even if they aren't really twins."

"We are blessed, every one of us," Grace said, "and it all started right here in the Devine Doughnut Shop. Like you said, love before business."

Dear readers,

Making bread, cinnamon rolls, and doughnuts from scratch has long been my "thing." I've perfected my recipe and given it to folks, but most of them say they can't get the technique down just right. I guess that part comes from years and years of practice. I thought it would be fun to write about a secret recipe for a shop, but I never realized just how invested I would become in the characters who run the place—or how much of my own past would make cameo appearances in the book when Raelene showed up at the door, looking for a job. I hope that you enjoy reading this and meeting the whole cast as much as I did when I was writing the story. I have a confession: sometimes at night, Audrey would wake me up to fuss at me for not getting a scene just right, and she wouldn't leave me alone until it was like she remembered it.

As always, there is a lot of work between the first few lines of an idea and the finished product you have in your hands. And as always, there is a whole truckload of thanks for all that hard work for the team that has made this book possible. My thanks go out to my agency, Folio Management, and my agent, Erin Niumata. Erin and I have been together now for almost a quarter of a century. That's longer than most Hollywood marriages, folks. Also, to Montlake for continuing to believe in me, with special thanks to Alison Dasho, my acquiring editor, and Krista Stroever, my developmental editor, who pushes me to tell my best story. And to my family for understanding what a deadline is all about, and my husband, Mr. B, who is my biggest supporter. But most of all, thank you to my readers. Your notes, reviews, and support mean the world to me.

Until next time,
Carolyn Brown

About the Author

Carolyn Brown is a *New York Times*, *USA Today*, *Washington Post*, *Wall Street Journal*, and *Publishers Weekly* best-selling author and RITA finalist with more than 125 published books. She has written women's fiction, historical and contemporary romance, and cowboys-and-country-music novels. She and her husband live in the small town of Davis, Oklahoma, where everyone knows everyone else, knows what they are doing and when, and reads the local newspaper on Wednesday to see who got caught. They have three grown children and enough grandchildren and great-grandchildren to keep them young. For more information, visit www.carolynbrownbooks.com.